PRAISE FOR THE CUTTHROAT BUSINESS SERIES

"Move over Stephanie Plum, there is a sassy, sexy sleuth in town! If you enjoy your cozy mysteries with a good shot of romance, and a love triangle with a sexy bad boy and a South[...] mix, then you will love this. Very re[...] [b]ooks, but the laughs are louder, the [...] [th]at murder mystery to top it off."

—[...] [Myster]y Book Reviews

"...a frothy girl drink of houses, hunks and whodunit narrated in a breezy first person."

—Lyda Phillips, The Nashville Scene

"VERDICT: The hilarious dialog and the tension between Savannah and Rafe will delight fans of chick-lit mysteries and romantic suspense."

—Jo Ann Vicarel, Library Journal

"... equal parts charming and sexy, with a side of suspense. Hero and heroine, Savannah Martin and Rafe Collier, are a pairing of perfection."

—Paige Crutcher, examiner.com

"...hooks you in the first page and doesn't let go until the last!"

—Lynda Coker, Between the Pages

"With a dose of southern charm and a bad boy you won't want to forget, A Cutthroat Business has enough wit and sexual chemistry to rival Janet Evanovich."

—Tasha Alexander,
New York Times bestselling author of Murder in the Floating City

"A delicious and dazzling romantic thriller ... equal parts wit and suspense, distilled with a Southern flavor as authentic as a mint julep."

—Kelli Stanley, bestselling author and Bruce Alexander award winner,
Nox Dormienda

Also in this series:

Savannah Martin has always been a good girl, doing what was expected and fully expecting life to fall into place in its turn. But when her perfect husband turns out to be a lying, cheating slimeball—and bad in bed to boot—Savannah kicks the jerk to the curb and embarks on life on her own terms. With a new apartment, a new career, and a brand new outlook on life, she's all set to take the world by storm. If only the world would stop throwing her curveballs...

When Shelby Ferguson, Savannah's ex-husband's new wife, begs Savannah's help in figuring out what's going on with Bradley, Savannah can't in good conscience say no. Shelby has no one else to turn to, no one to whom she can admit that her marriage is on the rocks and that Bradley may be straying.

But helping Shelby turns out to be just the tip of the iceberg. With two different sets of buyers vying to purchase Mrs. Jenkins's house, and an escaped prisoner targeting Savannah, she has more than enough to deal with. And that's before TBI rookie Manny Ortega is shot down in cold blood.

With Savannah's boyfriend Rafe Collier, and homicide detective Tamara Grimaldi, along with the combined forces of the Tennessee Bureau of Investigations and the Metro Nashville Police Department, all busy looking for Manny's murderer, it's up to Savannah to juggle buyers and adulterers and vandals and murderers, and come out on top... without losing her Southern Belle poise or her life in the process.

KICKOUT CLAUSE

Jenna Bennett

KICKOUT CLAUSE
SAVANNAH MARTIN MYSTERY #7

Interior design: April Martinez, GraphicFantastic.com

ISBN: 978-0-9899434-4-4

MAGPIE INK

One

In real estate, a kickout clause is something that allows a seller—under certain circumstances, after accepting an offer—to accept another offer and kick the first one to the curb.

In life, an equivalent would be something like accepting an offer of marriage from a gentleman of means, while reserving the right to accept an offer from another gentleman of bigger means, should he happen to come along before the marriage is consummated.

Rafe finished the renovations on his grandmother's old house on Potsdam Street the first week in March. After three days on the market, we had an offer to purchase that included a sale-of-home contingency. In other words, the potential new owners already had a condo they had to sell before they could buy Mrs. Jenkins's house. And although there wasn't really much doubt that they'd find someone to buy it—Nashville's real estate market was reasonably brisk, and the location, in the downtown area called the Gulch, was hot—we still ran the risk of something going wrong, and of having to wait month after month while hoping and praying that things would work out.

So being the smart and savvy real estate agent that I am, I advised my client—and boyfriend—to accept the offer but to attach a rider known as 'seller's right to continue to market property.' That's what set up the kickout clause. And it was a good thing I did, because two days later we received another offer, this time without the sale-of-home contingency. The second set of potential owners had no house or condo they had to sell before they could afford to buy Mrs. J's house.

At that point, I notified Brian, the agent for the first potential buyers, that his clients had 48 hours to decide whether they wanted Mrs. J's house badly enough that they were willing to take a chance on ending up with two properties for a while if they couldn't sell the condo in a timely manner, or whether they wanted to withdraw their offer and let the other people have the house.

While they were thinking about it, I received a phone call from Shelby Ferguson asking me to meet her for coffee.

Shelby is my ex-husband Bradley's wife. She was his paralegal while we were married, and she became his wife less than two weeks after our divorce was final.

In other words, I had no reason whatsoever to like her, and none at all to agree to meet her.

And I must have made my feelings clear, because she said, "Please, Savannah. There's nobody else I can ask."

I found that very hard to believe, and told her so. The last time I'd seen her, in November, she and a girlfriend had stopped by an open house I was hosting, and they had whispered about me behind my back. I was pretty sure I'd overheard the word 'chunky.' To add insult to injury, Shelby had been pregnant and glowing, while I'd been battling morning sickness and weight gain and wondering whether Rafe would be happy or upset about knocking me up.

"It's true!" I could hear panic lacing through her voice. "I can't tell any of my friends that my husband... that Bradley..."

She ran down before she could get the damning information out, but I could read between the lines. She couldn't tell her friends and family that her husband was a jackass, but she could tell me, because I'd been married to Bradley too, and was only too familiar with that fact.

I allowed myself a few seconds to gloat—silently—before I took pity on her and agreed to meet.

She must really be desperate, because she said, "Now?"

"Sure," I said, throwing caution to the wind. And hey, this way I got it over with. No need to fret about it until tomorrow if I took care of it today. "There's a Starbucks on Hillsboro Road, right?"

"We can't meet there!"

We couldn't? I was trying to do her a favor, by picking a meeting place close to Bradley's townhouse—the one I'd shared with him before Shelby entered the picture—so she wouldn't have to drive so far in her condition.

"I'll come to East Nashville," Shelby said. "Nobody will recognize me there."

Oh, sure. These days, people from all over town come to East Nashville to eat and shop, even from Shelby's snobby Green Hills. But if she preferred to believe she'd be safely slumming in my neighborhood, she was welcome to.

"There's a coffee shop on the corner of Tenth and East Main," I told her. "Brew-ha-ha."

"That's the name of it?"

I told her it was, and resisted the temptation to ask whether she didn't think it was a cute name. Between you and me, I find it a little too cute, but the coffee's good. "It's just after you pass the gym."

"I'll find it," Shelby said. "Three o'clock?"

I checked my watch. Less than forty five minutes from now. "That's fine."

"I'll see you there." She clicked off before I had the chance to respond. I arched my brows and dialed Rafe.

"Something funny just happened," I told him when he answered.

I could almost see one eyebrow arch. "Strange funny? Or ha-ha funny?"

A little of both, actually. "Shelby Ferguson called. You know, Bradley's new wife?" Or not exactly new—they'd been married for almost three years—but new since me.

There was a moment's pause. "Why?"

"She didn't say. Just that she needed to talk to me. And that she couldn't talk to anyone else."

"Maybe she found out you had dinner with him back in December," Rafe said.

Dear Lord. I could feel myself turn pale. I had had dinner with Bradley in December. And he'd been very concerned that Shelby not learn about it, too.

But surely, since we were into March, if she was going to hear about it, she would have heard by now? "You don't really think so, do you?"

"Dunno," Rafe said. "What'd she say?"

"Just what I told you."

There was a pause. "He cheating again?"

"I wouldn't be surprised," I said. "He cheated on me. There's no reason he wouldn't cheat on her."

In fact, I've never understood women who marry cheaters—men they've been sleeping with while he was married to someone else. If he cheated on his first wife, do they really think he won't cheat on them?

"You gonna meet her?" Rafe asked.

"Three o'clock at Brew-ha-ha."

"She ain't wasting any time."

No, she wasn't.

"You want I should go with you?"

"I don't think I need a bodyguard," I said, "do you? She must be at least eight months pregnant by now. I don't think she'd risk a fistfight." And if she did, I could probably take her.

"Prob'ly," Rafe agreed. "You worried?"

"Not at all. Even if she has found out about that dinner back in December, it wasn't like it meant anything. I just needed some information about Bradley's uncle. It's not like I'd want him back."

"No?" I could hear the grin.

"Absolutely not. Why would I want Bradley when I have you?"

"I can't imagine," Rafe said.

I couldn't, either. "And anyway, it isn't like Bradley would be interested in taking me back even if Shelby weren't in the picture. If he's cheating again, he's moved on. To someone who isn't pregnant and who can still do it on top of the desk."

There was a beat. "I thought you said he was boring in bed."

"He was boring with me. But I'm sure he and Shelby did it on the desk. Or in the broom closet. They worked together, after all."

Rafe didn't say anything for another second. "I have a desk," he told me.

My boyfriend works for the TBI, the Tennessee Bureau of Investigation. For the past ten years, from the time they sprang him from prison at twenty until last December, he worked undercover, doing his best to eliminate a far-reaching SATG—South American Theft Gang—with fingers in a lot of pies all over the southeastern United States. In the process, he blew his cover sky high, and had to retire from undercover work. He retired from the TBI altogether for about two months, until civilian life drove him crazy and he decided to accept the position they offered of training other undercover agents. These days, he spent most of his time in the gym, teaching rookies how to become Quick Draw McGraw and excel at hand-to-hand combat, and the rest of the time in the field, teaching them surveillance and how to evade capture. But he did have a desk, for whenever he had to do paperwork. It was located in a cubicle, on a floor full of other cubicles, and I draw the line there.

"I'll make to love to you anywhere there's a door I can close," I informed him. "But not in a cubicle at the TBI. You'd probably get fired if we got caught."

"Might be worth it," Rafe said.

"No, it wouldn't. You love your job."

"Not as much as I'd love to get you naked on top of my desk."

I blushed. "You can get me naked on top of the dining room table instead. Unless you're working late tonight?"

He'd only had the job for a few weeks, and so far he had worked late a couple nights a week. That was when he took one or more of his charges into the night to play cops and robbers. They'd practice following each other around, on foot or by car, and see who could get away without being caught. It must be fun, because he always came home with a big grin on his face.

"Not tonight. Tonight I'm all yours."

I don't think I imagined the innuendo in his voice. In fact, I'm sure of it. When I didn't answer, because I was too busy fanning myself, he grinned. I could hear it in his voice, even if I couldn't see him. "Have fun with Shelby, darlin'. Think about me."

"Sure thing," I managed.

The last thing I heard before he hung up was a chuckle, low and ripe, the kind of sound that trickles down your back and leaves goosebumps in its wake.

I GOT TO BREW-HA-HA BEFORE SHELBY, but only by a minute or two. I'd barely planted my posterior at a table by the window when I saw an eggshell white minivan pull up outside. Bradley had threatened to get her one for Christmas, and I guess he'd come through. After a moment the door opened and Shelby got out and waddled toward the entrance to the coffee house.

I did my best not to stare—staring is rude—but it was hard.

Last time I'd seen her, three or four months ago, she'd looked great: dressed in snug jeans and a shirt that draped becomingly over her baby bump, positively glowing with health and pregnancy hormones.

That woman was nowhere to be seen today.

She must have gained thirty pounds in the time since I'd last seen her, to where her butt was now the size of a doublewide trailer, and clad in something that looked suspiciously like polyester. The shiny blonde hair that used to hang like a curtain to her shoulders, looked stringy and thin around her much rounder face. And it was mousy brown. I guess maybe she couldn't bleach it while she was pregnant, so she'd gone back to her natural color for the duration.

She scanned the room until she found me, and then waddled over to pull out the chair on the other side of the table. "Thanks for coming out, Savannah." She dropped down on it with an unladylike groan.

"Swollen ankles?" I asked sympathetically, while inside I was grinning like mad.

She made a face. "Pregnancy sucks."

I hadn't felt that way about mine. I'd struggled with morning sickness and worry, and with sleeping more than usual and gaining weight, but I hadn't thought that being pregnant sucked. Being pregnant without knowing whether my baby daddy was alive or dead or would ever come back to Nashville... now, *that* had sucked a bit. But I had rather enjoyed the pregnancy itself, or would have, if it hadn't been for that other thing.

"What can I get you?" I asked and got to my feet. "I guess coffee is out?"

She nodded. "Hot chocolate, please. And some kind of muffin or scone."

"Just a minute." I headed to the counter, where I placed an order for two hot chocolates—I ordered mine out of solidarity, and also because it sounded good—and an orange cranberry muffin for Shelby. That sounded good, as well, but I resisted the temptation to indulge. I wasn't eating for two, after all, and the hot chocolate had calories enough.

The barista told me she'd bring the drinks to the table once they were made, so I paid and took the muffin and headed back to Shelby, who was scanning the room, a nervous look on her face. When I stopped beside her, she jumped.

"Here." I put the plate with the muffin down. "Orange cranberry. The hot chocolate is on its way."

"Thank you." She started picking at the muffin while I took my seat on the other side of the table again. I waited for her to begin the conversation with something that mattered, but when she looked up and addressed me, what she said was, "You look good."

"Thank you." I should have known better. Like me, Shelby was raised a Southern Belle, and we excel at small talk. Flattery. Beating around the bush. Putting people at their ease before getting to the point.

"Have you lost weight?"

"Since the last time you saw me? Probably. I was pregnant then."

The way she looked down at my stomach was impossible to miss, as was the question scrolling across her eyes like a marquee.

"I had a miscarriage," I said. It had taken several months to get to the point where I could say those words out loud without dissolving into tears, but my voice was even. "Just a week or so after the open house in Green Hills where you stopped by."

"I'm sorry," Shelby said. "Brad..." She trailed off, blushing.

Surely she didn't think I'd mind if she brought up Bradley's name? "What about him?"

"Brad told me you had a miscarriage while you were married to him, too."

I nodded. "I seem to be prone to them." And that was one of my biggest fears, that I'd never be able to carry a baby to term. I did my best not to let it show in my voice, though. "I'm hoping I'll get lucky the third time."

She slanted another glance down at my midriff. "Are you expecting again?"

I shook my head. "Not yet. We haven't really been trying."

Of course, we hadn't really been trying to avoid it, either. But in spite of all the sex we'd had, somehow I hadn't ended up getting pregnant in the past two months. But that was fine with me, honestly. I wanted Rafe's baby, but our relationship was still very new, and on top of that, I was nervous from the last miscarriage. Having a little extra time before I had to deal with another pregnancy didn't bother me. It would happen when it did. So far, I hadn't had any problems conceiving, after all; it was what happened afterwards that was the problem.

"Brad told me you were thinking of getting remarried." Shelby's eyes lingered on the ring on my finger, with a stone just about the same shade of blue as her eyes.

I twisted it self-consciously. It had been a Christmas gift from Rafe. Not an engagement ring, he'd informed me, because he hadn't thought we were ready for that level of commitment the day after he showed back up in my life. I'm pretty sure a little part of him had been worried that I wouldn't want him. But at the same time, he'd wanted to claim ownership of me, and to do that, he needed me to wear his ring. I was happy to do it because there was nothing I wanted more than to belong to Rafe, and to know that he belonged to me too.

"We're thinking about it," I told Shelby. "We're not quite there yet, but we're getting closer."

At least I hoped we were. We hadn't talked about it again, but things were settling down between us, into a nice, comfortable way of life. Rafe's new job helped. He hadn't liked being unemployed.

"I'm happy for you," Shelby said formally, just as the barista crossed the floor with a steaming cup of hot chocolate in each hand. The conversation ceased while we both got busy stirring and (in my case) spooning the whipped cream and white chocolate shavings off the top of the cup and into my mouth with the dark chocolate stick.

"So what's going on?" I asked eventually. Mother brought me up as a Southern Belle, too, but I'm recovering, and besides, we'd already done the preliminaries.

Only we didn't seem to have done them well enough, because Shelby glanced up at me. "What do you mean?"

I was going to have to drag—or more likely tease—every tidbit of information out of her, it seemed. "It's nice to see you." A slight white lie. Although I didn't mind so much, actually, now that she looked like hell while I looked pretty good. "But we're not exactly friends. So what can I do for you?"

She looked at me as if she couldn't quite believe I'd cut to the point so quickly, and for a second it seemed like she didn't know what to say. Then she looked down at her cup again, as if the motion of stirring was beyond interesting. "It's Brad."

No kidding.

I bit my tongue and didn't tell her I'd assumed as much. "What is he doing?" Not that I couldn't make an educated guess.

The guess must have echoed in my voice, because Shelby glanced up and said, "He isn't cheating. He wouldn't do that to me."

"He did it to me," I said. And added, "Oh, wait. You know that. You were there."

She had the decency to blush. "Brad loves me."

Sure. I thought it, but I managed to bite back the word.

Although the thing is, he probably did. I'd believed he loved me, back when we were married. Back when I didn't know better, and I didn't realize that what we had didn't come close to being love.

But maybe he did love her, the best he was able. They'd managed to stay married longer than Bradley and I had, anyway. If not by a whole lot. And toward the end of our just under two years together, Bradley had been getting Shelby naked on top of the desk at Ferncliff & Morton with regularity. She might not want to believe he was doing it again, but I had no problem imagining it.

"He's not!" Shelby insisted.

I wanted to ask how she knew, but I didn't get the chance. The bell above the door tinkled, and Shelby glanced in that direction. And turned pale.

"What?" I glanced over my shoulder.

She lowered her voice. "That man who just came in..."

"What about him?"

"He looks... dangerous."

He did, rather. My lips curved.

"Oh, no!" Shelby breathed.

"What?"

Her eyes were huge, and unless I missed my guess, terrified. "He's coming this way!"

Of course he was. I looked up again just as Rafe stopped beside the table and gave me the kind of smile that curled my toes inside the suede boots. "Afternoon, darlin'."

Two

"Hi." The sight of him took my breath away, as usual. "What are you doing here?"

"Had an hour to kill," Rafe said. He put one hand on the back of my chair and one hand on the table in front of me, and leaned in.

There was a time when I would have been horrified at the thought of him kissing me in public. Not because of the kiss—I wanted that—but because of who might be looking and what they might think and whether or not they would call my mother and tell her that I'd been kissing LaDonna Collier's good-for-nothing colored boy in broad daylight.

Those days were long gone. I tilted my head back and closed my eyes, the better to enjoy the feel of his mouth on mine.

He took his sweet time, and by the time he straightened, my stomach had turned to liquid. It had nothing at all to do with the hot chocolate. If he had suggested it, I might almost have considered getting naked on top of this table, right here and now.

Almost.

Shelby hadn't said a word, and I decided to ignore the social niceties as I concentrated on smoothing out the wrinkles in Rafe's T-shirt, where I'd held on for dear life. She probably wouldn't want an introduction anyway, and he wasn't here to meet her. To have a look at her, maybe, and to send the message back to Bradley that I was well and truly spoken for—assuming Shelby had any plans of telling Bradley about our conversation—but Shelby herself was of secondary interest to him.

Besides, I had a hard time tearing my gaze away.

He knew it, too. I could see it in his eyes when he trailed his fingertips down my cheek. "Hold that thought," he told me, his voice laced with laughter and a bit of residual heat. Apparently he wasn't entirely unaffected either, which was nice to know.

And then he straightened and glanced at Shelby. "Sorry to interrupt."

She squeaked something. I'm not even sure what it was.

Rafe turned back to me. "I'll see you later, darlin'."

I nodded. Like Shelby, I couldn't quite get my voice to cooperate yet. All I could do was sit there, mesmerized, as he leaned in for another kiss, this one just a soft brush of his lips across mine. But I did manage to refrain from turning to watch him saunter away when he headed across the floor to the counter and ordered his coffee to go. I even managed to keep my back to him after he took the cup of coffee out the door. I could hear the roar of the Harley Davidson starting up—how on earth did he plan to drive that and drink coffee at the same time?—but I didn't turn to watch him drive away.

Shelby did. She watched him every step of the way across the floor, and she made sure he was well and truly gone before she leaned closer, across the table, and breathed, "Who was that?!"

I opened my mouth. But before I could tell her, she'd added, "Wouldn't your boyfriend mind that you were kissing someone else?"

"That *was* my boyfriend," I said. And had the pleasure of seeing Shelby struck dumb. At least for a few seconds. She stared at me, and at the door where Rafe had disappeared, and back at me again.

"You're dating *that guy*?"

Yes. Although— "We've gone a bit beyond dating."

Shelby's eyes widened and her voice lowered. "You're sleeping with him?"

Well, duh. That kiss, coupled with the promise that he'd see me later... surely there hadn't been much doubt? "Every night," I said. "We live together."

It took a few moments, or more than a few, but eventually she found her voice again. "I thought you were thinking of marrying some man you grew up with."

"We did grow up together." Although Shelby was probably thinking of Todd Satterfield, the son of my mother's gentleman friend, Sweetwater sheriff Bob Satterfield.

Todd was my mother's choice of second husband for me. He also happens to be my brother Dix's best friend, and we had dated for a year in high school. It was mostly because Dix dated my best friend Charlotte, but my mother had fixated on Todd from that moment on. She had approved of Bradley, who had been another tall, blond, Southern lawyer, but since that hadn't worked out, it would set her world to rights if I married Todd on my second go-round. Needless to say, she does not approve of my relationship with Rafe. For a number of reasons, but Todd features large. "Rafe is from Sweetwater too," I said.

"His name is Rafe?"

"Rafael Collier." And while I'd grown up in the Martin Mansion—what Rafe refers to as 'the mausoleum on the hill'—he'd spent his formative years in the Bog, the mobile home park on the other side of town. But we did both hail from Sweetwater, and we'd gone to high school together for one year, until he graduated and moved on, first to Alabama for the summer, and then to Riverbend Penitentiary for two years.

"Wow." She stared at me. And then—I should have known—she lowered her voice until it was just above a whisper. "So is it true what they say? You know, about black men...?"

In case you don't know what it is they say about black men—I didn't, the first time I heard the expression—it's that they're well-endowed. Physically.

And I should have resisted. I know I should. I just couldn't. I stuck my tongue firmly in my cheek and told her, "I don't have a lot of scope for comparison." Only Bradley. "But from what I can tell... yes."

In other words, my boyfriend blows your husband out of the water.

Shelby stared at me. "Wow."

I nodded and refrained from telling her that size isn't everything. Because while it isn't—it can't possibly be—there was no doubt that my sex life had improved about a million percent when I took up with Rafe. I'm not sure the size of his personal equipment was the reason, though. I fell for him before we got naked together, before I'd ever laid eyes on the equipment in question, and the fact that I'm in love with him surely has something to do with the fact that our sex life is good. And also, he's had rather a lot of practice, so he knows how to use said equipment. I think it's more about that, than about the size.

Although I had no complaints about the size of his personal package.

But it was probably time to get the conversation back on track. "We were talking about Bradley. And how he's not cheating."

Shelby nodded.

"If that's not it, what's the problem?"

"I don't know!" Her voice rose, and she immediately adjusted it, with a guilty look around. As if anyone cared. This was East Nashville, and we're made of sterner stuff out here. "He isn't talking to me."

"At all?"

"Of course not at all," Shelby said impatiently. "But he isn't home much. He goes in to work early and stays late. Sometimes he works at night. And when I ask him what's going on, he just tells me not to worry about it."

Not to worry her pretty little head about it, most likely. He'd told me that once, as well. I hadn't objected, but considering that we'd been divorced for almost three years now, yet the memory still had the power to make me want to kick him where it hurt, I probably should have.

"I see," I said.

And I did. Back when I'd been the one worrying my pretty little head about Bradley's whereabouts, he'd been busy banging Shelby in the broom closet at work. He was probably doing the same thing now, with whoever his new paralegal was. Or the mailroom girl. Or one of the other junior partners. Or a client. There wasn't much I would put past him. Once a cheater, always a cheater, as far as I'm concerned.

And let's face it, all the signs were there. The very same signs that had alerted me. He stayed out late, citing work. He came home after I'd fallen asleep and didn't wake me. Or he was so tired that he was just going to relax in front of the TV for a while, and then he conveniently fell asleep on the sofa so he could spend the night in the living room instead of sharing the bed with me.

Classic guilty conscience brought on by diddling someone other than his wife.

"Are you still having sex?" I asked, point blank.

Shelby blinked once, as if I'd inadvertently splashed her with cold water. Several seconds went by before she found her voice. "It's been a couple of weeks."

My face must have given me away, because she scrambled to reassure me that, "It's just because of the baby. The doctor said that relations in the last six weeks could bring on premature labor."

Sure.

I mean, I'm sure the doctor did tell her that, if that's what she was telling me. She had no reason to lie about it. But if Bradley wasn't getting any at home, that made it all the more likely that he'd gone out and found some elsewhere. As he'd told me once, he was a man and men had needs.

"I don't mean to harp," I said, "but how do you know he's not cheating?"

"Bradley loves me! He wouldn't do that to me!"

Right.

We sat in silence for a minute while I tried to come up with something to say. To me it was obvious what was going on, but if Shelby was unwilling—or unable—to see or acknowledge it, what was I supposed to do? I couldn't force her to believe.

"What is it you think I can do for you?" I asked eventually. She must have had a reason for wanting to get together, after all. And if it wasn't to commiserate over a cheating husband, what was it?

She looked up at me, her eyes miserable. "I need you to help me figure out what's going on."

Whoa.

"How do you want me to do that?"

"I don't know. Follow him around?"

Oh, sure. Because I had nothing better to do than stalk my ex-husband. "Why me?"

"There's no one else I can ask," Shelby said, and burst into tears.

Things went downhill from there.

I understood where she was coming from, of course. There really was no one else she could ask, not without letting all her friends know that something was going on with Bradley. She might not be willing to admit it, not to me, but I think she knew that any one of her friends would jump to the same conclusion I had. Or maybe she just didn't want anyone else to know that she and Bradley hadn't had sex for weeks.

She'd attempted to stake out her husband herself, she told me, but she had run into the twin problems of needing to visit the bathroom every thirty minutes because of the pregnancy, and the fact that Bradley had recognized her car.

I had dealt with the bathroom problem myself once, when I was parked outside a warehouse waiting for someone to show up, so I could relate. And I'd also gotten caught, although not by Bradley. "What happened?"

"He got angry," Shelby sniffed.

Another blatantly obvious sign of a guilty conscience. Bradley was far too well-bred to raise his voice under most circumstances. In my case, I'd gotten caught by Rafe—whom I hadn't been looking for—but he hadn't been angry at all. Sometimes he seemed angry, but I'd come to realize that it was only because he was worried about me. It wasn't that he was worried about himself, or about what I might discover.

I knew I had no reason to feel bad for Shelby. I owed her nothing. She'd stolen my husband. But the truth was, if she hadn't, I'd never have met Rafe again, and I wouldn't now be deliriously happy. I'd still be miserably married to Bradley, and it would be me sitting on the other side of the table needing help. By now I might have had a child or two, tying me even tighter to the bastard.

"I suppose it wouldn't hurt for me to take a look," I said.

Shelby brightened immediately, although the damage was already done. I'd thought she looked bad when she walked in, thirty pounds overweight and frumpy. Now she was thirty pounds overweight, frumpy, red-faced and soggy from crying. Her mascara had run, her eyes were rimmed with red, and she looked awful.

"What do you want me to?" I added and pushed a napkin across the table toward her. "Here. Blow your nose."

Shelby dabbed delicately at her face, but didn't blow. Much too unseemly. Southern Belles only blow their noses in the privacy of their own bathrooms.

"Can you find out where he's going? And what's going on?"

"I can try," I said. "I mean, I can try to catch him after work one day and see whether he goes home."

Shelby sniffed. "Today?"

I thought about it. Rafe was working until six. Bradley would most likely leave the office at or before five. I could leave Brew-ha-ha, head over to Ferncliff & Morton, and park myself outside for an hour or two. If he came out by five thirty, I could follow him and see where he went. If he didn't... well, then I would just go home to Rafe, and no harm done.

"I suppose."

"Thank you," Shelby said.

"Just as long as you understand that I may not discover anything at all. Or if I do, that you may not like what I discover."

She nodded, but I could see in her eyes that she really didn't believe I'd discover that Bradley was running off to some fleabag motel to meet another woman. Shelby actually trusted him. I wasn't sure whether to laugh or cry, so I did neither, just pushed my chair back. "I should go. Just in case he leaves work early."

Shelby nodded. "You know where he works?"

"Has he left Ferncliff & Morton?"

She shook her head.

"Then I know where he works."

Shelby heaved herself to her feet. I waited for her to trundle toward the exit, but she pointed the other way. "I have to... um..."

Visit the restroom. Right.

"I'll call you later," I said, and left her to take care of business.

THE FIRM OF FERNCLIFF & Morton specializes in family law, which has to do with marriage and divorce, adoption, paternity testing, surrogacy and the like. In other words, I married a divorce attorney, and I daresay that should have tipped me off as to Bradley's true nature. I can only say in my defense that I was young and stupid.

Ferncliff & Morton is located in the Germantown area, an urban regentrification neighborhood north of downtown. It took me less than ten minutes to get there. I knew exactly where it was, since Bradley had started working there straight out of law school. I'd visited Ferncliff & Morton before. And I was still driving the same car I'd been driving then: a pale blue Volvo, six years old, that Bradley had bought me just after we got married.

This mission would have been easier had Ferncliff & Morton been located in downtown. I would have had an easier time disappearing among the other cars and people. Up here, it was more likely that Bradley would catch me spying on him.

Then again, in downtown, he'd probably keep the car in a parking garage, one he'd access from inside the building, so I wouldn't see him at all until he came driving out. At least up here he had to park in plain view.

Germantown is an old industrial area, full of old warehouses and turn-of-the-last-century architecture. Ferncliff & Morton was located in one of the old Victorian homes: a two story brick beauty with a mansard roof and arched windows. The employee parking lot is in the rear, but I drove down the street in front of the building first, just to make sure the BMW Bradley had been driving in December wasn't parked out front.

It wasn't. I peered up at the building itself as I drove slowly past.

Unless Bradley's office had been moved along with his promotions, he worked on the second floor, on the right as one came up the stairs. That would put him on the left hand corner of the second floor from where I was. There was a light on in the corner office.

I took the next right and then pointed the Volvo down the alley behind the buildings. About halfway down was the Ferncliff & Morton employee parking lot. And there was Bradley's navy blue SUV parked near the back door.

Of course I couldn't stay there. I couldn't park in the lot and hope he wouldn't notice the car he'd bought me six years ago. I had to find somewhere else to wait, somewhere out of the way, where I could still keep an eye on the SUV but without being seen.

The answer turned out to be on the next block. If I parked at the curb, there was about a ten foot gap between two buildings where I could look directly at the back door to Ferncliff & Morton.

And that's where I sat, while the seconds and minutes ticked by, with agonizing slowness.

All around me, people were coming out of buildings and getting into cars, driving away. It was getting close to the end of the workday and I'm sure a lot of people were hoping to get a jump on the traffic. With all the people moving to Nashville lately, our traffic problems have exploded.

The first time the back door at F&M opened, I sat up straight in my seat, my hand already reaching for the keys in the ignition. But it wasn't Bradley. It was a blonde, dressed in a navy business suit, with a briefcase. Diana Morton, one of the senior partners. She was into her forties, so past the first bloom of youth, but still attractive, in a cool ice-queen sort of way. If Bradley was messing around with anyone at the office, it probably wasn't Diana. Unless something had changed in the past couple of years, she had a husband, and anyway, I doubted she'd give Bradley the time of day.

She got into a white Mercedes and drove away down the alley. I went back to keeping watch.

The next time the door opened, a man came out, but it wasn't Bradley. Tall, gray hair, dark suit. Nathan Ferncliff, another of the senior partners. His car was a BMW.

After that came someone I didn't know, who must be new. Young, handsome, male. Another BMW. Not Bradley's type.

The receptionist left, the same receptionist Ferncliff & Morton had employed for as long as Bradley had worked for them. Carolyn

Wilkins. Middle-aged, overweight, a single mother of two. Bradley definitely wasn't cheating on Shelby with her.

Carolyn didn't have a Mercedes, nor a BMW. She got into a prosaic Toyota and drove away. It was a nice Toyota, just a few years old, but not on the same level as the luxury cars.

I waited some more, and finally the door opened and Bradley came out.

Last time I'd had occasion to spend time with him, I had reflected that married life—to Shelby—must agree with him, because he'd gained about twenty pounds since we got divorced, and he'd looked smug and self-satisfied.

This afternoon, that excess weight was nowhere in evidence. He must have gone on one hell of a diet to drop that much weight that fast.

Shelby hadn't mentioned the sudden, rapid weight loss. Then again, she didn't know I'd seen Bradley in December, so maybe she hadn't thought it necessary.

It struck me as interesting, though.

And not only did he look almost gaunt, inside an oversized suit that hung from his shoulders, but he looked pale and drawn, too.

Granted, it was the time of years when we all looked pale. Winter was just ending, and it had been a cold one by Nashville standards. Sometimes we have temperatures in the 60s and 70s through the cold months, rendering them not cold at all, but this winter we'd had snow and sleet and just general ickiness since before Christmas. It was still a little unseasonably cold. Sometimes, by mid-March, spring is in full swing, with flowers blooming and sunny, warm weather.

Not this year. I was still wearing a jacket over my blouse and skirt, and boots instead of pumps on my feet. Sandals were just a fond memory.

Anyway, Bradley looked thin and pale. Unhealthy. Like something was wrong, either physically or emotionally.

A guilty conscience could do that to a man. I didn't remember it happening when he'd been cheating on me with Shelby, but she was expecting a baby and things were different now.

He stood for a few moments on the steps outside the door looking around, before heading down to the SUV. I watched as he unlocked the door and got in. And then I watched as he reversed out of the parking spot and drove off down the alley. In the opposite direction of the way I was parked.

I had to scramble to get the car turned around. In fact, I was still in the middle of a highly illegal U-turn when Bradley came around the corner and saw me.

So much for hoping he wouldn't notice I was there. There was no way he could avoid it, with the way I was skidding across his lane so he had to slow down to let me get out of the way.

And because he was already familiar with my car, of course he slowed to a stop and powered down his window. "Savannah?"

I got the Volvo straightened out and into the proper lane—except it was the improper lane now. And there was no way I could make another U-ie and fall in behind him without being transparently, blatantly obvious.

So I did the next best thing and pretended this was a coincidence. "Hi, Bradley. Sorry."

"No problem," Bradley said, glancing around. "Is everything OK?"

"Fine. I just had to turn the car around. And since nobody was coming, I thought I'd make it easy." I took a breath and added, innocently, "Are you on your way home from the office?"

Bradley nodded. "You?"

"I had an appointment—" I caught sight of a sign out of the corner of my eye, "—at the internet dating agency."

Bradley looked worried. "If you're looking for company, Savannah, I'm sure there are safer ways to find a date."

"I'm not." Sheesh. "I was just... um... dropping off some paperwork. For a client. A real estate client."

"Oh," Bradley said, his face clearing.

"I don't have a problem getting a date. I'm practically engaged."

His eyes glanced off the ring on my finger, where my left hand was resting on the steering wheel. "Congratulations."

"Thank you. How is Shelby?"

"Fine," Bradley said. I wondered whether he truly believed it, or he had no idea that she wasn't.

"How long before the baby comes?"

"Less than three weeks." He looked tense at the thought.

"Are you all right?" I asked.

He met my eyes for a second, before looking away. "Fine."

"You look..." I hesitated, "tired."

"I'm fine," Bradley said again and put the car in gear. "It was good to see you, Savannah." He made no effort to sound like he meant it.

"You, too," I said, although he was already driving away.

There was absolutely no point in trying to follow him. He'd notice me, especially now that I was already on his mind. And he knew where I lived, and that it was in the opposite direction of the one he was going, so I had no excuse for going his way. I'd be better off trying again tomorrow, and seeing if I couldn't borrow another car before I did, one he wouldn't recognize.

So I watched in the rearview mirror while he disappeared down the street, before I headed in the direction of the Jefferson Street Bridge and East Nashville myself.

Three

Rafe wasn't there yet when I came home, so I started dinner while I waited for him.

When he first moved in with me, the day after Christmas, I'd gone overboard on the domesticity. I'd been so happy to have him with me full time, and so worried that he'd get tired of me and leave, that I'd done everything I could think of to make myself indispensable. Home cooked meals on the table when he walked through the door, fresh laundry every other day, sex whenever and wherever he wanted it—not that that last one was a hardship. After months of never knowing when I might see him again—if ever—being able to touch him whenever I wanted was a gift from God.

But I digress. As it turned out, the attempts to domesticate him were having the opposite effect of the one I intended.

Oh, he'd enjoyed the food and the clean laundry and especially the sex, but he was going crazy trying to be the man he thought I wanted. Someone safe and settled and out of harm's way. We were both much happier now that he'd gone back to work for the TBI and I had stopped trying so hard to hold on to him.

So I cooked, but I didn't worry too much about it. And I also didn't use the downtime between stirring the pot to slip into the bedroom to change into 'something more comfortable.' I'd met him at the door in lingerie before—not that there's anything comfortable about the kind of lingerie men like—and it had usually ended with him carrying me to bed while the food burned. But I had learned that it didn't take lingerie to achieve that effect, and that he knew I was available even if I didn't make it blatantly obvious. It also didn't matter if we stopped to eat first. He knew I wanted him either way, and I was in no doubt whatsoever that he wanted me.

In short, I stopped trying so hard and let things just develop the way they wanted to. And we were both happier. Incidentally, I also felt safer about our relationship, perhaps because I was less obsessively concerned about every minute expression that flitted across his face. He loved me. He was here. I could relax a little.

So instead of changing out of skirt and blouse into stiff and scratchy satin and lace, I changed into yoga pants and a T-shirt instead, and spent the time setting the table and stirring the pot and wondering what was going on with Shelby and Bradley.

She'd looked horrible, but he surely hadn't looked much better. Was he ill, maybe? Dying of cancer, but he just didn't want to tell Shelby about it when she was less than a month away from giving birth?

It was hard to believe that the man I'd been married to had it in him to be that considerate, but maybe his and Shelby's relationship was different from the way his and mine had been. He hadn't loved me; I was well aware of that. I hadn't loved him either, even if I'd kidded myself into thinking that maybe I did, a little. But he might love her. And if he did, he might actually be selfless enough to keep something like that from her, so as not to ruin her last month of pregnancy.

Or it could be something else. Something going on at work? Some sort of case that was taking its toll on him?

Or maybe I'd been right the first time, and he was just catting around. Just because Shelby assured me it was impossible, I wasn't as sanguine. He'd cheated on me. As far as I was concerned, that meant he could cheat on Shelby.

I heard the key in the lock about twenty minutes after I came home. Then the door opened, and I heard the thud of Rafe's boots hitting the floor. He padded into the kitchen on stocking feet and slipped his hands around my waist, under the T-shirt and up, his hands hot and hard against my skin. "Mmmm." He nuzzled my hair aside to kiss the side of my neck. "Smells good."

I wasn't sure whether he was talking about the food or me, but it didn't matter. I just leaned back against him, his front against my back, and closed my eyes. "Did you have a good day?"

"I got to kiss you halfway through it, so yeah." His breath was warm and his lips soft against my skin.

"I enjoyed that," I told him.

"I know." There was amusement in his voice. "You been waiting for me to come home so I could do it again, haven't you?"

No sense in denying the obvious. "Of course."

He turned me around—or maybe I turned around—in his arms, and then he kissed me. And as usual when he did, the world went away and all that mattered was the feeling of his mouth on mine. I looped my arms around his neck and hung on, hardly even aware of the heat of the stove against my back.

"Oops."

Rafe was aware, though, and pulled me aside, to lean against the cool front of the refrigerator instead. Before he went back to kissing me.

I was pretty sure we'd end up in the bedroom, but he must have been hungry, because after a minute—or an hour—he lifted his head. "What's for dinner?"

"Chicken casserole," I managed.

"What about dessert?"

"Me?"

"Sounds good." He let me go, but not without a last lingering brush of lips. "Can I take a shower?"

"Of course." I turned down the burner.

"Five minutes." He blew me a kiss and headed down the hall. A minute later I heard the shower kick on.

"So what did you think of Shelby?" I asked later, when we were sitting across from one another at the dining room table. His short crop of espresso-colored hair was still damp from the shower, and he was dressed in a T-shirt and a pair of jeans, with his feet bare.

"Bradley's an idiot," Rafe said.

It was the exact same thing he always said when I brought up the subject of my ex. Usually, the unspoken ending of the sentence was "Bradley's an idiot... for cheating on you," and I took it to mean the same thing now, except it must be a reflection on Shelby and not me, since that's what I'd asked him.

"She's usually better looking than she was today," I told him.

He shrugged, and muscles moved smoothly under the soft cotton. I took a sip of water. "What'd she want?"

"Something's going on with Bradley. She wanted me to help her figure out what."

He arched a brow, and I added, "There's no one else she can ask. She doesn't want to tell her friends and family that her husband's stepping out on her."

"Is that what he's doing?" He conveyed a chunk of chicken to his mouth and chewed.

"I assume he is," I said. "It's hard to imagine what else could be going on. Although..."

When I didn't continue, he twitched a brow at me.

"He didn't look good. When I saw him before Christmas, he had put on about twenty pounds since I was married to him, and he looked settled and self-satisfied. You know?"

Rafe just looked at me, and I added, "It happens sometimes, when men settle down and get comfortable."

He glanced at the plate of food, and then glanced down at his stomach, before looking back up at me.

"You don't have to worry," I said. "The way you look, you should be walking around naked all day, every day."

His lips curved. I added, "What was that all about, anyway? Showing up at Brew-ha-ha this afternoon?"

"Just curious," Rafe said and went back to eating.

And we were back where we started. Much as I would have enjoyed another reassurance that he found me more attractive that Shelby and that he thought Bradley was an idiot, I resisted the temptation to ask and forged on. "Well, if you think she looked bad, you should have seen him."

"I'm more interested in when you saw him," Rafe said.

Ah. Yes, I hadn't mentioned that, had I? "She asked me to help her figure out what was going on. So I drove up to Germantown, where the Ferncliff & Morton office is. I thought I'd try to follow him when he left work for the day, to see if he went home or somewhere else."

"What happened?"

I made a face. "He caught me. I was parked on the next street, looking at the parking lot in the back of the building, and instead of doing the logical thing and driving down the alley in the direction of home, he drove in the opposite direction and came around the block."

"And saw you."

I nodded. "He bought me the Volvo. I guess it was too much to expect he wouldn't recognize it."

There was no need, no need at all, to mention my crazy U-turn maneuver that had brought Bradley's attention to me.

Rafe's eyes narrowed. "You never told me that."

"What?"

"About the car."

What about it? "He bought it for me just after we got married. Or I guess I should say that *we* bought it for me, since Bradley's money was my money back then. When I left him, I got a settlement and the car, and he got the townhouse and everything in it, except for the few things that were mine."

"You need a new car," Rafe said.

I wouldn't mind a new car. There were times it rankled to still be driving the car my ex-husband had bought me. But at the moment, I didn't have the money to buy myself a new cashmere winter coat, let alone a new car. "It'll have to wait until I can afford it. Anyway, Bradley saw me and stopped. And he looked awful. In the past couple of months, he's lost all the weight he'd gained, plus more. He looked ill."

"Maybe he is ill."

"Or maybe it's just a guilty conscience."

Rafe nodded. "What happened?"

"We spoke for a minute. I made an excuse for why I was there, one that had nothing to do with him. And then he drove off in his direction and I drove off in mine. I didn't think I'd better follow him."

"No," Rafe said, lips twitching, "that was prob'ly a good idea."

"Now I don't know what to do."

He contemplated me for a second. "You call Shelby and tell her you tried and it didn't work out."

I nodded. That was probably what I should do.

"What?" Rafe said when I didn't immediately tell him I would.

"I guess I got sucked in. I'm curious now." And in spite of myself, and my suspicion that Bradley was simply up to his old tricks, I was a little worried. I didn't owe him any concern, not after the way he'd treated me, but I didn't wish anything too bad on him, either.

"He's Shelby's problem," Rafe said, pushing back from the table, "not yours."

"I know that. It's just..."

"Just what?"

"I feel bad for her. She's so worried. And he really didn't look good."

Rafe hesitated. And then he picked up his plate and walked into the kitchen. It wasn't what I expected him to do. From the look in his eyes when he'd pushed his chair back, I had assumed he was about to pick me up and take me to bed to remind me that I was supposed to have forgotten about Bradley.

"I'm sorry," I said when he walked back in.

He shook his head. "It's obvious I ain't gonna get any until we figure this out."

"You can have some whenever you want."

"Yeah," Rafe said, "but I don't want you thinking about Bradley while I'm inside you."

"I would never think about Bradley while you were... you know." I hadn't even thought about Bradley while Bradley was... you know.

"Who d'you think about?"

He sounded halfway between shocked, intrigued, and amused.

"Oh." I blushed, both at the realization that I'd spoken out loud, and at the confession I was about to make. "I... um... You, I guess. I mean, I guess I was fantasizing about one of Barbara Botticelli's romance heroes, you know, and since Barbara—I mean, Elspeth— probably thought about you when she wrote those books..."

Elspeth Caulfield, AKA historical romance author Barbara Botticelli, had grown up in a little town called Damascus not far from Sweetwater. She'd gone to Columbia High at the same time as Rafe and me, and she'd had a thing for him. He'd kept his distance from her, until one night when he didn't. The result was a twelve-year-old boy named David Flannery, who lived with his adopted parents in the West Meade section of Nashville.

None of us had known he existed until Elspeth died in September, and left everything she owned to the son no one knew she had. My brother Dix was her attorney, so it fell to him to track David down, and since he turned out to be Rafe's son as well, let's just say I took an interest.

I had always adored Barbara Botticelli's romance heroes, and after I met Rafe again, I saw him in every tall, dark and dangerous highwayman, sheikh, Indian brave and pirate I read about. It wasn't until after Elspeth's death that I realized I hadn't been the only one to imagine Rafe during the love scenes, which sort of killed it for me. I haven't picked up a Botticelli book since.

His smile widened. "No kidding?"

I shook my head. "I wasn't thinking about you specifically, since I didn't really know you when I was married to Bradley, but I thought about Barbara's—I mean, Elspeth's—romance heroes, and since Elspeth probably thought about you too..."

He tilted his head. "You ain't just saying this to make me feel better?"

"No." Why would I have to make him feel better? He had nothing to worry about. "Bradley was bad in bed. You know that. And we're divorced. You know that, too."

"And yet you're worried about him."

"He looked ill. And now that I have you..."

I trailed off.

Rafe arched a brow. "Now that you have me?"

I flushed. "I guess I don't care so much about Bradley and Shelby anymore. If he hadn't slept with her and divorced me, I wouldn't have become a realtor, and we wouldn't have met, and you wouldn't be here now. I wouldn't, either. I'd still be married to Bradley. So I can afford to be worried, you know?"

He didn't say anything for a moment, just looked at me. Then— "You want I should help you?"

"With what?" I got to my feet as well, to take my plate to the kitchen. He trailed behind me as I passed out of the dining room and into the hallway.

"With Bradley. Figuring out what's going on."

I glanced at him over my shoulder as I stopped in front of the sink. "How are you planning to do that?" I turned on the water and rinsed the plate before putting it in the dishwasher.

He leaned in the doorway, folding his arms across his chest. "I'll use it as an exercise. Me and Manny are supposed to train tomorrow anyway. Instead of following me, we'll both follow Bradley."

"You'd do that for me?"

"Ain't much I wouldn't do for you, darlin'. And since it looks like I ain't gonna get any until this is taken care of..."

"I told you," I said, "you can have some any time you want."

He quirked a brow. "Now?"

"It's after dinner. That means it's time for dessert, right?"

"Works for me," Rafe said and grabbed me.

HE WENT TO WORK AS USUAL the next morning, and so did I.

I work at LB&A, a real estate firm half a mile from my apartment and a few blocks from where I'd met Shelby for coffee yesterday afternoon.

It was early, earlier than usual. Not as early as when I'd caught my broker, Tim Briggs—the B in LB&A—rinsing blood off his hands in the bathroom sink a few weeks ago, but early enough that mine was the only car in the lot when I pulled in behind the building. Rafe has to be at work at eight, and the bed had been lonely without him, so I was up and out early, too.

I parked and made my way over to the reinforced steel door, only to stop in my tracks a few feet away, keys dangling from my hand, when I realized that it was open a crack.

My first thought was that someone had forgotten to shut the door all the way last night. Brittany the receptionist had still been in the office when I left, and people sometimes come and go late at night. You never know when you might have need of a purchase and sale agreement.

However, the scratch marks on the door itself gave the lie to that explanation. Someone had forced the door open, and busted the lock, so it didn't latch anymore.

I stepped away, carefully. Chances were that whoever had been here was long gone, but I wasn't about to take any chances. I'd found a dead body once before, and wasn't keen to repeat the experience.

Instead, I pulled out my phone and dialed a number I knew by heart, hoping and praying it wasn't too early for the detective to be up and about.

I should have known better. The phone didn't have time to ring more than once before it was answered. "Metropolitan Nashville Police Department. Homicide. Detective Grimaldi speaking."

"It's me," I said.

"Ms.... Savannah."

I couldn't help it, I grinned. "You're getting better."

"You should talk," Grimaldi said. And she had a point. I had just as hard a time calling her Tamara as she did calling me Savannah.

I had known her since August, after walking in on that dead body I mentioned. In Mrs. Jenkins's house, as it happened. It was a body that belonged to my former colleague Brenda Puckett, queen bee of LB&A, or Walker Lamont Realty as it was called back then, and Tamara Grimaldi was the detective who ended up catching the case. We didn't get off on the best foot, she and I. I found her hardnosed and intimidating, while she found me girly and annoying.

But we kept running into each other as people kept dying, and in November, she ended up investigating the death of my sister-in-law, Sheila; my brother Dix's wife. By then, Grimaldi had decided that I wasn't as annoying as she'd first thought, and she had stopped intimidating me. And somehow, she and Dix took to one another. Not in a romantic way, since Dix's wife had just died and he wasn't in a position to be looking for another, but they clicked somehow.

Yet Grimaldi and I kept calling each other by our last names and titles. We'd slowly been working our way around to first names, but it was a lot harder than you might think.

"What's going on?" she asked now.

"I just got to the office and the back door is open. It looks like it was forced."

"Have you been inside?"

I said I hadn't. "I can go in if you want."

"No!" She took a breath and said it again, more calmly. "No. I want you to stay where you are. Don't go anywhere near that door. Someone will be there in a few minutes."

"You?"

"I work homicide, remember? Unless there's a dead body inside, it's not my jurisdiction."

I gulped. "You don't think there's a dead body inside, do you?"

Her voice remained calm. "I hope not. But if there is, I don't want you to find it."

If there was, I didn't want to find it, either. Once was enough.

"Just wait," Grimaldi said. "There's a patrol car a few minutes from you. I'm rerouting them in your direction. They should be there shortly. In the meantime, just stay on the line with me. And stay where you are."

"You don't have to babysit me," I said. "I'm fine."

"I'm sure you are. But it's standard procedure. If you called 911, they'd do the same thing."

Fine. I stepped away from the building and leaned my back against the side of my car. "So what's going on with you? Anything exciting?"

"Just the usual," Grimaldi said. "A gang-related shooting in Bordeaux overnight. An overdose the night before. Nothing new."

Just the usual crop of dead bodies. I changed the subject. "Have you seen Dix lately?"

"No," Grimaldi said, in a tone that didn't invite to further questions.

I asked anyway. "Did you have an argument?"

"No," Grimaldi said.

"So things are going well?"

She didn't answer. I guess she couldn't very well say no again, since then I'd ask why, but at the same time she didn't want to admit that things were going well.

"Any sign of the cruiser?" she asked instead.

I took my eyes off the back door and looked around. "Not yet." There was a steady stream of cars headed down the street toward downtown, the beginnings of rush hour, but none of them were police issue.

"Any movement from inside the building?"

"None I can see." But I wandered over to the wall, where there was a window, and peered in. With the lights off inside, it was hard to tell whether anything was wrong. All I could see were shadows: a chair, a desk, and filing cabinets. There was no sign of movement. "Do you want me to go around to the front and look through the windows there?"

Grimaldi hesitated. "No," she said eventually. "Stay where you are until the car comes. Just in case."

I didn't ask her to elaborate on the 'just in case,' since I could imagine several scenarios, none of which appealed. Another dead body, a man with a gun, or a man with a knife, or a man with a baseball bat...

"The cruiser's here." I watched as it pulled off the street into the lot and came to a stop.

"Good," Grimaldi said. "I'll get a copy of the report, but I'd appreciate an update."

"Of course." I hung up as the doors to the cruiser opened, in synchronicity, and two officers got out.

They turned out to be my old friends Lyle Spicer and George Truman, whom I'd also met that fateful day in August. When I'd called 911 to report a murder, Spicer and Truman had been first on the scene, and they had transported Rafe and me to downtown for the interview with Grimaldi.

Yes, Rafe had been there, too. For a few days I'd been worried that maybe he had killed Brenda.

Spicer, Truman and I have met many times since then. They often catch me doing things I shouldn't be doing, like breaking and entering and kissing Rafe outside the privacy of our own bedroom. They're by way of being Tamara Grimaldi's favorite minions, or maybe it just seems that way to me, since they patrol East Nashville, where I spend most of my time.

Spicer nodded. "Miz Martin."

I nodded back. "Officer."

"What's going on?"

I pointed to the door. He sidled closer, while Truman gave me a nod of his own on his way past. Spicer is the senior partner, while Truman is a rookie, twenty-two or twenty-three years old. He blushes if I smile at him.

They exchanged a look over the condition of the door, and then, without a word, they both pulled their weapons. Spicer nudged the door open, and they pushed inside, Spicer going high and Truman low.

I stood where I was and waited, nervously gnawing my bottom lip.

There were no indications of what was going on inside; no shots and no sounds of struggle. No furniture breaking, no yells or raised voices. After a few minutes, Spicer came back, holstering his gun. "The place is clear. C'mon in, Miz Martin."

Four

stepped gingerly through the door and inside, looking around as I
did.

Everything looked normal. I had been afraid the office would be a
mess, but it wasn't. The toilet paper hung sedately from the roll, and the
refrigerator was closed and the counter clean. Nobody had vandalized
anything that I could see.

On the other side of the hall, Tim's office looked the way it always
did. His computer was still on the desk, with his printer, scanner, and
shredder where they always were. The electronics hummed softly,
comfortingly.

The conference room looked untouched. So did the other offices
along the hall.

I stepped into the reception area at the front of the building, and
looked around.

It looked the way it always does, too, with the exception of
Brittany, who wasn't here yet. Usually she sits at the desk chewing
gum and reading the most recent issue of Cosmopolitan or Marie

Claire. Today it was too early. But—I checked my watch—in an hour she'd be here.

Unless, of course, the office turned into a crime scene, and then I'd have to call and tell her.

But so far that didn't seem likely.

"I don't see anything missing," I told Spicer and Truman.

Spicer looked around. "Nothing?"

I shook my head. All the computer equipment was here, and if someone had broken in to rip us off, surely that'd be the first thing they'd take. The paperwork wasn't worth anything, aside from the fact that it had signatures all over it, and it wasn't as if we kept money sitting around, other than some petty cash in Brittany's desk drawer.

I walked over and pulled it out. "The petty cash is gone."

"How much?"

"I have no idea," I said. "You'd have to ask Brittany. Or Tim. There might be a regulation for how much was supposed to be here."

It didn't make sense, though. Petty cash was under a hundred dollars, surely. Probably under fifty. The office equipment was worth many times that. So why would someone take the petty cash but leave the equipment, after going to the trouble of forcing the door?

Spicer looked around. "Is this all of it?"

"Other than my office." I gestured to the door on the other side of the reception area. "It used to be the coat closet." And still looked like one.

"You wanna go look," Spicer asked, "or you want me to?"

"I'm sure everything is fine." But I walked across the reception area anyway, and reached for the door knob. Only to stop when Spicer tutted at me. "What?"

"Fingerprints."

I rolled my eyes, but wrapped a fold of my coat over my hand before I twisted the knob. "See? Everything's..."

I stopped when I saw the state of my desk. Because no, everything was not fine.

While the rest of the building looked untouched, someone had been inside my office. And hadn't left it the way they found it.

The papers that had been neatly stacked on my desk were now strewn everywhere, across the desktop, chair and floor. It was a couple of folders worth, and it would take me a bit of time to sort and organize everything again.

My pencil cup had been emptied and hurled at the wall, or maybe it had been full when it was thrown. At any rate, there were pens and pencils everywhere, and the cup itself lay in a couple of pieces on the floor, while the wall had a dent in it. It also had black and blue speckles, from where a couple of pens had broken open and the ink had spattered. Everything had been ripped from the little cork board above the desk, thumbtacks scattered, and worst of all—to me, anyway—was that the framed photograph on the desk—of Rafe and me on New Year's Eve; the only picture I had of us—was broken. The glass was shattered, the frame cracked, and someone had taken the photograph itself and torn it into about a million teeny-tiny pieces, and tossed them like confetti.

I could organize the paperwork and glue the pencil cup together, but there was no way to save that photograph.

I reached out without thinking, and Truman put out a hand to stop me. He blushed when I turned to him. "Don't touch anything."

By then I'd realized my mistake, so I just nodded and stepped back, out of the doorway. Spicer, meanwhile, had already gotten on the phone to request a crime scene tech. "Fingerprints," he was telling the phone, "and fibers."

"You OK?" Truman was looking at me. Maybe he was afraid he'd have to catch me if I fainted.

I nodded. "I'm fine, thank you."

Or maybe not fine, exactly, but I wasn't in danger of fainting. I did feel violated. Someone had come into my space, uninvited, and destroyed it. I was angry. A little afraid. Nauseous. My hands shook. And I felt unsafe.

"Burglary," Spicer said into the phone.

I turned to Truman. "Why would someone go to all this trouble just for what was in the petty cash?"

He blushed, of course, as always when I gave him my undivided attention. "Not sure."

Spicer hung up the phone and offered a theory. "Maybe they thought there'd be more money here. They went through the whole place looking, and when all they found was the petty cash, they took out their frustration on your office."

Maybe. If they—whoever they were—had come in through the back door, as it appeared they had, my office would have been the last thing they encountered. It made sense that, after a buildup of frustration at finding nothing, someone might be led to have a temper tantrum. However— "Why my office? If they wanted to make a statement, wouldn't it make more sense to wreck the reception area? They could have thrown the computer at the wall and broken the glass on everyone's real estate licenses, and so forth."

There were a lot of things in the reception area it might be tempting to break, including the two plate glass windows out to the street.

Then again, breaking those would have set off— "The alarm isn't on," I said.

Spicer looked around. "There's an alarm?"

"Just inside the back door. Last person out at night is supposed to set it."

"You come and go out the back?"

"It's where the parking lot is." And most of us drive to work. "Brittany makes sure the front door is locked before she leaves at five, and the last person out the back door sets the alarm." Sometimes that's Brittany, sometimes it's someone else. It depends on who's in the office at closing time. Real estate isn't a nine to five business—for anyone but Brittany—so most of us work late at least some of the time.

"Who was the last one out yesterday?"

"I don't know," I said. "I left early. I was meeting a... friend for coffee."

And that reminded me, I had to call Shelby to tell her that my attempt to follow Bradley had come to nothing. I hadn't called her last night, since I figured Bradley would be home and I didn't want her to have to explain away my phone call.

But I could also tell her that starting today, I'd have help figuring out what was going on. And that reminded me... "I have to call Rafe." He'd want to know about this. "And Grimaldi."

"Go ahead and call the detective," Spicer said. "I'm gonna have another look around, but so far it looks like your office and the petty cash took the brunt of it."

It did. I watched him walk off while I stood in the middle of the reception area and dialed Tamara Grimaldi.

This time she didn't even bother with a greeting. "What's wrong?"

"Someone vandalized my office," I said, and to my—and Truman's—consternation, saying it out loud made me burst into tears. The young man beat a hasty retreat, following his partner down the hall.

Grimaldi waited a few seconds for me to get myself back under control, and then she said, "Tell me what happened."

I did, up to and including the missing petty cash and the photograph of Rafe and myself torn to pieces.

She didn't say anything for a moment. "I know you won't want to hear this, but that sounds personal."

She was right: I didn't want to hear it. "Spicer thought maybe whoever broke in here was frustrated by the lack of profit and took it out on my office."

"And that's possible. But the thing with the picture... that sounds personal."

It did. Much as I didn't want to admit it, it did.

"What have you been up lately?" Grimaldi asked.

"Nothing!"

Her voice didn't change. "No trouble in paradise? No secret admirers coming out of the woodwork?"

"I had coffee with my ex-husband's current wife yesterday. The one he cheated on me with. She met Rafe, but it didn't seem as if she developed a sudden illicit passion for him, that would cause her to break into my office and shred our picture." And that brief meeting with Bradley surely hadn't caused him to do anything that stupid, even if he had realized I was trying to follow him, and I didn't think he had.

But since Shelby and Bradley's marital problems weren't any of Detective Grimaldi's business, I didn't mention that little incident.

"Anything work related? Have you stolen a listing from anyone recently? Beaten anyone out in the real estate game?"

"Mrs. Jenkins's house is in limbo." I explained about the two offers and the kickout clause. "They're supposed to get back to me at the end of business today with their decision. Even if they're angry with me—or if the other potential buyers are—wrecking my office wouldn't make any difference as to who gets the house. The two are unrelated."

"No conflict in the office? You didn't use anyone's stapler or their last manila envelope? Nothing underhanded going on that you have knowledge of, like that net deal of Mrs. Puckett's last year?"

"Nothing I know of." If I had known that someone was bending the law, I would have told Tim Briggs, our broker, and he would have handled it. But I hadn't, so no one had any reason to wish me ill.

"Did Spicer call for backup?"

I told her that a crime scene tech was on his way. "Do we have to close the office?"

"It's not my field," Grimaldi said, since there was no dead body involved in this one, "but I doubt it. They'll probably fingerprint the petty cash drawer, and the back door, and the security pad, but if nothing else looks like it's been touched, there's no sense in wasting time and manpower on it. Unless something is missing?"

"The only thing I noticed was petty cash," I said. "My office is such a mess that I couldn't tell whether everything was there that was supposed to be or not, but I didn't notice anything in particular that was supposed to be there and wasn't. If you know what I mean."

"Then I suggest you take the morning off. The tech will stay out of everyone else's way, but he'll have to go over everything in your office. It'll take a few hours, at least."

"Will you let me know what he finds out?"

"Someone will. But I'll try to keep an eye on things, as well."

I thanked her and hung up. And then I dialed Tim's number and told him what was going on.

Timothy Briggs has been our broker since the founder of the company, Walker Lamont, went to prison in August. Walker was the L in LB&A—Lamont, Briggs and Associates.

Tim and I have always had a semi-adversarial relationship, as opposed to me and Walker, who always got along well, right up until the moment he apologized for having to kill me. I went to see him in prison once, and he was nice to me then, too.

As for Tim, our relationship has gotten better recently. I helped him evade a murder rap last month, and also saved him from being shot by the real killer, so he owes me. And he has a crush on Rafe, which alternately amuses and annoys me.

At any rate, I called him and told him what was going on. He instructed me to deal with it since I was there and I was used to dealing with the police, and then he said that Brittany was on her way and that he'd be in later.

"Of course," I said, reflecting that he was probably still jumpy about the police after his recent debacle. He had been guilty of disposing of a body, even if it wasn't one he had killed, so they could have thrown the book at him. I guess maybe he was afraid they'd change their minds and haul him off to prison if he didn't watch out.

I informed Spicer and Truman about what Tim and Grimaldi had said, and then I dialed Rafe's cell phone and got his voicemail. He was probably in the middle of some sort of class or other, and it was just as well, since there was nothing he could do here, and since he might worry. I left a message telling him we'd had a break-in at the office overnight, and that the police were here and CSI was on their way, but that it looked like petty cash was the only casualty. In other words, I lied, or adjusted the truth enough that I wouldn't have to mention what had happened to my own office. There was nothing at all he could do about it, and no matter how I looked at the event, and twisted and turned the angles, I couldn't come up with any reason why anyone would target me specifically. I hadn't annoyed anyone recently. And unless Rafe had another ex-girlfriend hidden in the woodwork—which he swore to me he didn't—I couldn't imagine who might want to destroy my stuff. The last woman he'd slept with—Carmen Arroyo— was still in prison, and no threat to me.

And at any rate, whoever had been here had either been very lucky in that whoever had been last out the door last night had forgotten to set the alarm... or the intruder had had the code.

The crime tech arrived about fifteen minutes later, and got busy fingerprinting the back door and keypad. Spicer and Truman, meanwhile, canvassed the area around the parking lot, opening dumpsters and kicking at trash, just in case they lucked out and found whatever the burglar had used to force the door open.

"Some sort of crowbar or wrecking bar," Truman told me. "Have you seen anything like that sitting around?"

I hadn't. Not specifically. "But a lot of the agents here work with renovators, so there are lots of tools floating around. I'm sure anyone who works here had access to a crowbar. Although they wouldn't need one. If they work here, they have a key."

"Maybe they were trying to make it look like a burglary when it wasn't," Truman said.

Maybe. "But why would they turn off the alarm? Only people who work here, or have worked here, have the code."

"Maybe they weren't thinking straight," Truman said.

Maybe not. But if I'd been standing there with a crowbar in my hand, that I had used to open the door because I wanted it to look like I had broken in, I would have used that same crowbar to smash the alarm system to smithereens before I gave myself away by using the super secret code.

At any rate, they didn't find any crowbar, or anything else that might have been used to open the door. Whoever our unknown intruder was, he or she must have taken the implement away with him after use.

Just as the tech left the door and keypad and got ready to start on the front desk, Brittany arrived, and blinked at the activity. I told her what had happened while the crime tech dusted her desk for fingerprints, and then I left Brittany to hold down the fort while I took myself off. I had no desire to watch the crime tech sift through the remnants of my office.

I went to Brew-ha-ha instead, got myself a cup of coffee, and called Shelby.

She picked up on the first ring, so she must have been expecting the call. "What did you find out?"

"Nothing," I said with a grimace. "He caught me."

"He did?!"

"Don't worry. I don't think he realized I was there to follow him. But after he saw me, I couldn't follow him, since he'd be suspicious if he saw me again."

Shelby murmured something. I hoped it was agreement, and not a pointed comment on my stupidity.

"But tonight I've got help," I said.

She brightened, or her voice did. "Who?"

"I can't tell you that. Just that it's a friend of friend. But it's someone Bradley has never seen before, so even if he notices this person, he won't think anything of it."

"That's good," Shelby said.

When she didn't say anything else, like 'Thank you, Savannah,'—I continued. "How were things last night?"

"What do you mean?"

"Did he come home from work? At the usual time? He left the office before five."

"He got home at five thirty," Shelby said.

Ah. Either my presence had rattled him sufficiently that he hadn't gone to visit his girlfriend after all yesterday, or it hadn't been their day to meet.

"What about later? Did he go out again?"

"No," Shelby said. "We stayed in."

Unless she was lying—and I wouldn't put it past her—it hadn't been either of them who vandalized my office. Not that I could imagine either the pregnant-to-bursting Shelby or the uptight Bradley wielding a crowbar at the back door to the office. Besides, what would be the point? While I wouldn't put lying past her, there didn't seem to be any reason why she would lie about this.

"Did Bradley go to work today?"

He had. Or at least he had left the townhouse to go somewhere, dressed in his usual suit and tie, and Shelby assumed he was going to work. She hadn't asked, and he hadn't said, not specifically, but since going to work was what he did—or was supposed to do—every day, he had probably gone to work today too.

"I've got a few hours free," I told her. "I'll drive up there and take a look. I'll let you know if I see anything interesting."

Shelby thanked me, and I put the car in gear and rolled out of the parking lot and in the direction of Germantown and of Ferncliff & Morton.

I was on my way down the street in front of the F&M building, like yesterday, when my phone rang.

"What the hell happened?" Rafe wanted to know.

I forgave him for the lack of greeting because his voice was tight with concern. Not with anger, as I would have assumed before I knew him as well as I do now. Or at least not anger with me. "Not sure. When I got there, the lock was busted and the back door was open."

"You didn't go inside, did you?"

"I called Grimaldi and she told me to wait for backup. She sent Spicer and Truman over. They called for a crime tech. He's there now, looking for fingerprints."

There was a beat. "Where are you?"

I thought back over what I'd said, and realized I'd used 'there' instead of 'here,' thus tipping him off to the fact that I wasn't at LB&A any longer. "My office took a little damage. It's going to take the crime tech a few hours to finish. Grimaldi suggested I make myself scarce. So I'm in Germantown to keep an eye on Bradley for an hour or two."

There was another beat. I guess maybe he wasn't sure which subject to tackle first. "Tammy told you to leave?"

My boyfriend is the only person in the world who gets away with calling Tamara Grimaldi Tammy. Her own mother doesn't even call her Tammy, or so she's told me. Rafe does, and there's nothing she can do to stop him.

"Brittany got there," I said. "She's manning the front desk. And you know how small my office is. There isn't enough room inside for both me and the crime tech."

"What happened to your office?"

I crossed my fingers. Not an easy task while driving with one hand and juggling the phone with the other. "Nothing big. Just some paperwork on the floor and things right that."

He didn't say anything for a moment, but when he spoke again it was about something else, so I assumed I'd gotten away with something. "What's Bradley up to?"

"Nothing, as far as I can tell." The lights had been on in his office again, and his car was parked in the back lot, just like yesterday. I rolled past, down to the next cross street, preparatory to staking out the same spot at the curb I'd occupied then. "What about you?"

"Between classes," Rafe said. "I got your call."

"I figured you would." And I'd figured he'd worry. "I'm sure it's not a big deal. These things happen."

"I got Manny on tap for this afternoon. He'll follow Bradley home—or wherever he's going—and hang around awhile."

"That sounds great," I said. "I won't sit here long. Just until my office is clear and I can get back in. We should hear something about Mrs. J's house by five this afternoon."

"Sounds good," Rafe said. "I gotta go. Another class is about to start."

Of course. "I'll talk to you later."

He hung up, and I settled in to watch the rear of Ferncliff & Morton.

I wish I could report that something exiting happened, but it didn't. The same young business-suited guy I'd seen yesterday arrived—a new hire, taking it easy this morning, I guess.

Nobody left, not until lunch. I'm sure a few people came and went through the front door—clients, the mailman, the Fedex or UPS guy—but I couldn't be in two places at once, so I didn't see them. It crossed my mind that maybe I ought to be out there instead of here... but then I might miss Bradley leaving.

Except he didn't leave. Eleven o'clock rolled around, and then eleven thirty. Diana Morton left, clad in a polka-dotted dress and blue jacket. She got into her car and drove away, I assumed to what was either a business lunch or a personal ditto.

A few minutes later, Nathan Ferncliff did the same thing, minus the polka-dotted dress. Maybe the two of them were carrying on. I'd never seen any sign of it, but then it was almost three years since I divorced Bradley. Things change.

The new guy didn't come out again, nor did Carolyn. She was there, because I saw her car parked in the lot, but I guess the people who were left inside ate at their desks, or in the little lunch room. Bradley was one of them, because he didn't exit the building. Maybe that was how he had lost so much weight: by working through lunch every day.

Or maybe he'd gone out through the front door and had walked somewhere to eat lunch. At any rate, his car stayed in the lot.

By twelve thirty I was getting antsy—and desperate for a bathroom. Shouldn't have had that cup of coffee.

There was nothing going on at Ferncliff & Morton that I could see. Bradley hadn't stirred. Nathan came back, but Diana didn't, so I guess the two of them weren't carrying on. Or if they were, they were being more than discreet about it. Carolyn finally left, on foot; I guess maybe she was on her way to the Germantown Café or somewhere like that to eat.

She cut across the parking lot and the alley, and then straight through the lot adjacent to the building I was parked in front of. I crouched down in my seat when she reached the sidewalk, but she didn't glance my way, just continued straight across the street to the other sidewalk before turning right. I watched in the mirror as she disappeared around the corner on her sensible two inch heels.

By now my bladder was screaming for relief, and I figured my office was probably my own again. I gave the back of Ferncliff & Morton one last look before putting the car in gear and rolling away from the curb.

I was halfway to the office when my phone rang. The caller ID said MNPD—Metro Nashville Police Department—which usually means Tamara Grimaldi's office phone, but because of today's events, I thought there was a chance it might be someone else instead. "This is Savannah. How may I help you?"

"It's me," Grimaldi said. "Are you sitting down?"

Uh-oh. "In a manner of speaking. I'm in the car."

"Do you want me to call you back?"

"No," I said. "If you don't tell me whatever it is you were going to tell me now, I'll just worry about it until you do. So just spit it out."

"We don't know anything for certain. The fingerprinting was inconclusive. But I played a hunch and made a call to the department of corrections."

"OK." I maneuvered carefully through the intersection of Spring and First. Up ahead, I could see my building, on the corner of Fifth and East Main, outlined against the sky.

"Your former boss got leave to go to his mother's funeral yesterday. He isn't back yet."

"What?"

She didn't answer, obviously recognizing my exclamation not as a request for information so much as disbelief.

"Someone let Walker out of prison? He killed two people!"

"More than that," Grimaldi said.

"It's only been seven months. How could he get out?"

"They gave him a 24-hour furlough," Grimaldi said, "to go to his mother's funeral. Under guard."

"I thought his mother was dead."

Which sounded stupid, I realize. What I'd meant to say was that I thought she'd been dead longer than this.

"She is," Grimaldi said. "Four years."

"So how could he—? Never mind. He planned it. Somehow."

"So it seems. He didn't come back last night. Nor did the guard who went with him. We've mounted a search. I just wanted you to know who to keep an eye out for."

"No problem." I was looking around so diligently I neglected to keep an eye on traffic. A car horn at my rear made me jump and realize the light had turned. I inched across the intersection and took a left onto Main Street.

"I'll let you know what I hear," Grimaldi said.

"I'd appreciate that." I kept glancing side to side, as if expecting to see Walker standing on the sidewalk, which of course I didn't. "You don't think he'll come looking for me, do you? Last night was just a fluke, right? My picture was there, and it reminded him that it was my fault he's in prison, and he got angry?"

Grimaldi hesitated. "I don't know," she said eventually. "Just... be careful. Stay where there are other people. Make sure your boyfriend sticks around home tonight."

"He's supposed to play cops and robbers."

"Cops and...?"

"Surveillance and counter-surveillance. Training."

"Tell him to call it off," Grimaldi said, "and to stay home with you. I don't think Lamont will do anything stupid, but better safe than sorry."

Indeed.

I promised her I'd put Rafe on alert, and then I drove the rest of the way to the office wishing I had eyes in the back of my head.

Five

I had to leave another message for Rafe, which was just as well, because I could imagine the kind of reception my news would get, and I was already rattled enough.

Back at the office, things were pretty much back to normal. Brittany sat at the front desk with her bubble gum and her copy of Cosmo, and Tim was in the rear wringing his hands. Other people kept coming and going as if nothing was wrong.

And nothing was, except in my office. It still looked like a whirlwind had blown through, scattering everything. By now, the gray fingerprint powder the crime tech had left added insult to injury. I knew he'd had to do it—I wanted him to do it—but it was still annoying to have to clean it up.

It took me the next couple of hours to set everything to rights, and every minute I spent, I felt more violated, nervous and upset.

When Rafe called, just the sound of his voice set me off. All he had to say was, "What the hell?" and the mixture of anger and worry in his voice had me sobbing into the phone.

"Talk to me, darlin'." I could hear the tightness underlying the words, and pulled myself together. When his voice goes tight like that, it's never a good sign.

"I'm fine. I just... I heard your voice and figured it was safe to break down."

He didn't say anything to that.

"I'm fine," I said again, focusing on breathing evenly. "Nothing happened to me. Just to my office." I couldn't keep myself from adding, "He destroyed the picture of us from New Year's Eve."

"Bastard."

"It was the only picture I had of us. Together." And because I'd lost it, I started crying again. I didn't want to, but the tears just came.

"I'm gonna kill him," Rafe said, conversationally.

"The police will find him. I'm sure they will."

"Not if I find him first," Rafe said, which was such a movie cliché thing to say that I giggled, in the middle of the tears. "What?" he added.

"Nothing." He'd meant it seriously, I knew. I sniffed, and got myself under control. I had to, for his sake as much as for my own. "Don't worry about it. I'm fine. Really."

He took a breath. A long, very audible one. When he came back, his voice was calmer. "You sure?"

"Yes. I'm sure. I'm fine. Just a bit overwhelmed with cleaning up the mess, and it's upsetting that it happened, you know? You feel violated. But it's just stuff. And I can get another picture of us." I hoped. Rafe wasn't big on picture taking. He'd spent so much time keeping a low profile that being photographed worried him.

But I had Rafe himself, after all, so losing the picture wasn't really that big a deal. Or so I tried to tell myself.

"I spoke to Tammy," he said.

"You called her?" Before he'd called me?

"She called me. And told me to cancel anything I was planning to do tonight." Something I had left out of the message I'd left for him. A fact he'd obviously noted.

"She didn't have to do that," I said. "I was going to ask you."

"Sure." He made no attempt to sound like he believed me.

"I just didn't want to leave Shelby in the lurch. She's worried about Bradley. I wanted someone to follow him to see where he went."

"And someone will," Rafe said. "It just won't be me."

"Who?"

"I'll give it to Manny as an assignment. Follow the SUV from work to home, make note of any stops the driver makes along the way, and stay there long enough to make sure he's settled for the night, then report in. He won't know Bradley is anyone you know. I'll make out it's just a random choice."

"Thank you."

"Manny needs to train," Rafe said. "He might as well train on Bradley."

True.

And this would actually work out better, as far as I was concerned. Bradley and Rafe had met once, briefly, on the sidewalk outside the condo when Bradley was bringing me back from dinner in December. I wasn't sure whether Bradley had gotten a good look at Rafe, and whether he would recall him or not. Given the circumstances, he might. And if he recognized Rafe today, after recognizing me yesterday, he might suspect that something was up. But Bradley would never recognize Manny, since it was unlikely they'd ever crossed paths.

"Did Tammy... Grimaldi say anything else?" I asked. Between the two of them, they had a habit of trying to protect me from some of life's more unpleasant facts.

"The idiots let him go," Rafe said, his voice disgusted. "His mother's been dead for years, and nobody bothered to notice."

"They sent a guard with him, though. What happened to the guard?"

"Ain't been answering his phone. Dead in a ditch somewhere, most likely." Rafe's tone indicated that he thought it was no more than the unfortunate guard deserved for being stupid enough to go anywhere with Walker Lamont.

"You think Walker killed him?"

"Don't you?"

Considering that he'd killed several other people, and tried to kill me and Mrs. Jenkins to cover it up, let's just say I wouldn't put it past him.

"Call me when you're ready to come home," Rafe said. "And don't park in the garage. Find a spot on the street. I'll meet you."

"Are you sure that's necessary? I mean, if he killed the guard and got away, and found whatever he came here for—which probably wasn't to trash my office—don't you think he has more important things to worry about than me? Won't he be trying to get as far from Nashville as he can before anyone starts looking for him?"

"Prob'ly," Rafe admitted. "But it don't make sense to take stupid chances."

It didn't. "I'll call you."

"Thanks, darlin'." There was no mistaking the relief in his voice. He must be more worried than he wanted me to realize. "Gotta go. Duty calls."

I listened to the click as he hung up, and then the silence, before shaking myself off and getting back to work.

I SPENT THE REST OF THE afternoon cleaning up the office. My coffee mug slash pencil holder was a total loss, so I had to dump all the pens and pencils into the desk drawer until I could bring another from home, but other than that, everything else could be returned to normal. I pinned all my reminders and comics back up on the cork board and sorted the paperwork into piles. It gave me an excuse, or incentive, to organize my files too, so I spent some time doing that. And then I wiped off all the fingerprint powder, wondering whether that was what had given Grimaldi her hunch to call the Department of Corrections to check on Walker. If his fingerprints had been here, seven months after he went to prison, that'd be something of a dead giveaway.

When the phone rang a little after four, it startled me. My heart jumped, but when I looked at the display, I realized it was just the call I'd been waiting for, the one I'd forgotten all about in the tumult.

"This is Savannah."

"It's me," the agent for the buyers said. "They can't take the contingency off." He sounded a bit angry, although I wasn't sure whether it was with me, with them, or with the situation in general.

"I'm sorry," I said, since I was a little unhappy about the situation in general myself. I had really hoped the first couple who wanted Mrs. J's house would be able to buy it, condo notwithstanding. You're not supposed to play favorites, of course, but I had shown them the house, only learning once I got there that they had a realtor in mind that they wanted to work with, and I had really hoped things would work out.

"Sure."

There was a distinct edge of 'yeah, right,' in the single syllable. It put my back up, even though I knew what had happened wasn't my fault. I mean, we could have taken their offer without the sale of home contingency and kickout clause, I guess, and just taken the risk that the condo would sell in a timely manner... but experience and common sense dictated otherwise. I shouldn't have to feel guilty about that.

My no doubt loud silence must have spurred Brian into speaking again. He sounded a mite more conciliatory this time. "Will you let me know if something changes?"

"Of course," I said graciously. "The other buyers still have their inspection and financial contingencies to get through, so there are no guarantees that things will work out. I'll keep your number and let you know the minute something happens. If it does."

"Thank you." He hung up without saying goodbye and without giving me the chance to.

I blew out a breath, feeling like a tiny gray raincloud had settled right over my head, and dialed Rafe. "I'll be ready to go in a few minutes."

"Gimme fifteen to get in place."

No problem. "We heard from the agent for the buyers. They're withdrawing their offer."

"Damn," Rafe said.

"We still have the backup offer."

"I know. But I liked them."

I had, too. "I have to call the other agent now, and let him know that his clients just moved up into first position. Hopefully they haven't changed their minds."

"If they have, it's too late," Rafe said.

"I know. But there are ways they can get out if they're not serious. They have an inspection contingency and a financial contingency. If they want out, they can get out."

He didn't answer.

"I'll be outside the condo in fifteen minutes," I told him. "I'll park on the street."

"If you don't see me, stay in the car till you do."

I promised I would, and then I hung up and called the other agent to tell him his clients had just become the primary offerers for Mrs. Jenkins's house. That done, I said good night to Brittany and headed out into the parking lot.

I did look around a little extra carefully on my way to the Volvo, but nobody was in the parking lot. And while I kept an eye in the rearview mirror on the half dozen blocks down to Fifth and East Main, I didn't pick up a tail, either.

Of course, Walker wouldn't have to follow me to know where I was going. He'd had access to the employee roster last night, and could have looked up my address. It was in the same drawer as the petty cash.

I imagined getting out of the car in front of the condo complex and being picked off by a long-range hunting rifle. Walker had told me once that his father used to take him hunting, until the unfortunate accident that killed him. An accident that killed the father, I mean. Walker hadn't said it in so many words, but I'd gotten the distinct impression that he was behind the sad occurrence.

Yes, I knew it was ridiculous to imagine being gunned down on the street in front of my building in what was almost broad daylight, but I couldn't shake the idea. And then I thought of Rafe standing there waiting, to make sure nothing bad happened to me, and of Walker picking him off first. I thought about arriving home to find him on the ground, his blood running across the pavement, and I stepped on the gas.

That was an equally ridiculous notion, of course, but fear is a funny thing. I didn't start breathing again until I got close enough to see him standing—upright and whole—on the sidewalk beside an empty parking space. I pulled in behind the Harley Davidson and cut the engine. Before I could open the door, he was already there, shielding me with his own body.

"C'mon." He kept a hand on my back and himself between me and the openness of the street on the way across the courtyard. I felt my neck prickle—he probably did, too—but nothing happened.

"This is ridiculous," I informed him when we were inside the stairwell and on our way up to the second floor. "Walker has better things to do than spend time and effort getting back at me."

Rafe didn't answer, just kept an eye out, forward and back, as we emerged on the second floor and halted in front of our own door.

"We got along well," I continued as I fitted the key in the lock. "Even after I put him in prison. He understood that he got caught fair and square. He didn't blame me. And he undid all the damage from Brenda's net listing and gave the house back to your grandmother."

"That don't mean I'm gonna let him hurt you," Rafe said and moved into the hallway behind me. He closed and locked the door, then stuck his head into the kitchen and opened the door to the half bath to make sure it was empty. "Stay," he told me over his shoulder as he moved farther into the apartment.

"I'm not a dog," I threw after him, but he'd already passed into the living room, gun in hand.

I spent the time shrugging out of my lightweight spring coat and kicking off my shoes, while I listened for sounds. None came. Rafe can move soundlessly when he wants to, and he obviously did.

It took about a minute, and then he called out. "C'mere."

Another command, short and to the point. I was grumbling as I skirted the dining room table and padded across the living room carpet to the bedroom door. "You know, I don't appreciate being talked to like I walk on four legs and pant—"

And then I stopped in the doorway, struck mute by the sight of Rafe, flat on his back on the bed, arms tucked behind his head. Stark naked. And grinning.

The apartment must be secure.

Part of me wanted to ask how he'd managed to strip down so quickly, but to be honest, I couldn't get my vocal chords to cooperate. Never mind panting: my tongue was practically hanging out and I was a second away from drooling. We'd been together every day (and every night) for two and a half months now, so I should be used to looking at him, even in the nude. But the truth was, he never fails to take my breath away. Part of me hopes he never will.

But of course I didn't want him to see that—as if there was any chance at all he didn't already know the effect he has on me—so I put my hands on my hips and surveyed him. arching my brows. "What? You're going to throw me a bone?"

The grin turned into a full-blown laugh, and my own lips curved in appreciation. It's been happening more often recently, but I still celebrate every time I coax a spontaneous, unguarded moment out of him.

"C'mere, darlin'." He patted the bed next to him. I walked over and sat down. Demurely, with my hands folded in my lap.

And then I thought, to hell with it, and reached out to smooth my hand over his skin. He tumbled me down on top of him, and the rest, as they say, is history.

The phone rang just after seven.

"Must be Manny," Rafe said, reaching for it. We were still in bed, and I watched with appreciation as muscles moved smoothly under his skin as he sat up against the pillows and put the phone to his ear. "Yeah?"

The phone started quacking.

"Is it him?" I mouthed. He nodded. "I want to hear."

"Hang on a sec, Manny. I'm gonna put you on speaker." He put a finger to his lips to indicate that I needed to be quiet. I nodded. I just wanted to hear what Manny had to say, I had no need to let him know he hadn't been involved in a TBI training exercise.

"Sure, Rafe," Manny said. He had a light, smooth voice with a hint of a Spanish accent, and he sounded young. "So like I was saying, I followed the dude from the office through downtown and onto Church Street. He stopped at the post office."

"Mailbox?"

"Post box. He got something out of it, or put something in, I'm not sure. I couldn't follow him inside, or he'd make me."

"That's fine," Rafe said. "Don't worry about it. Then what?"

"He got back in the car. Started driving west on Church, toward the park. But he only went a couple blocks, and then he turned left and left again on West End. Back the way he came."

"Maybe he forgot something at the office."

"He didn't go to the office," Manny said. "He took a right on Fourth and drove down to a bar off Nolensville Road in Tusculum."

Tusculum? That was half a world away from Bradley's townhouse in Green Hills, both financially and socially.

"Place have a name?"

"Shortstop," Manny said.

I grimaced, and Rafe shot me a warning look. I nodded, rolling my eyes. I wasn't going to say anything. But I remembered the Shortstop. He'd taken me there once, when we'd been on that side of town and after I'd asked for a place where no one would recognize me.

"D'you go in?" Rafe asked.

"Yeah. I figured it'd be safe. No way I'd stick out in a place like that."

Indeed not. Rafe hadn't stuck out when we'd been there. No more than he does anywhere else, by being above average height and nice-looking.

No, I'd been the anomaly at the Shortstop. Other than me, it had been all men and a couple of waitresses, both of whom had been common as dirt, as my mother would say. Rafe had known several of the men, and they'd all been petty criminals. And Tusculum was located on the south side of town, in an area that had seen a lot of immigration from Mexico in the last few years. If Manny looked like a Manuel, he'd fit right in.

While I'd been remembering my own experience at the Shortstop, Rafe had assured Manny that it was fine that he'd followed Bradley inside, and Manny had told Rafe about how he'd sat at the bar drinking a beer and eating peanuts while keeping an eye on Bradley in the mirror.

"He looked like he didn't wanna be there, you know what I mean?"

I could imagine. I'm sure I had looked like I hadn't wanted to be there too, back in the fall.

"So what was he doing?" Rafe asked.

"He was meeting somebody."

"Who?" I said.

Rafe scowled at me, and Manny hesitated, obviously thrown by the sound of my voice.

Rafe cleared his throat. "Who?" he said again.

"Um..." Manny must have decided he'd either made a mistake or it didn't matter who Rafe had with him. "I don't know, man. Just another dude in a suit. He was there when the subject walked in, and he stayed when the subject left. All you told me to do was follow the subject home and call you. So I'm calling."

"Sure." Rafe's voice was easy. "No problem. I thought maybe, since you saw him, you'd wanna gimme a description."

I'm pretty sure Manny was rolling his eyes, but he complied. "Older than the other dude. Maybe forty, forty-five. Black suit, white shirt, striped tie. I wasn't close enough to see eyes, but his hair was going gray."

"Any idea what he was driving?"

"He was inside, man!"

"In the lot," Rafe said. "Did the target's car stand out?"

"Yeah. So?"

"Did anything else stand out? Guy in a suit prob'ly isn't gonna drive a truck, you know what I mean?"

Manny thought about it. "Coulda been a Mercedes. Think I saw one. I'm not sure, though." He sounded worried now, like he was afraid he was going to receive a failing grade.

"Don't worry about it," Rafe said easily. "I'm just reminding you to look around, is all. So the target's home now?"

"Thirty minutes ago," Manny confirmed. "He left the dude in the bar and drove straight to a townhouse in Green Hills. Pregnant woman inside. He opened the garage door with a remote and parked inside. I figured that was the end of the line. They're eating dinner."

If Manny thought Bradley had been a random assignment, just a guy or a car Rafe had picked out of thin air, it wouldn't do to let on that we knew just who Bradley was and where he lived. But a townhouse in Green Hills with a pregnant woman inside—that was definitely Shelby and home.

"Good work," Rafe told Manny. "Go home. We'll talk more in the morning. If you want something to do tonight, you can start on the report."

"Oh, man..."

Rafe chuckled and hung up. "Where were we?"

"Here." I snuggled up next to him, with my head on his shoulder, just as I'd been when the phone rang. "Looks like I was wrong and Shelby was right. Bradley isn't cheating."

"No." He put his arm around me. "Or at least he wasn't cheating tonight. Looks like he's up to something, though. You've been to the Shortstop. It ain't the kind of place Bradley'd go if he didn't have to, is it?"

No, it wasn't. "I guess that means the other guy must have called the meeting."

Rafe nodded. "And he's got enough pull that he can get Bradley to go outside his comfort zone to meet him."

I glanced up at his profile. "What do you think is going on?"

He turned his head on the pillow to look down at me. "Dunno. But if they're hiding in a corner of the Shortstop, I don't imagine it's anything good."

I didn't imagine so, either, and the implications worried me. Bradley was no longer my responsibility, true. He was Shelby's problem now, and she deserved him. But that didn't mean I wanted anything bad to happen to either of them. I hadn't wanted anything bad to happen to them even when they were fooling around behind my back.

True, the knowledge that Bradley was battling a persistent case of genital warts might have gone a long way to salving my feelings, but that was the extent of it.

When I said as much, Rafe nodded. "I know, darlin'."

"I'm not sure what to tell Shelby."

"Why don't you let me take a drive down to the Shortstop," Rafe said, "and see what I can find out before you tell her anything."

"You'd do that for Shelby? Or Bradley?"

"No," Rafe said. "But I'd do it for you."

"Thank you." I went up on my elbows to kiss him, and one thing led to another, and that, as they say, was that.

Six

The phone rang again before seven AM.

In fact, it was before six thirty, which is rarely a good sign, in my experience.

It was Rafe's phone, though, so I stayed where I was, warm and snug under the covers, while he stretched for the side table. "Yeah?" He kept his voice low, so he wouldn't disturb me any more than necessary.

There was a pause, during which the phone quacked. Rafe cursed. "Where?"

The phone sounded again. By now I was wide awake, but I wasn't able to make out the words on the other end of the line.

"Something wrong?" I asked when he hung up.

"Yeah." He ran a hand over his head. There's not enough hair there to actually run his fingers through, but it comes to the same thing. A gesture of resignation and frustration. "I gotta go."

I watched as he got to his feet and padded over to the chest of drawers. Obviously he wasn't going to take the time to shower, which reinforced my impression that what was going on was serious.

"Does it have something to do with Walker?" I asked.

"Shit." He turned to look at me, his eyes wide.

"What?"

"I forgot. Get up."

"Forgot what?" But I swung my legs over the side of the bed and got to my feet. Instead of watching me, he turned back to the drawers to rummage, another sign something was seriously wrong. Usually, when I'm standing nearby, naked, he's looking at me.

"Here." He tossed underwear at me. "Hurry."

I hurried. And because it was early, and because something was wrong, I didn't bother to dress up, just slipped into the pair of yoga pants I'd worn the other day, along with a fresh T-shirt. My only concession to makeup was a smear of lipstick. Mother would have been horrified to learn that I'd gone beyond the front door without my 'face' on, but needs must and all that. Rafe was almost crackling with suppressed energy, and I didn't want to take any more time than I absolutely had to.

He kept his gun in his hand and his body between me and any comers on the way to the car, and I didn't distract him with small talk. Thus it was that we were in the Volvo, peeling away from the curb, by the time I asked, "Where are we going?"

He shot me a glance out of the corner of his eye as he crossed Fifth Street at fifty miles an hour. "Antioch."

"Why?"

"Manny's place," Rafe said, taking the corner onto Interstate Drive on two wheels and gunned the engine for the freeway.

"Was that him on the phone?"

He shook his head. "Tammy."

"Grimaldi?"

He nodded.

Uh-oh. I sat back in my seat.

Rafe drove, his face grim, dodging and weaving through the early-morning traffic on I-24. Thank God it was too early for rush hour.

The trip from my condo to Antioch, a middle class suburban neighborhood on the southeast side of town, usually takes somewhere between twenty five and thirty minutes, depending on traffic. We made it in seventeen. By the time we squealed to a stop at the curb outside what I assumed was Manny's place, I had to pry my fingernails out of my seat, and I felt like my hair was blown straight back. It wasn't, of course—the windows had been up the whole time—but that was how fast we'd been going.

Rafe didn't wait for me. He pulled up behind a MNPD cruiser and had the door open almost before we'd come to a full stop. And he covered the distance between the car and the door to the condo almost at a run, not even stopping to flash the cop at the door his ID. By the time I had disentangled myself from the seatbelt and followed, he was well inside the building.

I stopped in front of the guard. "Hi."

He nodded.

"What's going on?"

He hesitated. But of course he'd seen me arrive with Rafe, and Rafe had breezed right in like he belonged here—I could hear his voice from inside as I stood on the stoop—so I guess Officer Lowrie must have decided he could give me at least the bare bones. "Homicide."

I had already surmised as much. When Tamara Grimaldi calls, unless it's a personal call, that's usually the reason.

"Who died?"

He hesitated again, but eventually told me. "Someone named Manuel Ortega."

Damn. I mean... darn.

My stomach clenched. I'd never met Manny, had only heard his voice on the phone yesterday, but I knew Rafe liked him. He'd been responsible for a handful of TBI rookies, putting them through their paces and teaching them hand to hand combat and such, and I knew he thought Manny was the one who showed the most potential. This must be devastating for him.

"What happened?"

It took another second before Lowrie answered. "Single gunshot wound to the chest."

God. "When?"

"Sometime last night. The M.E. will have to make the determination."

"When was he found?"

"An early riser saw the door standing open at five AM," Lowrie said. "She called 911."

And by six Grimaldi had been here and had called us. "Any idea who did it?"

Lowrie shook his head. "Sorry, ma'am." He glanced over his shoulder. "You wanna go in?"

It was my turn to hesitate. "Is the body still here?"

Lowrie nodded.

I shook my head. "No thanks. I've seen someone shot before. That was enough. I'll wait in the car." I headed back to the Volvo and closed myself in.

The van from the medical examiner's office showed up a few minutes later. I watched as two men dressed in coveralls moved a gurney up the walkway and into the condo. Then I watched as they came back out a few minutes later, trailed by Rafe and Tamara Grimaldi, looking grim.

Manny was zipped into a body bag, the way you see on TV, and that was fine with me. I had no need to look at him. Nor did those of the neighbors who were hanging out on their stoops, watching the show. Two uniformed officers were slowly making their way from door to door, taking statements. Hopefully someone had seen or heard something useful last night.

I was in the process of watching the two paramedics—or morgue employees—load the gurney into the back of the van when suddenly there was a knock on my window. I jumped, and so did my heart, right up into my throat.

"Morning," Tamara Grimaldi said.

She left off the 'good,' which was probably a smart omission.

I glanced out the windshield and saw that Rafe was on his way toward the two officers who'd been doing the canvassing. The morgue van was driving off, slowly. I got out of the car so I could talk to Grimaldi without making her stoop. "Do you have any idea what happened?"

She shook her head. "Best as we can figure it, he opened the door to someone who shot him. Point blank, right in the heart. He fell backwards into the entry. Death would have been instantaneous."

That was good news, anyway. No suffering. "Nobody saw or heard anything?"

"No one we've found so far. One of the neighbors saw the door standing open when she was out with the dog early. By then, the shooter was long gone."

"I don't suppose this place has security cameras at the entrance?"

There'd been no other security. No gate, no guard house, no security pad with a code. This wasn't a closed community. The entrance was wide open onto the road for anyone to come and go as they pleased.

Grimaldi shook her head. "Afraid not."

I glanced at Rafe again, now in conversation with the two uniformed officers. "He's pretty upset, isn't he?"

"Yes," Grimaldi said, "he is."

"He really liked Manny."

Grimaldi nodded. "He said Mr. Ortega spent the evening following your ex-husband around?"

There was no censorship in her voice, but I flushed anyway. "It wasn't the whole evening. Just a couple of hours. But yes, he did. He and Rafe were supposed to do it together. Part of their cops and robbers training. But then, when this thing with Walker happened, Rafe didn't want to leave me alone. He said you called and told him not to?"

"I thought you might not want to do it yourself," Grimaldi said.

"Thank you." Because, yes, the thought of coming across as clingy had crossed my mind, and the last thing I wanted to do, was make Rafe feel smothered.

"What's going on with your ex?"

"Not much. Not that I know of." Certainly nothing that would explain this.

She didn't answer, and I felt compelled to explain. "His wife called me the other day. She said Bradley wasn't acting right, and asked my help to figure out why. I assumed he was cheating again, but I told her I'd follow him around for a day or two to see where he went. But he gave me this car, so the first time he saw me, he recognized me. Rafe said he and Manny would do it instead. As a training exercise. But then Walker broke out of prison, and it ended up being just Manny following Bradley yesterday afternoon."

Grimaldi nodded. "What happened?"

"Didn't Rafe tell you?" I didn't wait for her to answer. "Manny followed him to the post office, and then to some dive on Nolensville Road, and home. Once he saw that Bradley was settled with Shelby, he left."

"When was that?"

I told her it had been just after seven when Manny called.

"He didn't say where he was going?"

I shook my head. "I have no idea where he went. I assumed he was going home, but that's just because I'd go home at seven o'clock on a weeknight. It doesn't mean Manny would. I know nothing about him, aside from the fact that the TBI took him on."

"He's got something of the same story as your boyfriend," Grimaldi told me. "Early brushes with the law, and then a stint in prison for robbery. The TBI recruited him while he was inside."

No wonder Rafe had gotten along so well with this guy. That was exactly the same path he'd taken to come to work for the TBI, with the only difference being that he'd served two years of a five year sentence for assault and battery when they arranged to have him released early.

"Do you think this had something to do with Manny's previous profession?"

"It's likely," Grimaldi said. "He associated with some unsavory characters. Both before and after the prison sentence. That's the thing about these undercover agents. They get out of prison and go back to their old lives. The only difference is that their allegiances have shifted."

She thought for a moment and added a judicious, "Hopefully."

Right.

I glanced at Rafe, still in conversation with the two patrol officers. "He's going to want to get whoever did this. He'll feel responsible."

"He's not," Grimaldi said.

Maybe not, but he'd still feel that way. "He'll want to be a part of the investigation." And knowing him, there was absolutely nothing Tamara Grimaldi or anyone else could do to keep him out.

"I imagine it'll be a joint effort with the MNPS and the TBI," Grimaldi said calmly. "Mr. Ortega was one of theirs. They'll want to be part of it."

Good. Even if it meant I'd probably see very little of Rafe the next few days. And that reminded me... "Any news of Walker?"

Grimaldi shook her head. "Not as of last night. Sorry. I haven't been in to the office yet this morning, to read the reports."

"The prison guard hasn't turned up?" Dead or alive.

"Not so far."

"Is anyone looking for him? I assume it's a male, right?"

"Never assume," Grimaldi said. "There are plenty of female guards in all-male prisons. But in this case, yes. The missing guard is male."

"I don't expect it would matter much to Walker, actually. Both Brenda and Clarice were women, and he had no problem killing them. He wouldn't have had a problem killing me or Mrs. Jenkins, either."

Grimaldi nodded. "We're going on the assumption that the guard is dead and that we just haven't found the body yet. Truth is, we don't know where to start looking. Lamont got leave to go to his mother's funeral in Kentucky, but since she didn't die—or rather, since she's been dead for years—there was no reason for him to go there."

"He might have had to, though. The guard may have kept him in the back of the car or something until they got to where they were supposed to be going. That might have been the first chance Walker had to get away."

Grimaldi nodded. "I had someone check the cemetery where Mrs. Lamont is buried after I figured out what was going on. There was no sign of the guard or the car they traveled in."

So they could have been there and left, or they might not have gotten there at all.

"It's a desolate sort of place," Grimaldi added. "Lots of fields and forest. Easy place to hide a body, especially for someone familiar with the area. The local PD had a look around yesterday, but didn't find anything. They said they'd take another look this morning, but again..."

I nodded. "You don't even know if Walker and the guard made it there."

We stood in silence a moment and watched Rafe talk to the uniformed officers. One of the crime scene investigators walked to her van with a Ziploc baggie she locked away in the back.

"You've checked Walker's house," I asked, "haven't you?"

A few weeks ago, I'd found Tim Briggs holed up there, avoiding the police, so Walker's place had been on my mind recently. If it hadn't been for that, I would have assumed that he'd lost the house when he went to prison.

Tamara Grimaldi nodded. "I asked the Oak Hill cops to check on it. They said it was empty. And they've been doing drive-bys all night, just in case."

"What about the guard? If Walker killed him, he might have taken the guy's keys and gone there."

Grimaldi smirked. "Trying to take my job, Ms.... Savannah?"

"God forbid. But if Rafe's going to be busy working this case, he won't have time to babysit me. And I certainly don't want to make him choose between working the case and babysitting me. So the sooner you—or someone—can get Walker back where he belongs, the better it'll be."

There was no arguing with that, and Grimaldi didn't try. "There's an APB out on him. And on the car they were driving. We'll get him. Just be careful."

I promised I would, and watched her walk up to Rafe and the officers and engage them in conversation. Rafe glanced at me over his shoulder and held up a finger. *One minute.* I nodded and folded myself back into the car to wait.

"I'M SO SORRY," I TOLD him ten minutes later, when we were on our way back out of the neighborhood.

He glanced at me. "Thanks."

"You liked him a lot."

There was a pause while his hands tightened on the steering wheel until the knuckles showed white, before he relaxed again. "He was me, ten years ago."

"Grimaldi told me he was drafted in prison, the way you were. Do you think someone from his old life did this to him?"

"Hard to imagine what else it could be," Rafe said. "He hadn't started working anything big. It takes time to establish a cover and work your way in deep."

He should know, having spent ten years doing it.

"How long did it take you?"

He glanced at me again. "Nine years. I told you that. They recruited me while I was inside—"

"Both the TBI and the bad guys, right?"

He nodded. "The bad guys first, and then, when they figured out what was going on, the TBI. But it was just small stuff at first. Then a little bigger, and a little bigger. It took until last fall before I finally made contact with Hector."

Hector Gonzales, head of the biggest—former—South American Theft Gang in the southeast, now a guest of the Georgia Department of Corrections. Thanks to Rafe.

"Grimaldi said there'd probably be a joint investigation. TBI and MNPD."

"Good," Rafe said grimly. "I want the guys who did this."

I didn't doubt it.

"I asked her about Walker, too. There is no news. He's still out there."

"You worried?" He shot me a look as he merged with traffic heading north on I-24. By now, rush hour had started, and we were headed toward downtown in a glut of fifty other cars.

"Not too much. I think he's probably miles and miles away by now. And even if he isn't, I think he has more important things to worry about than me." Such as saving his own skin. I mean, I may have been responsible for putting him in prison, but he was out now. And he wasn't stupid. Surely he'd realize that the best thing he could do for himself would be to get as far away from Nashville as he could as quickly as possible, and not linger to even the score with me?

Rafe muttered something.

"What?" I said.

He shook his head and focused on driving. After a few minutes, and a few miles, he glanced over at me again. But not at my face this time. "What are you wearing?"

"Yoga pants," I said. "And a T-shirt."

He didn't say anything, and I added, "I'm sorry. I just didn't want to take the time to put on all the things I usually wear when it was so early and we were in a hurry. Pantyhose and high heels and everything. I thought it was more important that we get out of the house quickly. But if you don't like it, I won't do it again."

"Why would I care what you wear?"

He sounded honestly baffled, and I blinked. "I thought..."

"Cause Bradley gave you a hard time about going outside dressed down, you thought I'd do it, too?"

Something like that.

"I told you before," Rafe said, "I ain't Bradley."

"I know. I just..." I'd fallen back into old habits, thinking the man I was with, and the people surrounding me, judged me based on whether or not I looked polished and acted perfect at any given time. "Why did you ask, then?"

"Wondering whether I need to take you home before I take you to the TBI with me."

Oh. "Yes, please. I wouldn't want to go to your workplace dressed like this."

"Too bad," Rafe said and merged with traffic on I-40.

"What do you mean?"

"You're wearing exactly what I want you to wear."

I was? "How so?" If he wanted to take me to the TBI and introduce me to his coworkers, I wasn't likely to impress anyone dressed like this.

"I could tell you," Rafe said, "but..."

"You'd have to kill me?"

"Not really. But I don't feel like listening to you argue."

Ah.

We sat in silence for a few more minutes. He headed north on I-24 and took the exit for Ellington Parkway.

"How about if I promise not to argue?"

"We're just a few minutes away," Rafe said. "Just be patient."

Fine. I stuck out my lower lip and folded my arms and did my best.

Seven

The Tennessee Bureau of Investigations' headquarters is located in Inglewood, just off Ellington Parkway and quite close to the medical examiner's office.

I'd never been there before.

At the medical examiner's office, yes. It was where my sister-in-law, Sheila, had ended up after being fished out of the Cumberland River back in November. And it was where Tamara Grimaldi had had me meet her to give a preliminary identification of my friend Lila Vaughn in September.

But I hadn't been to the TBI yet. My only knowledge of Rafe's desk and his cubicle had been from description.

Now I got to see it up close and personal, if not quite as personally as Rafe had hinted he wanted me to.

He scanned his ID card at the front desk, and signed me in as a visiting guest. Then he took me through the jungle of hallways and cubicles down into the basement. Nobody stopped us, not even to ask questions about Manny. Either they hadn't heard the news yet, or the look on his face—grim determination with a hint of don't-mess-with-me-unless-you're-prepared-for-the-consequences—warned them off.

I looked around, at the gray concrete walls and utilitarian floors. "What's down here?"

"Gym."

I glanced up at him. That expression on his face made me a little wary myself. "Why are we going to the gym?"

"If you're gonna be out there on your own, with an escaped murderer looking for you, I want you to be able to protect yourself."

Ah.

And then I realized what he'd said. "What are you going to do to me?"

"Teach you unarmed combat," Rafe said.

"You're joking."

He looked at me. "No. Why?"

"I don't think I'll be very good at that. I wasn't brought up to be violent."

"I don't want you to be violent, darlin'. I want to you protect yourself."

"How am I going to do that without being violent?"

Rafe pushed open a door halfway down the corridor and gestured me inside. "Try to think of it as self-defense. Not violence."

I stepped through the door into the TBI gym and looked around.

It was big and utilitarian, with lots of mirrors along all the walls. Dumbbells and benches and other strength training equipment took up one half of the room, and the other half consisted of a bunch of mats and a boxing ring. At this time of the morning, it was empty except for the two of us.

Rafe steered me toward the mats. "We'll start with some stretches to get you warmed up."

I did my best not to look at myself in any of the mirrors. I knew I looked awful. My hair was a mess, I was sans makeup, and my

T-shirt wasn't long enough to cover my butt in the tight yoga pants. "Why do I have to warm up? If someone attacks me, I won't have stretched."

He arched a brow. For a second he didn't say anything, but then he nodded. "Just don't blame me if you pull any muscles."

"If someone attacks me, I won't be wearing these clothes, either. Maybe we should do this sometime when I'm wearing a skirt and heels." Heels I could dig into someone's foot.

"Sure," Rafe said accommodatingly. "Maybe we can wait until the place is full, too. That way, when I throw you down on the mat and your skirt flies up, everyone can enjoy the view."

I blinked. "You're going to throw me down on the mat?"

"That depends on you," Rafe said, "and how good you are at getting away from me. But yeah, I imagine your back'll hit the floor a few times before we're done."

I looked away. Met my eyes in the mirror and looked back. "I don't want to do this."

His voice gentled. "I know, darlin'. And I wish you didn't have to. But if I ain't gonna be there to protect you, I wanna know that you can protect yourself."

I suppose I did have a certain propensity for getting myself into situations where a few basic self defense moves might come in handy. "Fine. What do you want me to do?"

"I want you to fight me off," Rafe said and lifted his hands.

I didn't lift mine. I was afraid of looking stupid. "I don't want to hurt you."

He grinned. "You won't."

He reached for me. I dodged, but he must have read my mind and known which direction I was going to go, because he was right there, spinning me around and into his embrace. His arms closed around my ribcage like a steel band, squeezing the air out of me. Turns out it's hard to fight when you can't breathe.

It took him a second to kick my feet out from under me, another to force me to my knees and then onto my stomach. He spared a last second to flip me over onto my back before landing on top of me. I blinked up at the florescent lights, trying to catch my breath. Not an easy task between having the air knocked out of me in the fall, and the two hundred pounds of muscle sitting on my diaphragm.

"That," Rafe said, looking down into my face, still keeping my hands pinned to the mat above my head, "was pathetic."

He, of course, wasn't breathing hard.

"If I'd had high heels on," I informed him, "I would have stepped on your foot."

He shook his head. "Wouldn't have done you any good."

Maybe not. But it would have been something to do. As it was, I hadn't had a chance to do anything at all.

He vaulted off me. "C'mon."

I took the hand he extended and let him haul me to my feet. "I don't think this is going to work."

"Give it a chance." He brushed me off, with a little extra attention to my butt. "You just have to learn what to do."

"I think there's probably a little more to it than that. You're much bigger than I am."

If it was Walker Lamont coming at me, it'd be a different story. He was shorter than Rafe by several inches, and weighed probably thirty pounds less. Still bigger and heavier than me, but considerably smaller and slighter than Rafe. I'd have a chance against Walker, at least as long as he wasn't carrying a gun or a knife. Against Rafe, I had no chance at all.

"It ain't just about size. A smaller, lighter guy can take down a bigger, heavier guy every time if he knows what to do."

"So what do I do?"

"The target points are knees, groin, throat, nose, and eyes." He pointed to them as he spoke. "Hit me in any of 'em, and I'm gonna be distracted. Hit me hard enough and you might get away."

"I told you. I don't want to hurt you."

"And I told you you won't." He stepped in close behind me. "Let's try this again. If I grab you like this," he slipped both arms around my waist, but without tightening the grip to cut off my air this time, "what're you gonna do?"

I hesitated. The first time he did it, he'd had me on the ground in a couple of seconds. This time he was giving me time to think.

However, as soon as I shifted my weight onto one foot to stomp his foot with the other, he yanked me off balance and then I was back on the mat with him on top of me again. This time he didn't even bother to turn me right side up, just landed on my back.

I grunted, in a very unladylike fashion.

"This is getting monotonous," I informed him once I'd gotten my breath back.

"You made it easy for me. I outweigh you to begin with, and then you made it easier by compromising your own balance." He lifted me to my feet. "Try again. This time, don't make it so easy."

Easier said than done, no pun intended.

But trying to stomp on his foot hadn't worked, so this time I threw my weight backwards, and came pretty close to having the top of my head connect with his nose; one of those target areas he'd shown me. But he must have been expecting it, because while he rocked back on his heels, he didn't fall or so much as stumble. And then his arms tightened around my midriff again. "Good try," he told me while I struggled to catch my breath, "but not good enough. Try again."

He put me on my feet and gave me a second to get my balance.

I thought about my options. Stomping hadn't worked. Going backwards hadn't worked. How about going forward?

I tensed, but that just caused him to tighten his arms again, and to move his knee to the outside of mine, preparatory to knocking me down. "Don't telegraph your moves, Savannah," he murmured against my ear, his breath stirring the hairs at my cheek. "Surprise me."

Sure.

I fought back the shiver that warm puff of air had caused. If going backwards didn't work, and going forward wouldn't work, how about going limp? It went against every inclination to fight—or at least every inclination I would have had to fight, had it been anyone but Rafe behind me—but it might be the most unexpected thing I could do. And unexpected was good, right? If I couldn't throw him off balance physically, maybe I could do it emotionally.

I sagged against him. He didn't falter, as I had hoped, but his hold changed to support instead of restrain me. To hold me up instead of keeping me from getting away. I took the opportunity to twist in his arms, and looped my own around his neck, so we were stomach to stomach and face to face.

His mouth softened into a half smile. "That's one way to do it."

"It wouldn't work on anyone but you," I informed him, a little breathless, although not so much because he was holding me too tightly this time.

"Sure it would."

"It wouldn't work on Walker." Since Walker didn't swing my way.

"Maybe not." He made no move to let me go. I shifted a little, just enough to rub against him, and watched his nostrils flare.

I lowered my voice to a whisper. "You know…"

"Yeah?"

I stroked the back of his neck with my fingertips. "Right now, I wouldn't have any problem at all putting you on the ground."

He opened his mouth to argue, but closed it again when he realized I had my knee between his legs and was a tenth of a second from being able to knock his crown jewels up into his abdomen. A flicker of chagrin crossed his face, followed by amusement. "Damn."

"I know." I preened, just a little.

"Oh, well." He shrugged. "Since you got me…" His arms tightened and his gaze dropped from my eyes to my mouth. As he lowered his head, my eyes fluttered closed. Only to fly open again, in shock, when instead of the expected kiss, my back hit the mat.

"I told you," Rafe said, two inches from my face, his arms braced on either side of my head, "don't telegraph your moves."

The unspoken part of that sentence? Don't believe other people when they do.

He'd certainly managed to surprise me.

He also felt very good where he was. His weight pushed my body into the mat, and he was warm and hard against me, his mouth just a few inches from mine. I'd been primed for a kiss, and I hadn't gotten one. I wanted it. He must have as well, because when I looped my hands around the back of his neck and tugged, he didn't resist.

Things might have gone on from there, had it not been for the rather insistent clearing of a throat that cut through the rosy clouds a minute—or five—later.

Rafe rolled off me and to the side. "Oh," he said after a second, "you're here. Good."

I blinked up at Wendell Craig, Rafe's handler from back in his undercover days. And I didn't share Rafe's assessment that it was a good thing. Wendell didn't seem happy, his eyes flat and his lips set in an uncompromising line as he looked from Rafe to me and back.

"I'm sorry." I scrambled to my feet, my cheeks flaming. I'd never gotten caught making out in high school, probably because Todd and I hadn't really made out, ever. But here I was at almost twenty eight, caught in the act, and by my boyfriend's boss, no less. It was beyond embarrassing.

Rafe didn't seem to have any such qualms. "I was teaching Savannah self-defense," he said.

"No offense," Wendell told him dryly, "but it didn't look like she was fighting very hard."

"We got a little carried away," I murmured.

Rafe glanced at me, and then put an arm around my shoulders. "With Lamont out there," he told Wendell, "I wanna make sure she can take care of herself."

Wendell's expression showed what he thought of that excuse. "She know how to handle a gun?"

"I've touched one," I said, "if that's what you mean."

Wendell shook his head, possibly in amusement but more likely in disgust. Rafe grinned, and I realized a little too late that 'gun' is also a euphemism for something else.

"I don't want a gun," I told them both. "I don't have a permit. And I'd be afraid to use it. If I wouldn't use it, I don't need one."

Wendell didn't argue with me. "You got anything else you can use to protect yourself?"

"Knife and pepper spray."

They both looked at me like they thought I might be joking, so I went to retrieve my purse and pulled both knife and pepper spray out and held them up for inspection. They looked like lipstick cylinders, but one opened to a little 1.25 inch serrated blade, the other to a tiny nozzle. I hadn't yet had occasion to use the knife, but I'd given my sister-in-law Sheila's murderer a snootful of spray back in November. There was still enough left to douse someone else, though.

Wendell looked at them both with brows elevated. Maybe I'd managed to surprise him.

He's an older man, mid-fifties maybe, African-American and with a grizzled military haircut. I first met him in August, just a few days after I met Rafe again. For a while, I'd been under the impression that they were criminal accomplices. It took me a couple of months to figure out the truth, that appearances to the contrary, they were both on the side of the angels.

I turned from him to Rafe. "Now that we've established that I have weapons at my disposal, can I go? I'm sure you and Wendell have more important things to do."

"Dunno about more important," Rafe answered. "If something happens to you on my watch, your mama's gonna have my head."

No doubt. "Nothing's going to happen to me. Walker is probably in Bermuda by now. Or Oregon." Somewhere he could drive.

"Not enough time for him to get to Oregon."

"New Hampshire. Whatever. The point I'm trying to make is that he wouldn't hang around here. I'm not important enough for that. He's hundreds of miles away by now."

"Unless he's waiting for something."

"What would he be waiting for?"

"Dunno," Rafe said. "But I ain't discounting it."

"Well, you have more important things to deal with today than me. I'll be careful. I'll park on the street, and I'll make sure I don't stay at the office by myself." I didn't really think I was in danger, but just in case I was wrong, it wouldn't hurt to take precautions.

"See that you do." He turned to Wendell. "I'll walk her out and meet you in your office."

Wendell nodded. "Nice to see you again, Ms. Martin."

"Likewise," I said politely. Though he and Rafe had worked together for ten years, and I'd met him multiple times before, I hadn't ever really spent enough time with Wendell to be comfortable with him. "Good luck today."

He nodded, and watched us walk out.

Eight

"That was embarrassing," I said, as soon as we were outside.

He glanced at me. "What?"

"Getting caught making out, like two randy teenagers."

Rafe grinned. "Never been caught in the act before?"

I shook my head. "With you a couple of times, but we were always standing up, at least."

The grin widened, and I blushed. "You make it sound like it's an everyday occurrence for you."

He shrugged. "Not anymore. But I got caught a lot when I was a kid. Doing all kinds of stuff, including some of that."

"Who did you get caught with?"

"None of your business," Rafe said and opened my car door for me. "I'll get a ride home tonight. Don't wait up for me. Until we know what happened to Manny, this is gonna be my more than full-time occupation."

"I understand," I said, because of course I did. Manny's murder had to take precedence over everything else, that was obvious. "Just be careful. And let me know what's going on."

He nodded. "You too."

He kissed me again, but only lightly. I didn't mind, since it was just a couple of minutes since he'd curled my toes down in the gym. And then he waited for me to drive away before he headed back inside the TBI building.

I parked on the street outside the condo complex again, and sat in the car for a minute, looking around, before I opened the door. My heart was beating a little extra fast as I closed it behind me, and I scurried across the courtyard and through the door like a scared rabbit. Once upstairs, I kept the pepper spray in my hand while I searched the apartment.

Yes, I know I'd told Rafe and Grimaldi and anyone else who'd listen that I didn't think I was in danger. If Walker had any sense at all—and he does—he wouldn't hang around Nashville just for a shot at me. Frankly, I didn't think I was important enough to him for that. He'd make tracks instead, and get to somewhere where it was less likely that someone would recognize him. He was a fugitive, after all, and it didn't make sense to stick around a place where people knew him.

But I wasn't so sure I was right that I neglected to take precautions. Both Rafe and Grimaldi are smart people, and are used to dealing with the criminal element. If they both thought I should be careful, I was perfectly willing to listen. Better safe than sorry, and all that.

I made sure the deadbolt and security chain were on the front door before I went in the shower, and I took my cell phone with me, safely enclosed in a Ziploc bag, just in case.

I didn't need it, of course. When I turned off the water and pushed the shower curtain aside, no one was there. Even so, I made another circuit of the apartment, while water dripped on the floor from my hair.

It was empty. Still. That didn't stop me from keeping the phone next to me on the bed while I dried my hair and put on clothes and makeup.

Then I made the trip down the stairs and across the courtyard into the car again, realizing as I closed myself in that if Walker was watching, he must be having quite a good laugh at my behavior. I'm sure I looked as much of an idiot as I felt.

That didn't keep me from making my way equally carefully across the parking lot behind the office and through the door.

Inside, everything was normal. Tim's office was empty, so he either hadn't made it in for the day yet, or he had business somewhere else. A lot of real estate is listing appointments and running around showing properties, so there was nothing strange in that. A few of the other medium-to-big shots were in their offices, talking on the phone or working on the computer, and Heidi Hoppenfeldt, Tim's assistant, was in the kitchen fixing herself a snack.

(For the record, I'm neither a medium nor a big shot. I'm a very small fry indeed, and no one even acknowledged me as I walked down the hall. Heidi didn't see me, and no one else cared.)

Brittany was behind the reception desk in the lobby. For a change she wasn't reading Cosmopolitan or Elle. Instead, her two inch long, iridescent green fingernails were clacking over the keyboard. The pink bubblegum was in full swing.

"Anything new?" I asked as I stopped by the mail center to check my box.

She shook her head and didn't look up from the computer screen.

"I'll be in my office."

She nodded and kept typing.

Everything in the former coat closet was just the way I'd left it yesterday afternoon. I'd cleaned up the mess Walker had made, and best as I could tell, no one had disturbed it since. So that was one good thing in the midst of everything else that was going on.

Truth be told, I had a hard time even wrapping my brain around what had happened to Manny Ortega. I hadn't known him beyond hearing his voice on the phone, but last night he'd been alive and well, and today he was dead. Rafe hadn't shown much emotion beyond cold anger and determination to find whoever did it and make that person pay, but he must be upset. Anyone would be, and my boyfriend wasn't anywhere near as hard as I'd originally thought. This had to be killing him inside. It hadn't been his fault, hadn't had anything to do with him, but the responsibility—not for what had happened, but for bringing the murderer to justice—must weigh heavily on him. It was personal, in a professional way, and that always makes it harder.

With everything that had happened, it was hard to concentrate on work. I did check my email, and found a message from the agent for the new buyers of the house on Potsdam telling me that they'd set up their home inspection for the following morning and that they were now in the process of finding a loan officer to qualify them for a mortgage. Since I had assumed they'd already prequalified for the mortgage, that piece of news was a little disconcerting, but legally they did have five days to take care of it, so I tried not to see it as the big, red flag it looked like. I shot him an email back saying I'd make sure the house was ready for inspection at nine the following morning, and that I'd see him then and there.

That done, I sat back and twiddled my thumbs.

I could have worked on some kind of mailing or something, I suppose. Some way to drum up more business. But my heart wasn't in it. I'd gone into real estate because I liked looking at houses, but it was hard to concentrate on houses when Walker might be gunning for me and when someone had shot Manny Ortega.

The possibility of a connection brought me up short.

But no. Surely not. If Walker wanted to hurt me, he would have shot Rafe, not Manny. Manny and I hadn't even met. There was no way Walker could have known that Manny even existed, let alone that I knew—or that my boyfriend knew—who he was.

Unless he'd followed Rafe from our apartment to the TBI and seen him with Manny.

But if he wanted to get at me, he would have been better off shooting Rafe.

Unless...

Was it a warning? Manny first, then Rafe, and then me?

The idea gave me heart palpitations. Literally. My heart skipped a beat before picking up the rhythm, a bit faster than before.

But again, why would he bother? I may have been responsible for putting him in jail, but he was out now. He'd be better off focusing on preserving his freedom than taking revenge on me. Nutcases get caught up in things like that, but unless Walker had done a total one-eighty during his time at Riverbend Penitentiary, he wasn't crazy. He'd been all about self-preservation. Everything he'd done—the two murders he'd committed and the two he'd tried to tack on—had been in an effort to preserve the status quo, his business and his reputation. I couldn't see him doing a total about-face now, and suddenly not caring about anything but getting revenge on me.

But just in case, I dialed Tamara Grimaldi's number.

I figured I'd get her voicemail, but she answered, her voice harried. "Grimaldi. Homicide."

"It's me," I said.

"Ms.... Savannah."

In deference to her obvious stress, I cut straight to the chase. "Any news on Walker?"

"His house is empty. There's no sign of him in Kentucky. We haven't found the guard, alive or dead. We haven't found the car."

"Is there any chance at all that Walker shot Manny?" I ran through my thought process, including all the reasons I thought I was probably wrong.

"It does seem unlikely," Grimaldi agreed, "but I'll keep it in mind."

"There's no news on Manny, I assume?"

"It's too soon."

Right. "I'll let you go," I said. "I just wanted to mention the possibility that Walker was involved, since it crossed my mind."

"No problem. Take care of yourself." She didn't give me time to answer, just hung up in my ear. I didn't take it personally. I was stressed out myself, and it wasn't even my job to figure out what had happened.

By ten thirty I was sick of sitting there, so I got back into the car—very carefully—and drove to Germantown. If I was going to sit and twiddle my thumbs, I might as well sit in my car and keep an eye on Bradley.

I hadn't heard from Shelby this morning, which was a bit of a surprise. She had known that someone was following him last night, and I would have thought she'd be interested to know how things had gone down.

Then again, she was pregnant. I remembered, from my own two truncated pregnancies, how hard it sometimes had been to drag myself out of bed in the morning. Maybe she was sleeping in.

I drove down the street in front of Ferncliff & Morton. Everything looked normal. Then I drove down the alley past the employee parking lot.

Bradley's SUV wasn't there.

I almost stopped, so I could stare stupidly at the empty space. But I caught myself in time, and kept going.

My mind went, too, into hyperdrive. Maybe he'd had an early appointment. Or maybe he and Shelby were both sleeping in. Maybe Shelby finally got some.

Or—my stomach clenched at the idea—maybe something was wrong with the baby, and they'd had to rush to the hospital.

It was that thought that made me pick up the phone and dial. I don't know why it should matter to me that Shelby and Bradley's baby was OK, but it did. After going through a few miscarriages myself, I knew just how devastating they could be. Mine had been in the first trimester. I could only imagine how horrible it must be to lose a baby you'd carried inside your body for seven or eight months.

The phone rang. And rang. And rang some more. Finally voicemail picked up.

"This is Shelby. I can't get to the phone right now. Please leave a message."

"It's Savannah," I said, concentrating on keeping my voice even. "I hadn't heard from you today, and I just wanted to check in. Call me."

And then, just in case Bradley had dropped his car off at the shop for an oil change and to have the tires rotated on his way to work this morning, I dialed Ferncliff & Morton. I'd ask for him, and if he was there, I'd just hang up before Carolyn transferred me. But that way at least I'd know one way or the other whether he had shown up for work today.

Unlike Shelby, Carolyn answered on the first ring. "Ferncliff & Morton Family Law. How may I direct your call?"

"I'd like to speak with Bradley Ferguson," I said, only realizing as I did it that maybe I should have done something to disguise my voice, since Carolyn had been working for Ferncliff & Morton since before Bradley and I were married, and there was a chance she might realize who I was.

Indeed, there was a hesitation before she responded, as if she might be trying to place me. If she recognized me, she didn't say anything about it, however. "Mr. Ferguson is out of the office this morning. Can I take a message?"

I thought fast. "He had an appointment here earlier..."

"Mrs. Vandervinder?"

No way was I claiming that.

"No," I said firmly. "I'm her assistant."

"What can I do for you, Ms....?"

"Walker," I said, since it was the first name that popped into my head. "We're a little concerned, since Mr. Ferguson hasn't arrived yet. Would you happen to know when he left?"

"He hasn't been in the office so far," Carolyn said, her voice shaded by concern. For Bradley, I guess, or maybe for the fact that he had stood up an F&M client. It made me feel a little guilty. I pushed through it.

"Have you spoken to him this morning? I hope everything is OK?"

"I'm sure it's fine," Carolyn said. "His wife is expecting. Maybe something happened."

"Ah." I made myself smile, because I knew it would show in my voice. "Of course. He mentioned that. I'll let my employer know."

"I'll leave him a note," Carolyn said, "for when he comes in."

I thanked her and hung up, pondering who Mrs. Vandervinder might be.

It wasn't a common name, for certain. And she must be one of the Ferncliff & Morton clients, if Bradley had an appointment with her this morning.

That's probably where he was right now. Maybe the guy he'd met with at the Shortstop yesterday had been a red herring, unrelated to whatever was going on in Bradley's life. Maybe he was getting it on with Mrs. Vandervinder.

With a name like that, she shouldn't be hard to find.

I called the office and got Brittany. "I need you to look something up for me."

"Can't you look it up yourself?" Brittany asked.

"I'm in the car." It was true. Even if I was parked and had both hands free.

She rolled her eyes, audibly. "What do you need?"

"Anything in the name Vandervinder."

"Spell it."

I did, to the best of my ability.

"There's only one," Brittany said after a half a minute. "Dale and Ilona Vandervinder. They live in Brentwood." She rattled off an address.

"Any information about the house?"

Another pause, and then Brittany came back on the line. "It isn't on the market. According to the tax records, it was built four years ago. Custom. No one else has owned it. It's appraised at 4.2 million. Seven thousand square feet, on three acres near the Brentwood Country Club."

"Wow."

Brittany didn't reply, but I heard the sound of a bubble popping. "Anything else you need?" she inquired.

"That's it for now. Unless you know who the Vandervinders are and what they do for a living?"

Brittany snorted and hung up on me. Couldn't wait to get back to this month's issue of Cosmopolitan, no doubt. I gave the parking lot behind Ferncliff & Morton another look—there was still no sign of Bradley's car—before starting my own and rolling away from the curb.

BRENTWOOD IS A SPRAWLING NEIGHBORHOOD south of Nashville and north of Franklin, in wealthy Williamson County. The roads are good, the schools are better, and people have a lot of money. From where I was, it took me about twenty minutes to get there. Another ten before I was rolling slowly up the road in front of the Vandervinder mansion.

And it was a mansion. Not in the sense that my ancestral home, the Martin Mansion in Sweetwater, Tennessee, is a mansion. The Martin Mansion was built in 1839, a true antebellum plantation home. As Brittany had told me, the Vandervinder mansion was brand spanking new. And huge. A typical, if hugely overblown, McMansion in pale pinkish brick with a lot of jutting gables and fake half-timbering. It looked bigger than seven thousand square feet, but the bank of five garages probably had something to do with that, as had the structure I suspected of being a pool house in the back of the main structure.

It looked like a compound, surrounded as it was by an eight feet tall brick wall and sturdy wrought iron gates that probably only opened at the touch of a keypad, from someone who knew the proper digits to input. I had no hope of being able to snoop.

I drove slowly down the road to the next corner, turned around, and drove back. This time, coming from the other direction, I caught sight of a dark SUV parked halfway out of sight on the east side of the complex.

It was difficult to be sure from where I was, down on the road, a half mile away, but it looked like Bradley's car.

So this was why he hadn't come to work yet today. He'd gone to his meeting with Mrs. Vandervinder.

That could prove to be a problem. When he went back to the office, Carolyn would surely mention that Mrs. Vandervinder's assistant had called to inquire why he wasn't there. She had said she would, and from what I knew about her, she was nothing if not efficient. No copies of Cosmo or Marie Claire in Carolyn Wilkins's desk drawer.

Bradley would tell her he'd been here, that there must be some mistake, and if I was very unlucky, Carolyn might mention that the woman who called sounded a lot like his ex-wife. Bradley would remember seeing me two days ago, and then the manure would hit the fan.

There was nothing at all I could do about it, though. I could deny it, sure, but that likely wouldn't make an iota of difference to what Bradley believed.

A car came up the road behind me, and I pulled over to the side and put my blinkers on to show the driver that he should go around me. He signaled to pull out and rolled by, a BMW. The profile of the driver looked familiar, and with a jolt of surprise, I recognized Nathan Ferncliff.

What on earth was he doing here? Checking up on Bradley? Suspicious that Bradley had something going on the side with Mrs. Vandervinder?

Or had Carolyn told him about my phone call, and he had driven all the way down here to make sure Bradley wasn't ignoring the company's no doubt wealthy client?

Nathan's BMW disappeared down the hill and didn't come back. There was nothing to see, so I put my own car in gear and rolled off, as well, returning in my thoughts to where I'd been when the appearance of Nathan's car had derailed me.

I could tell Bradley the truth, that Shelby had been worried about him and had enlisted my help in trying to figure out what was going on. Or I could lie, and come up with some other reason I was trying to get in touch with him.

Something to do with a law question, maybe? I could probably come up with some story, maybe of an embarrassing nature, to make him believe that I hadn't wanted Carolyn to realize who I was. It would take some quick thinking, since I'd obviously compounded that offense by claiming I was someone specific, someone I was not, and I'm far and away the worst liar in the world. And he might wonder why I didn't just ask one of my family members, most of whom are also lawyers.

But if, say, I told him I'd gotten pregnant, out of wedlock, and I was afraid my on-again, off-again, no-good boyfriend would refuse to take responsibility so I needed a DNA test to force him to take action, he might believe that. Paternity testing is part of what family lawyers do, and I could make him believe that I didn't want to ask my traditional, overbearing, Southern family for help. Bradley had even encountered Rafe once, at his domineering, possessive, dangerous best, so he'd probably buy it.

As I rolled off down the road away from the Vandervinder spread, I admitted to myself that I didn't like having to lie about it, though. Not about being pregnant when I wasn't, and not about Rafe being an on-again, off-again, no-good boyfriend who'd refuse to take responsibility. The lie would cut a little too close for comfort, honestly, since that was exactly what I'd believed the one time I had been pregnant with Rafe's baby. That he hadn't signed on for fatherhood and wouldn't want to have a baby with me.

As for the other thing, we'd been together every day—and every night—for more than two and a half months now, and I still wasn't pregnant again. We weren't really trying, true. But we weren't not trying, either. I wasn't on the pill, and we didn't use condoms. I had confidently believed I'd be pregnant again by now. I wanted to be pregnant again. It was surprising and a bit disconcerting that I wasn't. The first time had been beyond easy. So easy it had been unplanned. I'd never even considered the possibility. I'd fallen into temptation once, and spent the night with him, and had woken up pregnant.

Yet here I was, sharing my bed with the guy. Having sex with him almost every night. Still not pregnant.

It was enough to make me concerned. To make me go from worry about another miscarriage in the event I did get pregnant again, to worry that I couldn't get pregnant even if I wanted to.

Was it possible that something had gone wrong during that last miscarriage in November? Something inside?

It was a sobering thought. I'd never been someone who'd desperate wanted children, but I'd always assumed I'd end up with one or two. Most of the people I knew did. Catherine had three, Dix had two, my best friend from high school, Charlotte, had a couple. I hadn't ever considered that I might end up without any.

Although there was always adoption, I guess. A very nice couple named Sam and Ginny Flannery had adopted Rafe's son David when he was an infant, many years before Rafe found out he had a son, and I don't think they could have loved David any more if Ginny had given birth to him.

I really wanted to have Rafe's baby, though. Our baby. I'd gone through hell over my last pregnancy, trying to decide whether to keep the baby or not, and when I finally decided—and lost it anyway—it had been devastating. I wanted—I needed—to get pregnant again, and this time have the outcome be different.

I should probably schedule an appointment with a gynecologist, just to make sure everything was A-OK. Someone other than my previous OB/GYN, who was currently serving twenty to life in Maury County for murder and adoption fraud.

Maybe Shelby would give me the name of her doctor. It would give me an excuse to call her, too, now that I knew she and Bradley weren't in bed together.

I dialed and waited, while maneuvering the car up Franklin Road in the direction of Old Hickory Boulevard.

There was no answer, and I didn't want to leave a message, just in case Bradley got his hands on Shelby's phone and realized I'd called. Much better not to invite trouble. Instead, I just tucked the phone away and concentrated on driving.

Nine

The way from Brentwood to Green Hills lies through Oak Hill. Oak Hill happens to be where Walker Lamont's old spread is located.

Or maybe I shouldn't call it his old spread, since he was now out of prison, hopefully only temporarily, and it was sort of his current spread.

Not that he was there, of course. Tamara Grimaldi had told me the house had been checked out and was empty, so I fell into temptation and drove by, just because I was so close anyway.

It was actually just a few weeks since I'd been here. Tim had the key, and had been holed up at Walker's place while the police were trying to arrest him for murder back in February. I'd realized he might be here, and had stopped by for a chat.

Everything looked just the way it had then. The grass was a little greener and there were a few tentative buds on the trees, but apart from that, nothing had changed.

I pulled around the back of the house and parked in the spot where I'd parked last time I was here, with the nose of the car against a low stone wall separating the parking pad from one of the many flower beds surrounding the house. All that was in the bed right now were a few spindly sticks, and beyond was the back patio where a gas grill used to be. I'd attended a barbeque here last summer, shortly after getting my real estate license and signing on with what was then Walker Lamont Realty. Back before Walker started killing people, or at least before he started killing people I knew.

I got out of the car and stood for a moment, looking around.

There was nothing at all to see. Things were quiet. It's a settled neighborhood with large, well-maintained houses on enormous, parklike lots. The closest neighbor was a football field away, and didn't seem to be the kind who blasted music at earpopping decibels in the middle of the day. A demure off-white Chrysler was parked in their driveway.

The neighbor on the other side was even farther away, and out of sight behind a wall of bushes. I couldn't hear anything from that direction, either. Meanwhile, Walker's house backed up to the nature preserve surrounding Radnor Lake, so there were no neighbors in the back, just trees and brush.

I turned my attention to the house. It too looked deserted. The garage was empty. Walker's ranch house was low to the ground, and there was a window in the side wall of the garage I could reach. I peered through into the darkness, and saw nothing but wheelbarrows, garden hoses, and picks and shovels. Walker might not have seen the sense— or had the need—to put his house on the market when he went to prison, but he had probably sold his car. A house can sit for a while without anyone living in it, but a car needs to be driven.

It would have been fun to look through the big floor to ceiling window in the living room, but I would be safer in the back, where no one could see me. The last thing I needed was for one of the neighbors to notice me sneaking around, and call the police. The last time I'd been here—looking for Tim—officers Spicer and Truman had caught

Rafe and me breaking and entering. I wasn't eager for a repeat. Spicer and Truman had let us go, but I didn't think I could count on being that lucky again.

So I went around to the back, and past the door into the mudroom—locked—to the kitchen windows. They were high off the ground, and try as I might, I couldn't see anything but a wedge of the ceiling.

There were double doors, though, from the patio into the family room, but they were locked too. But at least I got a good look into the kitchen. It looked neat and clean. I moved on, across the patio.

Beyond the family room was what looked like a bathroom: another small window, high off the ground. Nothing to see there either; just a section of ceiling and half a ceiling light.

Next came a room that Walker must have been using for a home office. It was set up with a couple of desks, bookshelves, filing cabinets, etc. One of the file drawers hung open, which was interesting. Nothing looked out of place, though, so maybe it was just a front-loaded drawer that had slid out on its own.

I was past the patio by now, picking my way across the damp ground along the back of the house to the master bedroom on the far corner.

When I'd been here for the cookout last summer, I hadn't done much snooping. I was new in the office, and I didn't want to get off on the wrong foot with my boss. And in February, I'd stayed in the kitchen with Tim. As a result, I had never seen Walker's bedroom.

It was a big room, with a huge bed. Easily as wide as it was long. It faced a fireplace, with an elegant white surround and glazed porcelain tiles. On the wall opposite the window were a couple of double doors, probably closets. And a single open door through which I could see the tiled floor of the master bath.

The bed was rumpled. And not just rumpled as if a cat or small dog had jumped up on it. Rumpled as if someone had slept here and had gotten up, tossing the blankets and sheets aside.

There was the indentation of a head in the pillow nearest the window.

I stepped back, and almost twisted my ankle on the high heeled pump I had put on.

Three weeks ago, after Tim left, there had been no sign that he'd ever been here. All the beds had been made, and pristine. The only anomaly was a wet shower curtain I overlooked, that only Rafe noticed.

Sometime since then, someone had spent the night in Walker's bed.

I dialed Grimaldi's number. "When you sent people to Walker's house yesterday, did they check the bedrooms?"

"Nice to hear from you, too," Grimaldi said mildly. "What do you need to know?"

"Whether any of the beds looked like they'd been slept in."

I heard the riffling of pages. "No," Grimaldi said. "Why do you ask?"

"I'm here now. Looking through the windows. And someone's definitely been using the bed in the master bedroom. The covers are upset and there's the imprint of someone's head on the pillow."

There was a beat. "What are you doing?" Grimaldi asked. I opened my mouth to answer, but before I could, she'd added, "Get out of there. Now."

"There's no one here—"

"You don't know that."

"You told me no one was here."

"That was before I knew the bed had been slept in," Grimaldi said. "Get out of there, Ms. Martin. Now!"

"I'm getting, I'm getting." I made my way back toward the car. I didn't think anyone was inside the house, but it was easier to do what she said than to argue. Especially since she was back to calling me by my last name. "You'll send someone down here, right? To see whether it was Walker or someone else?" To take fingerprints or gather hair samples or whatnot.

"Oh, yes." She sounded grim. "I'll have a CSI crew out there in twenty minutes. By then, I want you long gone."

"I will be." I was in the car by then, cranking the key in the ignition. "No sign of the car yet? Or the guard?"

"None. And I have a murder to solve, so if you'll excuse me...?"

"Of course." I put the car in reverse and started the process of turning around so I wouldn't have to back down the roughly quarter mile long driveway. "Will you let me know what you find out?"

"I'll do what I can," Grimaldi said, and hung up.

I CONTINUED ON MY WAY TO Green Hills and Shelby with my head buzzing.

So a day or two ago, the police had checked Walker's house and it had appeared empty and unused. This morning, it appeared as if someone had been in it and had spent the night. Unless Tim was up to something—and I couldn't imagine what—it was probably Walker himself. And that meant my comfortable assumption had been wrong. He wasn't three states away by now. He was still in Nashville.

But why?

I still couldn't believe it had to do with me. There was no point in his killing me, and Walker's other murders hadn't been pointless. He'd always killed to protect himself, his lifestyle, his reputation, his company... and I wasn't a threat to any of that. His reputation, lifestyle and company were out of his reach as a fugitive, and I certainly wasn't a threat to his life.

There must be something here in Nashville he needed or wanted. Something he was waiting for. Maybe he was simply waiting for interest in his escape to die down before he hightailed it out of town, but really, it would have been safer to make tracks immediately. Now all the cops were on high alert.

Had he been looking for something in the house? His passport, maybe? Or bank account information? A safety deposit box key?

If so, he was probably gone for real this time and I could stop worrying.

Maybe he had taken his car and left.

I had assumed Tim would have sold it after Walker went to prison, but maybe not.

I picked up the phone again and dialed Tim's number as I maneuvered my own car up Hillsboro Road toward Green Hills. He didn't answer, so I tried the main office number instead, just in case he was on the cell phone with someone else. "It's Savannah," I told Brittany. "Is Tim around?"

"Just a minute." Brittany went away, and then the phone clicked and buzzed. After just a second, Tim picked up and introduced himself.

"It's Savannah," I said, a little curious as to why he hadn't picked up my previous call when he obviously wasn't on the other line.

He didn't answer, and I can't swear to it, but I felt like I could hear—or sense—chagrin or guilt or something of that nature coming down the line toward me.

I added, "Is everything OK?"

"Fine," Tim said, but he didn't sound it. He sounded like he wished I hadn't called. "What can I do for you?"

"I just had a question."

"About real estate?"

That would be the logical assumption. I was a real estate agent and he was my broker. What was interesting, was that he thought he had to ask.

"I was wondering whether you remember whether Walker's car was in his garage three weeks ago, when you were camping out at his house."

"Sheesh!" Tim hissed. "Talk a little louder, why don't you? I'm not sure everyone heard you."

I glanced around. I was alone in the car, so who'd hear me? "I'm sorry. I assumed you were alone. Aren't you in your office? Did you put me on speaker?"

"No," Tim said. "The car wasn't there three weeks ago. I sold it for him in August. He wasn't going to need it for a while."

"But he kept the house."

"A house and a car are different," Tim said, as if I didn't already know that. "As long as the house is maintained, it'll be fine for years."

"Have you been down there lately?"

"To Walker's house?"

I waited for him to elaborate, because yes, it was obvious that I was asking him about Walker's house. When he didn't say any more, I spelled it out. "Yes. To Walker's house. Have you been there since you were squatting there last month?"

"No," Tim said, and I could tell from the tone of his voice that he was bristling.

"So you didn't spend the night in the master bedroom last night."

"Have you lost your mind?"

"Just checking," I said.

Tim sniffed. "Walker and I didn't have that kind of relationship."

Sure. Whatever. "I appreciate it."

I made to hang up, and Tim squealed. "Wait. Wait!"

"What?"

"Why do you want to know?"

"I was just down there. The bed had been slept in."

"What were you doing there?"

"Just curious," I said. "He trashed my office."

"Did you think you were going to trash his house?"

"Of course not." It was my turn to sniff. "I would never do that."

Tim was silent. It was a judgmental sort of silence. My mother is good at that sort of thing, so I've encountered it before. I resisted the temptation to babble, to reiterate that I'd never vandalize someone's house, no matter what they'd done to my office.

Finally Tim spoke again. "Did you need anything else?"

"Actually," I said.

"Yes?"

"When was the last time you spoke to Walker?"

Reluctance wafted down the line again. Eventually Tim said, "He called me yesterday."

"Did you tell the police?"

"No," Tim said.

Of course not. And since I could imagine the reasons—as well as the excuses—why he hadn't, I didn't push it. "What did he want?"

"Money," Tim said.

"Your money?"

"His money. Before he was arrested, he transferred most of his own money into the company accounts. He was afraid his personal assets would be frozen. Now he wants to draw the money back out."

"Was that what he was looking for at the office the other night?"

"Not the money," Tim said, "but statements and things. I guess he wanted to make sure I'd taken care of what he entrusted to me."

Yikes. I hoped for Tim's sake that he had, because an unhappy Walker wasn't someone I personally wanted to encounter.

"I suppose you'll have to get him the money. He can't go to the bank himself."

Tim didn't contradict me.

"And I suppose it takes a bit of time to get a lot of money in small, unmarked bills."

"He didn't mention unmarked bills," Tim said, sounding worried.

Too many action-adventures on my part lately, probably. I'm partial to romantic comedies, with the occasional romantic drama or historical thrown in for good measure. But Rafe likes action. And because I like Rafe, I'd sat through some of his movies, while he'd sat through some of mine. In his movies, the kidnappers always ask for the money in small, unmarked bills.

"Don't worry about it," I said. "If he didn't say anything, I'm sure he doesn't care. And it's his money, after all."

"Right," Tim said, sounding relieved.

I navigated the light at Hillsboro Road and Abbot Martin, taking a left in front of the Donut Den. "I assume you were planning to tell the police about this, so they can be there and take him back to prison?"

"Um..."

Just as I thought. "He killed two people, Tim. And then he tried to kill two more. And although they haven't found him yet, the police think he killed the guard who escorted him from prison to his mother's supposed funeral, too. Walker's a murderer. He belongs behind bars."

"Yes," Tim said, "but I don't want him to kill *me*."

"He won't kill you. Not if the police are there and catch him. Then he'll go back to prison."

"But what if they don't catch him? Then he'll be out there. And he'll be angry with me!"

Instead of with me. And next time it'd be Tim's office he tore to pieces.

"Call the police. They'll get him. And then we'll all breathe easier again." I turned the Volvo into the townhouse complex where Shelby and Bradley lived, the same place where I'd spent two years as Mrs. Ferguson.

"I'll think about it," Tim said and hung up. I pulled to a stop in front of Bradley and Shelby's townhouse and cut the engine.

It was strange to be back. I hadn't been here since Bradley and I divorced almost three years ago and he got the house as part of the settlement. I'd done an open house once, in a different part of the development, but I hadn't been here.

I sat in the car for a minute or two just looking at it.

It looked the same, except in subtle ways. The wreath on the door was Shelby's: shaped of twigs, with lots of spiky sunflowers and adorned with a little birdhouse. Very spring-like and cheerful. Mine had been an elegant concoction of yarn and felt flowers. It hadn't crossed my mind to take it with me when I left; now I kind of wished I had. I also wondered whether it was still inside somewhere, maybe in the hall closet, or whether Shelby had delighted in throwing it in the trash when she moved in.

The living room curtains were different too—a solid color, while mine had had stripes—and the mat in front of the door was different. I didn't care about that, though. I'd never been particularly attached to the mat we'd had, nor to the curtains.

The garage door was closed, and unlike at Walker's house, there was no side or front window I could look through. Shelby's minivan wasn't parked in sight, so it was either in the garage, or she had left. I got out of the Volvo and made my way up to the front door.

Ten

It took a while. Several minutes passed while nothing happened. There was no sound from inside, and no one came to the door. I was about to give up—maybe Shelby was out shopping or something—when the chain finally rattled.

Shelby opened the door, and for a second—or five—we stared at each other. She didn't say a word, and I didn't either. I was waiting for her to acknowledge me, but when she didn't, I smiled tentatively. "Hello."

Shelby blinked, and it was as if some spell was lifted. "What are you doing here?"

"I tried to call," I said, "but you didn't answer."

"I was..." She hesitated, "sleeping."

Sure. Only... she didn't look like she'd been sleeping. She was fully dressed, in maternity jeans and a blouse, with makeup on her face and big hoops in her ears. Surely, if she'd been lying down, she'd have taken those off, at least?

My doubt may have shown on my face because she flushed. "What do you want?"

Whoa. Not exactly the reception I had expected. We would never be best friends, but surely we'd been on better terms than this recently.

I tried to arch a brow the way Rafe does, and arched both instead. My voice was nice and cool, though. "I just wanted to make sure you were OK. You didn't answer the phone this morning. I thought you'd want to know how the surveillance went last night."

"Oh." She flushed again.

I waited in vain for her to invite me in. When she didn't, I took it upon myself to give her a little nudge. "Do you want to talk about this on the stoop?"

She finally took a step back. "Come in."

"Thank you," I said graciously, as if it had been her idea all along.

Walking into the townhouse was a little like stepping back in time. The interior hadn't changed much more than the outside had. The carpets were still tan, the walls still a toasty shade of oatmeal. The brown leather sofa Bradley had insisted on acquiring had worn well. Shelby had substituted solid panel curtains for the striped silk I had had, and the picture above the fireplace was a rather dull reproduction landscape, not the brightly colored print of people dancing I had talked Bradley into buying for me. But other than that, it was a lot like walking into my previous life.

"We can sit in the kitchen," Shelby said and led the way down the hall toward the back of the house. I followed, looking around.

She had updated the kitchen, anyway. When Bradley bought the place, it had had the old oak kitchen cabinets and laminate kitchen counter from the mid 1990s. Shelby had substituted white Shaker style cabinets and a marble counter, with glossy white subway tiles on the backsplash. It looked very nice, and I told her so.

"Thank you." She glanced around, negligently. I bit back... not envy, exactly, because to have this kitchen, I would have had to stay married to Bradley, and there was no part of me that wanted to be married to Bradley. Especially with what I thought might be going on between him and Mrs. Vandervinder. But at the same time, it seemed grossly unfair that Shelby, who had basically stolen my husband out from under me, should have gained this beautiful kitchen while I was stuck with 1980s cabinets and vinyl flooring.

And Rafe. Don't forget Rafe.

I relaxed, my priorities straight once more. "What can you tell me about Mrs. Vandervinder?"

Shelby looked surprised. "Who?"

"Vandervinder. Ilona. She's a Ferncliff and Morton client."

"Why?"

"I have no idea." And it was something I'd have to explore when I had more time. "Bradley's at her house right now."

"I know. He had a..." She trailed off, her eyes on the clock on the stove. The gorgeous stainless steel gas stove, far superior in every way to what I had in my apartment.

Not that I'd trade Rafe for a stainless steel gas stove, but still.

"He had a what?"

"Appointment," Shelby said, her gaze coming back to me. "With Mrs. Vandervinder. At nine thirty."

I glanced at the clock too. It was past twelve.

"He's still there?"

"He was there thirty minutes ago. At least I'm pretty sure it was his car I saw parked out back. And he wasn't at the office as of an hour ago."

Shelby blinked. "But that's not..."

Possible, I assumed. "Why not?"

She shook her head. "What happened yesterday?"

"He went to the post office and to a bar in South Nashville," I said. "He was meeting someone there."

Shelby looked like she was bracing herself. "Who?"

"Not Mrs. Vandervinder. Some guy."

"Did you recognize him?"

"I didn't see him," I said. "Middle-aged, going gray, suit and tie. Ring any bells?"

Shelby hesitated. "Nathan Ferncliff."

Now that she mentioned it, it might have been. The description fit him. I would have recognized Nathan, but of course Manny had no way of knowing who Nathan Ferncliff was. And now we had lost the chance to ask him.

Although why would Bradley and Nathan meet on the sly in a dive in Tusculum? They worked together all day. You'd think they'd have plenty of time to converse during business hours.

Unless this was something they had to keep outside the office. Something fishy that they didn't want Carolyn or Diana to find out about.

I made a mental note to pursue this line of thought sometime when I was alone, and filed it away. "Tell me about Mrs. Vandervinder."

"She's getting a divorce," Shelby said. "Bradley is her attorney."

"Is she attractive?"

Shelby gave me the evil eye. "My husband isn't cheating."

Fine. Whatever. "Why is she getting a divorce?"

"How would I know? Bradley doesn't talk about work. Attorney-client privilege, remember?"

Of course I remembered. I'd taken a year of pre-law before dropping out. I knew the basics. Bradley hadn't always kept completely mum while I'd been married to him, though. Sometimes he had talked things over with me, to get my opinion. But maybe he was more confident in his judgment these days, and didn't feel the need to double-check his instincts with his wife before acting.

"Have you met her?"

"No," Shelby said.

"I don't suppose Bradley told you what he was doing last night?"

"He said he was working," Shelby said. "And he didn't come home that late, you know. It was before seven."

I nodded. There was no reason why Shelby would have questioned it if he'd told her he'd worked until six thirty. I often work later than that. Bradley probably did, too.

There was nothing more Shelby could do for me, though. And she seemed eager to get rid of me. She was sitting on the edge of her chair, as if half a moment away from jumping up. I got to my feet. "I should go."

She didn't try to keep me, just began the process of rising. With an extra twenty five pounds right up front, gaining her feet wasn't as easy for Shelby as it was for me.

"I'll see myself out," I said. "I know the way." And I couldn't resist an extra parting jab. "I like what you've done to the kitchen."

Just a little reminder that it had been my kitchen first.

Shelby flushed but didn't answer. She also didn't get up. I made sure the lock clicked shut behind me, and then I got into my car and drove away.

By now it was lunchtime, and I was out and about, so rather than go home to be good and save money, I stopped at a restaurant on my way back to the office, picked up a salad to go, and ate at my desk at the office.

When that was done, I called Rafe.

I expected to get his voicemail, because I expected him to be busy investigating, or training someone, or doing something that would preclude him from answering the phone, but he picked up. "What's wrong?"

"Nothing," I said. "I mean... other than what was already wrong."

He waited, and I picked up the conversation again. "I spoke to Shelby. Turns out Bradley spent all morning with a client, a Mrs. Vandervinder. She's getting a divorce."

"OK," Rafe said.

"I told Shelby about last night. Not about Manny," that wasn't any of her concern, and besides, I was still struggling with it myself, "but about Bradley and the guy he was meeting."

"OK."

"She suggested it might be Nathan Ferncliff."

"Who's Nathan Ferncliff?"

"Bradley's boss. One of the senior partners."

"Another lawyer?"

"Yes."

"Don't they work together?"

"Maybe this is something they can't talk about in the office. Maybe they don't want Diana to find out. She's the other senior partner."

Rafe thought for a second. "Could be. Don't sound like either one of 'em would know how to find the Shortstop, though."

He was right about that. "You'll have to go talk to the people there, right? About Manny?"

"I don't think the Shortstop had anything to do with happened to Manny, darlin'."

"I don't either," I said, "but I thought maybe you'd have to—you know—trace Manny's movements last night, or something."

"Ain't no need to trace his movements," Rafe said patiently. "He told me his movements. He left the Shortstop, followed your ex-husband home, and went home himself. And seven or eight hours later, somebody shot him."

Right. "I thought maybe taking photographs of Bradley and Nathan to the Shortstop, to see if anyone could identify them, would be a good idea. I mean, I know Bradley was there. I just wanted to know if it was Nathan Ferncliff he was meeting. But if you're not going..."

I trailed off.

Rafe sighed. "I guess maybe I could make a special trip down there."

"You'd do that for me?"

"Ain't much I wouldn't do for you, darlin'. Just get me the pictures and I'll do my best."

"Could I... maybe come with you?"

There was a pause. "You didn't like it all that much the first time. Or did you forget?"

I hadn't forgotten. "I just thought it would be a way for us to spend some time together. With you being so busy today and all."

He sighed. "Hell, I'm prob'ly gonna have to do this on my own time anyway. And I could go for one of their burgers."

I couldn't. It had been delicious, but I swear I'd gained five pounds just from that one meal six months ago. However, I wanted him to take me with him, so I didn't say anything. "When will you pick me up?"

"At home at six o'clock," Rafe said.

I told him I'd be waiting, and then I let him get back to work.

There wasn't a whole lot more I could do—not to help figure out who killed Manny, not to try to discover where Walker was, nor to learn what was going on with Bradley—so I left the office again, and drove over to Potsdam Street, where Mrs. Jenkins's house is located. Tomorrow at 9 am, I'd have to be over there to let the other agent, his clients, and their home inspector in, and it was just as well to make sure there was nothing wrong with the place beforehand. Some little thing that maybe needed tweaking before the home inspector did his thing. Rafe had been over all of the house in the past few months, painting and redoing and replacing plumbing and electric, but you never know when a tree branch might fall and knock out a power line, or when the air conditioning system might cease to work because someone's stolen the condenser.

Or for that matter when someone might throw a rock through the front window.

That was the sight that greeted me when I drove up the circular driveway. The big window in the front of the house was shattered, shards of glass littering the ground below.

Mrs. Jenkins's house is an old 1880s red brick Victorian, three stories tall, with a tower on one corner and a ballroom across the entire top floor. The first time I saw it, in August, it was a dilapidated, run-down, overgrown mess, but since then, Rafe has sunk a lot of time and money into bringing it back to something of its former glory. He'd left the old, hand-blown windows alone, though. They'd been glazed and painted, of course, but the old glass remained. And now one of the panes was shattered. Not only would it cost a pretty penny to replace—we're talking a *big* window here—but there was no way to replace the original hundred and twenty five year old glass. That was lost forever.

I got out of the car and just stood, staring, for at least a minute. The senseless vandalism gave me a pain in my stomach. I know some people just enjoy ruining other people's hard work for the sake of their own enjoyment, but so far we'd mercifully avoided anything like this. Rafe looked like he belonged in this neighborhood, and no one had given him any trouble about fixing up the house and making it shine. Not that anyone would dare give Rafe trouble under most circumstances. He looks like he can take care of himself. But nobody had ripped out the condenser—which happens a lot in empty houses—and no one had crawled underneath the foundation to yank out the copper pipes, and no one—so far—had broken any of the windows.

After I finished fuming, I made my way onto the porch and over to the door, where a gray MLS lockbox hung from the handle. It was closed up tight, as opposed to the first time I'd been here, when the box had been hanging open. Then, Rafe and I had walked in to find Brenda Puckett dead on the floor in front of the library fireplace.

I won't claim that the memory didn't play with my mind as I fished the key out of the box, inserted it in the lock, and pushed the door open.

I stopped in the hallway just inside the open door and held my breath. The many times I've been here since then, with or without Rafe, I haven't really been nervous. Not about walking into the house. Or if I've been nervous, it's been for other reasons. Like, I was afraid I'd end up in bed with Rafe if I got too close to him.

But this time I was uncomfortable. It wasn't anything in particular that bothered me, nothing I could put my finger on, because there were no indications that anyone had been inside, but part of me (the intuitive part) was telling the moving parts to turn around and get out. I didn't listen to myself, because the logical part of me was busy telling the intuitive part that I had nothing to worry about. The door had been locked and the key had been in the lockbox. And although the window was broken, nobody had gotten in through it. Not unless he could vaporize. There was a jagged hole in the middle of the pane, about the size of a baseball, with a few jagged shards missing, but it wasn't like the rest of the pane was gone. The only living thing that would fit through the hole would be a bird, or if it could get up there, a mouse.

So there was no way anyone could be inside. It was just the memories of coming upon Brenda's butchered body that were playing havoc with my mind. Lying there in front of the fireplace, with her throat cut from ear to ear, and a surprised look on her face. And the blood...

I pushed the mental image aside and pulled the door shut behind me and, after a second, locked it. If anything were to happen to me, it was more likely to come from outside than in here.

That done, I looked around.

The house was not a perfect square, but it did have a central hallway. Directly in front of me, the hall headed straight back to the kitchen, along the stairs to the second and third floors. On the left, beyond the bottom step, was a formal living room or parlor, beyond that the library, where Brenda had met her demise, and then the kitchen across the back of the house.

On the right, a little further down the hall from where I was standing, was another formal living room or parlor, then the dining room, and again, the kitchen. There was a bathroom down there too, but all the bedrooms were upstairs, and then on the top floor was the big, open ballroom.

The baseball—or stone or brick—had taken out the window in the room to my left, so I headed in that direction first.

There were glass shards on the wood floor too, just as outside in the mulch under the window. The flying object—a broom?—lay in the middle of the floor.

I had expected something smaller and heavier—hard to imagine a broom flung from outside would sail all the way in here—but maybe whoever threw it had reasoned that I'd need it for the cleanup.

Still, it seemed like a strange sort of weapon. And where had it come from? Stones and bricks were plentiful, but it wasn't like brooms just lay around.

I left it where it was for the time being, and walked closer to the window. The glass crunched under my shoes.

The window needed immediate attention. Someone would have to come and replace the pane, or cover it with cardboard or plywood if they couldn't get to it immediately. We didn't want to leave the house unsecured like this, and besides, it was still cold enough in mid-March that I could feel a chilly draft on my face from the hole.

Dammit, it wasn't very long since I had spoken to Rafe, and now I had to call and bother him again.

Maybe I should just call the hardware store myself, and see if someone could come out and replace the glass. It would cost more than if we were to do it ourselves, but Rafe was busy. And it was the least I could do, to take a little worry off his mind on such a trying day.

Before I did that, though, I headed back past the bottom of the staircase into the hallway and down the hall toward the kitchen. I was here; I might as well make sure the broken window in the front was the only problem before I set about getting someone out to fix it.

The room to the right of the hall—another parlor or living room—looked fine. So did the dining room, when I stuck my head in. No broken windows or other problems in either of them. The furniture was all there, and nothing seemed disturbed.

I continued into the kitchen.

The first time I had been in this room, a few days after Brenda's murder, it had been a hideous mess, with cracked vinyl on the floor, lopsided cabinets, and avocado green appliances from the 1970s. Now it looked like a different room.

For all intents and purposes, it *was* a different room. The only thing that remained of the original was the ceiling, and even that had gotten a fresh coat of paint. The chipped vinyl was gone and the old hardwoods had been sanded and polished to a high gloss. The cabinets and appliances were new, and in the middle was a nice, sturdy kitchen table.

Once upon a time, Rafe and I had almost ended up making love on that table. I had put a stop to it, because the idea made me feel uncomfortable. And on our way down the hall and up the stairs to the bedroom, a gunshot had almost put a stop to both of us.

One of the windows had shattered then, as well. I had swept up the glass—a lot more glass than was on the parlor floor right now; it seemed as if most of the shards had fallen outside this time—and Rafe had boarded up the window, and eventually we had ended up upstairs and in bed.

That had been almost six months ago. We still hadn't made love on the kitchen table. Not here, and not anywhere else. I didn't have a kitchen table in my apartment—there wasn't enough room—and we had never spent the night here again. Now I guess we never would, since we were selling the house.

For a second I got lost in the memory of Rafe and me in this kitchen back in October, of my bare back against the coolness of the refrigerator and the heat of him against my front, before he swung me around and boosted me up on the table... and then I shook it off. Maybe we could come back here and finish what we'd started before the house sold. We—he—still owned it until then.

There was nothing noticeably out of place in the kitchen, and the back door was secured with a deadbolt. I headed back up the hall toward the front door.

The one room I hadn't checked yet was the library. I still avoid going in there whenever I can. It looks totally different now—the faded wallpaper with the big cabbage roses is gone and everything is neat and clean and tidy, with comfy furniture and a pretty rug. But I still can't look at the tile-front fireplace without imagining Brenda on the floor, her fat arms outflung, her skirt twisted around her hips, and that gaping wound across her throat.

I had to stop and steel myself before pushing open the door, and I was aware of my heart beating a little faster as I stepped across the threshold.

And then I wasn't aware of much of anything, except shock.

Eleven

No, nobody hit me over the head. The room was empty, just as it should be. But that was the only thing that was as it should be.

There were two windows in the library, and both of them were broken. All the books were tumbled onto the floor, along with the vases and other knick-knacks that had decorated the shelves. There were shards of glass everywhere, not just scattered in front of the windows, but all along the edges of the room. Clear glass in front of the windows, colored shards below the shelves.

Rafe had bought some very nice, comfortable furniture for this room: a pretty, overstuffed sofa and chair in nubby taupe fabric. Someone had slashed the seats of both of them, so the fabric hung in shreds. Same with the throw pillows: stuffing was spilling out, like organs out of a body.

Nasty metaphor, I know, but the feeling it gave me was a bit like that. A horrible clenching in my stomach. Someone hadn't just thrown a broom through the front window. Someone had been inside the house. And that same someone had taken a big knife out of the butcher block in the kitchen and used it to slash the furniture.

I knew that was the case, because the knife was standing upright in the floor right in front of the fireplace. In the same spot where Brenda's body had lain the first Saturday in February.

I MADE IT OUT OF THE house and into the car in record time. I didn't even lock the door behind me, nor did I put the key back into the lockbox. I just tumbled down the steps as quickly as my three inch heels would carry me, threw myself into the car, locked all the doors, and sat there, trying to get my breathing under control.

Nothing happened. I hadn't really expected it to. I assumed that whoever had done this—and I had a pretty good idea who—had done it either last night, or the night before. Either way, he was long gone.

Unless he was waiting for me on the second floor, of course. But surely he'd have realized that after seeing the tableau in the library, I wouldn't stick around to search the rest of the house.

Once my hands stopped shaking enough that I thought I could manage to push the right buttons on the phone, I fished it out of the purse on the passenger seat and dialed. While I listened to it ring on the other end of the line, I concentrated on steadying my breathing.

"M... Savannah?"

"Listen." I was pretty sure I could hear a hint of impatience in Tamara Grimaldi's voice, and I stumbled over my words trying to tell her that this was more than me just being curious and wanting to know what was going on. "You need to send a CSI team out to Mrs. Jenkins's house on Potsdam Street. Someone's been inside. I think it was Walker."

There was a beat while the detective processed this information. Then— "Are you all right?"

"Yes. Just scared."

"Are you there now? At the house?"

I told her I was in the car in the driveway. "I only walked through the downstairs. And when I saw the library—"

"What's wrong with the library?"

What wasn't? "Broken windows, slashed sofa pillows, books and knick-knacks and everything else on the shelves tossed on the floor…"

"What makes you think that's Mr. Lamont's doing? Broken windows and slashed furniture sounds like it could just be random vandalism."

"Two things." I took a deep breath, trying to get my voice to stop shaking. "There's no sign that anyone's broken in. All the doors were locked, and none of the windows were cracked enough that someone could get through. They're just small, jagged holes."

"OK," Grimaldi said. "So how do you think Mr. Lamont got in?"

"I think he opened the lockbox and took out the key. He may still have an MLS card he could have used. Maybe that's what he came to the office to look for. And that reminds me…"

"What?"

I recapped what Tim had told me about Walker contacting him to ask for money. "You may want to talk to Tim. Figure out wherever the drop point is for the money."

"I'll do that." Her voice was grim. "The issue with the lockbox doesn't prove that it was Mr. Lamont who broke into your boyfriend's house, though, Savannah. It could have been someone else picking the lock. A lot of people know how. And didn't you tell me you had two clients vying for this same property? Isn't it possible the losing bidder might have wanted to get even?"

I hadn't thought about that. I didn't really want to think about it now. I didn't want to believe that that sweet young couple I had liked so much could do something like this, out of spite for losing the house. But it wasn't impossible, at least not on paper.

I acknowledged as much. "I don't think so, though."

"Why not?"

"Because of the knife. A big butcher knife from the kitchen. The biggest knife in the butcher block. It was driven into the floor in front of the fireplace. In exactly the same spot where I found Brenda's body."

"The exact spot?"

"As far as I can tell. Right about where her throat was."

"Obviously Mr. Lamont would know where that was."

Obviously, since he was the one who had cut it.

"That could be luck," Grimaldi said. "The papers said that Mrs. Puckett was found in front of the fireplace in the library. The fact that the knife was in the exact same spot could be a coincidence."

Could be. I didn't believe it was, but I appreciated the attempt to make me feel better. "He trashed my office a couple days ago. This feels the same."

Grimaldi murmured something. It could have been agreement, or it could have been something entirely different.

"Whoever it was," I said, "it was someone. Someone was in the house, and someone vandalized it. Can you send a tech out here to dust for fingerprints on the knife and broom? Maybe that'll tell us something."

"I'll have someone out there in thirty minutes," Grimaldi promised. "Can you wait that long?"

"As long as Walker doesn't come running out of the house brandishing the butcher knife. If that happens, I'm driving away."

"Let's hope it won't come to that," Grimaldi said and hung up.

I leaned back in the seat, trying to relax, but I kept my eyes wide open and alert, just in case.

The crime scene tech—the same one who had smeared fingerprint dust all over my office a few days ago—showed up within a half hour, and I made him walk through the rest of the house with me. It was empty and untouched. And because I had company, I didn't linger over Rafe's bedroom on the second floor, overcome by the memories of waking up there with him next to me. We just walked through, opening doors and checking to make sure no one was there and nothing else was wrong, and then I made myself scarce while the tech went to work.

My first stop was Cumberland Hardware, down the street from the office. They do glass, and I ordered the panes I needed, along with someone to install them, to be at the house the next morning at eight. Maybe I could have the house cleaned up and the new glass in by the time the potential buyers and their inspector showed up at nine. No need to scare them off unnecessarily, after all.

While I was at it, I also picked up an old-fashioned coded lockbox. Not one of the new-fangled electronic ones that anyone with an MLS card can open, but one with a four digit code and thousands of possible variations, from 0000 to 9999 and everything in between. I had no proof—yet—that anyone had accessed the electronic lockbox, but it was just as well to be proactive.

Then I went down the street to the locksmith, and arranged for him to be there at the same time as the glazer to replace the cylinders in the locks. Not the locks themselves: they were original to the house, antique and practically priceless. I wasn't about to mess with those. But the cylinders for the keys, those we could replace. And would. Chances were there were no stray keys out there, but just in case Grimaldi was right, and the vandalism had been my sweet young buyer couple's work, I wanted to make sure the locks were changed and any key they may have made for themselves was useless.

The phone rang as I was getting back into the car. Rafe's number flashed on the screen. "Hi," I told him, surprised.

"Darlin'."

"What's going on?"

"Wondering why you haven't called."

"I spoke to you an hour and a half ago." Surely he didn't want me to bother him more often than that? Not on a day like today, with so many other things on his mind.

"About the house."

Oh. "How did you find out about that?"

"Tammy called me," Rafe said.

"Why?" Didn't she think I was capable of handling things on my own?

"I guess she thought you might not wanna bother me, and she thought I oughta know."

Right.

"So were you gonna call me?"

"I was planning to handle it myself," I said. "I've already got the glazer and the locksmith lined up for tomorrow morning. I figured you had enough on your plate and that it could wait until I saw you tonight. It's being taken care of."

"It ain't that I don't trust you to do it, darlin'."

"I know," I said. "It's your house. You have a right to know. I'm sorry."

I could hear him sigh. "You OK?"

"Fine. I was a little rattled at first, but I'm all right now."

"How bad does it look?"

"The house? Not too bad. The only damage is the broken windows. It's leaded glass, so we won't ever be able to replace it, but at least we can get new glass in. There are a lot of broken vases and things in the library. Everything breakable that was on the shelves smashed, pretty much, when whoever it was swept the shelves clean."

"Whoever?"

I took a breath. "I think it was Walker. Did Grimaldi tell you about the knife?"

"Yeah."

"It was driven into the floor just where Brenda was lying when we found her. Remember?"

"Not like I'm gonna forget," Rafe said mildly, and added, "It ain't every day a gorgeous woman faints into my arms."

"I didn't faint."

"You came close."

Maybe so. And he'd managed to take my mind off Brenda's death, which was probably what he'd intended.

"Anyway, the knife was there. Who else but Walker would have put it there? It was almost like writing a note. *You're next.*"

There was a pause, and when Rafe's voice came back, it was rather more alert than it had been. "You think he wants to kill you?"

"I'm not sure," I admitted. "When he first destroyed my office, I assumed it was just pique. He was there, my office was handy, and he took his frustrations out on it. But this... He went to the house deliberately. He went inside and found the broom and broke the windows and smashed everything else. He took a knife from the kitchen and slashed the sofa and chair. And then he drove the knife into the floor where Brenda died. Into hundred-and-twenty year old hardwood floors. Maybe I'm being paranoid, but I think it could be a message."

He didn't answer, and I added, "Maybe it isn't. But it could be. Couldn't it?"

He sounded reluctant. "It might could."

I hadn't expected that. I'd thought he'd tell me I was being silly and fanciful and it didn't mean anything. The fact that he didn't made me shiver, as if he'd drawn a very cold finger down the middle of my back.

While I was shaking off the feeling he asked, "Where are you?"

"Sitting in the car outside the locksmith's," I said.

"You being careful?"

I said I was. For good measure I looked around, and in the rearview mirror. There was nothing to see. No parked cars, and no lurking former brokers.

"Go home," Rafe said. "And stay there until I get there. I don't want you out on your own."

"But I was going to go back to the house to clean up the mess. The tech is going to leave fingerprint powder everywhere. Not to mention the pieces of glass. And we've got the new buyers and their home inspector coming at nine in the morning."

He thought for a second. "When's the locksmith coming tomorrow? And the window guy?"

I told him at eight.

"Then eight is soon enough for you, too. I'll take you there in the morning, make sure you're not alone, and then you can do what you need to do."

I guessed that would work. "I can do it now, though. Just in case something goes wrong tomorrow. We don't want to scare the buyers off."

"Nothing's gonna go wrong," Rafe said. "Go home. Wait for me."

I had my mouth open to tell him that I didn't take orders from him when he added, "Please, Savannah. I don't wanna fail you, too."

The catch in his voice took my breath away. After a second, I managed, "You didn't fail Manny. You had no way of knowing what was going to happen."

"Just wait for me. Please." He hung up before I had the chance to say anything else. Maybe he was ashamed of showing emotion, or maybe he just knew he had me where he wanted me. Either way, I pulled the car out of the parking lot and headed home.

Just as last time, I parked on the street and hurried across the courtyard to the building with the back of my neck prickling. And just like last time, nothing happened. I made it into the building unscathed, and nobody was lying in wait for me in the stairwell. Upstairs, I walked through the apartment with the pepper spray in my hand, making sure I was alone and that no one had been there, before taking off my jacket and shoes and hanging my bag in the hall.

The place was empty, of course, and untouched, and it was nice to feel safe.

Except I didn't, really. I didn't think Walker would try to get at me at home—then again, I hadn't thought he'd vandalize Rafe's house, either—but even if I was secure while I was inside these four walls, I would have to leave the apartment again at some point, and then I was fair game.

But surely—if it was Walker's doing— he was only trying to scare me. Wasn't he? Killing me would only make things worse when—if—when—the police caught up to him.

But there was no point in sitting and brooding about it, so I did my best to find something to occupy my time. It didn't make any sense to cook dinner, since we were going to the Shortstop when Rafe came home. But I changed from skirt and blouse into my only pair of jeans so I wouldn't stick out so much in the blue collar bar, and then I booted up the laptop.

The first thing I did was check my email, only to find I had one from my best friend from high school, Charlotte. *Are you going to the reunion?*

What reunion?

It took a few moments before I realized what she was talking about. Some three months ago, in late November, early December sometime, I'd received an email from the reunion committee for Columbia High. Come May, it would be ten years since we graduated from high school, and of course there was to be a party.

Back when the first email arrived, I'd been deep in the doldrums, trying to deal with my recent miscarriage and the fact that Rafe had walked out of my life without a word, while I was in the hospital losing his baby. I'd been in no position to consider whether or not I'd be going to a reunion six months in the future. Right then, all I really wanted to do was die.

I'd gotten over it, of course. And things had worked out. But I'd never done anything to respond to the invitation.

I'll be there, Charlotte's email said. *Would love to catch up.*

I would too, as it happened. Charlotte married a plastic surgeon and moved to North Carolina, so I hadn't seen her for a while. We'd sort of lost touch after Bradley and I divorced.

I could just imagine her reaction to finding out that I was living in sin with Rafe Collier.

I shot her an email back saying I would, and that we should try to meet for drinks the day before, and then I scrolled back through a couple pages of emails until I found the invitation itself, and RSVP'd to that, too.

That done, I signed out of the email program and set to work finding the photos we needed of Bradley and Nathan Ferncliff.

Google images are very convenient. You can find pictures of almost anyone there. Or at least of anyone who doesn't mind being photographed, unlike my boyfriend.

Nathan wasn't hard to find. He's been a prominent Nashville attorney for decades, and the internet was full of photos.

He did fit the description Manny had given of the man Bradley had met at the Shortstop yesterday. White, middle aged, graying hair, expensive suit. Unfortunately, it was a description that could fit probably a hundred thousand men in Nashville. We have a population of roughly a million in the metropolitan area, and I felt confident that a hundred thousand or more were middle aged and white, with graying hair. Put any one of them in an expensive suit, and he'd fit the same description.

There was a photograph of Nathan and Bradley together, that I sent to the printer. They were wearing golf shirts and were participating in some sort of charity golf tournament, so I also chose a recent picture of Nathan in a suit and tie and printed that as well, just in case the casual attire in the first picture threw someone off. Then I went looking for more pictures of Bradley.

There were less of those, and one of them stopped me dead.

When I divorced Bradley, I'd gotten rid of all my photos of the two of us, including the wedding photos. My sister Catherine had gleefully helped me create a little funeral pyre for my marriage, in which I burned my wedding pictures, my marriage license, and a few other things of sentimental value. Mother had removed them as well, of course, from the mansion, so this was the first time in several years I had seen a picture from my wedding day.

But there we were, on the steps of my childhood home, the Martin Mansion in Sweetwater: him in his tux and me in my virginal white dress, between two of the tall, white pillars.

(No, I wasn't a virgin anymore at that point. Bradley had been quite amorous before we got married. It was afterwards that he decided I was frigid and he needed to get his needs met elsewhere. Familiarity breeds contempt, and all that.)

Except for Bradley's thoroughly modern tux, the scene looked like something from out of *Gone with the Wind.* The mansion was finished in 1841, and my dress was classic 1860s Vivian Leigh, with a tight, beaded and embroidered bodice, small cap sleeves, and a huge, flounced skirt with actual, honest to goodness hoops. It weighed a ton, and the veil hadn't exactly been a lightweight, either. I looked something like a puffy cloud, and impossibly young.

Five years ago. I'd been twenty three. Back in the early days of the mansion, people married a lot younger than that. My great-great-great-grandmother Caroline—the one who slept with the groom—had been eighteen when she married the then Martin in residence, I think.

Nonetheless, looking at the picture, I couldn't believe how young I'd been. And not just how young I looked, but how innocent and unworldly and naive I had been. At that time, Mother had me firmly convinced that if I just toed the line and did everything I was supposed to do, my life would be perfect. It took marrying Bradley and having him cheat to realize that my mother didn't know everything.

That had been the beginning of the end, as far as my proper Southern Belle upbringing was concerned. Instead of crawling home to Sweetwater to lick my wounds, and in time letting mother convince me to marry Todd Satterfield, I had stayed in Nashville. On my own. I had sold makeup at the mall until I got my real estate license, and then, a month or two into that adventure, I had met Rafe, and he'd put the exclamation point on my life, as well as cemented my understanding that my mother had no clue about what I needed to make me happy.

But I digress. I printed out the wedding photo. I wasn't angry with Bradley anymore, and it was a nice reminder of how far I'd come. Besides, I thought Rafe might get some amusement out of seeing it.

That done, I started looking for a picture of Bradley I could take to the Shortstop—a more recent one, and one that didn't include me in my wedding gown.

I found one from last year, with Bradley looking fat-cat happy, the way he'd looked before Christmas when I'd had dinner with him. That was a few pounds ago. He was thinner now, and a lot more drawn, but it was the best I could do. In the earlier photos he looked too young and unfinished.

I printed it out and checked the time. I still had an hour to kill before Rafe came home. I turned back to the computer and started a Google search on the name Vandervinder.

I hadn't expected much, but as it turned out, Dale Vandervinder was something of a local celebrity. He was a producer in the music industry, and as such was 'somebody' here in Music City. There were several pictures of him, most with his wife on his arm. She was a buxom bottle-blonde in her forties, well-maintained but past the first bloom of youth. I couldn't imagine Bradley sleeping with her. I couldn't imagine her wanting to sleep with Bradley, either. After Dale Vandervinder— who was around fifty and exuded money and power, from his sterling-gray hair to his Armani suit—I'd have thought Bradley would be below her notice. I could imagine her frolicking with the pool boy or her personal trainer for a change of pace, maybe—she looked like she might be the type—but not Bradley.

Maybe their appointment had been purely business after all.

I did another search, this time on 'Dale Vandervinder + divorce.'

Family law, for your information, is about a lot of things besides dissolving marriages. There are paternity suits, surrogacy, adoption, and some other things, as well. But divorces are a family practice's bread and butter, so I started there.

And lo and behold, Country Music Today had a notice in the most recent issue saying that the acclaimed producer and his wife of fourteen years were splitting up.

Ferncliff & Morton must be representing Ilona Vandervinder.

Quite a coup for Bradley. And rather interesting how he, as opposed to one of the senior partners, had ended up representing such a high profile client. Maybe they really were sleeping together.

Although if they were, you'd think she'd make especially sure not to hire him as her legal representative.

Then again, it made a handy excuse for spending lots and lots of time together.

A sound at the door brought my head up. It was a scraping sort of sound, as if someone was fiddling with the lock. Maybe inserting something into it that wasn't a key.

I got to my feet, as soundlessly as I could, and made my way across the floor. My stocking clad feet were soundless on the carpet.

The scraping continued.

I peered down the hallway past the kitchen and raised my voice. "Who is it?"

The scraping stopped, with a sort of startled absence of sound. Or maybe that was just me reading something into the silence that wasn't there.

I took a few steps closer. "Hello?"

There was a scramble outside the door, and the sound of rapid footsteps retreating down the hall in the direction of the stairs. I started forward, but stopped before I got around to actually unlocking the door. Chances were there was no one left outside, but why take stupid chances?

I turned around instead, and headed for the window. I could have gone out on the balcony, I suppose, but that felt a little too exposed, so I kept the doors closed and just peered down at the street and sidewalk instead, craning my neck to try to catch a glimpse of someone who might come across the courtyard from my building. But since the human eye isn't designed to see around corners, I had very little luck. A few cars drove by, and a few people walked along the sidewalk—an elderly black man, a young couple of the hipster type in skinny jeans and with unwashed hair, and someone who looked like a bag lady pushing a shopping cart she must have borrowed from one of the local Kroger stores. It was full of soda cans. Empty, I assume, since they were all in a pile and not arranged in orderly rows.

I didn't recognize anyone. After a couple of minutes I gave up and went back to the computer.

Twelve

A little less than an hour later there was another sound at the door, bringing my head up and setting my spider senses tingling. This time it resolved itself into a key being inserted in the lock and after a second, the knob turning. The door opened a few inches and then stopped with a jarring sound.

"What the hell?" Rafe's voice said.

"I'm sorry. I'm sorry." I hustled down the hallway. "I forgot about the chain."

"Nervous?"

He waited for me to push the door shut enough to unhook the security chain and then open it again.

I took a step back to let him inside. "Someone was here, trying to get in."

He stared at me for a moment while the amusement in his eyes gave way to murderous intent, thankfully without veering off into doubt along the way. "You OK?"

I nodded. "I heard someone fiddle with the lock. When I asked who was there, he took off running."

"Did you run after?"

I shook my head. Rafe would have run after the intruder, gun in his hand and ready for use, but I'm not that brave.

"Good girl."

"I looked out the window. But I didn't see anyone. Or no one I recognized. Or anyone who acted suspiciously."

Rafe nodded. He was inspecting the lock. It had faint scratches on it. "After he's finished at the house tomorrow," he told me as he straightened, "get the locksmith over here to install another deadbolt."

"Are you sure that's necessary? I mean, whoever it was didn't even get past the first lock."

"Someone who knows what he's doing," Rafe said, shrugging out of his leather jacket, "can get through this door in a minute or less. Even with the chain on."

I blinked at him, doubtfully, until I remembered that he'd made his way in here once or twice without me opening the door for him first. "I'll do that."

"Thank you." He hung the jacket on the hook beside mine, and turned to look me over. "You look like you're ready to go."

I nodded.

"Hungry?"

Not for the kind of food the Shortstop served, but then I figured he knew that. I was hungry for information, though. I wanted to know who Bradley had been talking to the other night.

"Gimme five minutes." He walked away from me in the direction of the bedroom and—I assumed—the bathroom.

I went back to the dining room table, to turn the computer off and gather together the printed pages. By the time I was finished, Rafe was back, pulling a clean T-shirt over his head to hide all those beautiful muscles.

He grinned at me when his head popped free. "You sure you don't just wanna stay here tonight? We could order a pizza."

Tempting, but— "I'd really like to know who Bradley was meeting the other night. And don't you have to ask about Manny? I realize the Shortstop probably didn't have anything to do with what happened, but you should probably ask, right?"

"Prob'ly." He glanced at the papers in my hand. "What've you got there?"

"Photographs." I handed them to him and watched him rifle through. "That's Nathan Ferncliff, the senior partner at Ferncliff & Morton. The one Shelby said Bradley might have been meeting with."

Rafe nodded. "Fits the description." He flipped over to the next picture.

"That's Bradley," I said. "You probably recognize him."

"I didn't really get a good look at him," Rafe answered. "He was inside the car. And at the restaurant, I was watching you."

Nice to know. I had already known that when Bradley and I went out on that non-date before Christmas—dinner at Fidelio's so I could pick his brain about his uncle Joshua—Rafe had followed us. No sooner had Bradley pulled the car to a stop at the curb outside the condo after dinner, than Rafe had been there to remove me from the passenger seat. He'd been a little jealous, I think, at least until he realized who Bradley was. And then, of course, he'd realized that jealousy was ridiculous. There was nothing in the world that could induce me to go back to Bradley, and I was pretty sure Bradley wouldn't have wanted me back anyway. Back then he seemed plump and happy and thrilled about impending fatherhood.

"What the hell is this?"

I looked over, at what had prompted the outburst. "Oh. I thought you might enjoy seeing that."

He shot me a look. "A picture of you marrying someone else?"

I shrugged. "I burned all my pictures of Bradley after the divorce. Catherine and I had a bonfire in the backyard in Sweetwater. It's been years since I've seen that. And it doesn't make me angry anymore."

He went back to contemplating the photograph. Eventually he spoke. "Long time ago."

"Five years. In June." Long enough to get some perspective. And maybe just an ounce of wisdom.

"Why d'you print it out? You trying to tell me something?"

"What?... Oh. No." I shook my head. "I'm happy living in sin."

He quirked a brow. "You sure?"

"Positive. Bradley was different before we got married. He liked me better. Once we were husband and wife, everything went south. We stopped having sex, and he began sleeping with Shelby instead." And I would hate for that to happen to Rafe and me. All that lovely heat and passion—and fun—we had now might go away once we were shackled together wrist and ankle.

He was quiet for a moment. "I ain't Bradley. You remember that, right, darlin'?"

"Of course I remember it." Although part of me was still worried that once things were settled, all the magic would be gone. "I just don't want to jinx anything."

"Getting married ain't gonna change how I feel about you, darlin'."

Good to know. "I'm wearing your ring," I told him, and flashed the bit of blue on my hand. "That's good enough for now."

"If you say so. You ready?"

I nodded, and accepted the handful of print-outs from his hand. We got our shoes and jackets on, and a minute later, was on our way across the courtyard to the car.

Rafe put me inside and walked all the way around the Volvo, peering under the chassis, before he popped the hood. I sat there, with my hands folded in my lap and my heart knocking against my ribs, and watched him inspect the car for anything untoward. I was pretty sure it was unnecessary, that whoever had been upstairs—be it Walker or someone else—wouldn't have the gall, or for that matter the knowledge, to blow up my car. So far, nothing that had happened had been anything but petty and vaguely threatening. But I'd had a car catch fire while I was driving it before, and I wasn't eager for a repeat, so I was glad he wasn't taking any chances. He was carrying his gun, too, and I appreciated that, as well.

Everything must look as it should, because after a minute he closed the hood and slid into the drivers' seat. "Looks fine."

"I'm sure it is. It was parked on the street, in broad daylight. It would take a bold criminal to sabotage it in front of everyone."

"Not that bold." He turned the key in the ignition and listened to the engine catch. It sounded normal, at least to my untutored ear. Presumably to his as well, since he moved the gearshift before he continued, "All you'd need to do is bring a tow truck and a tool box. People would assume you were making a house call."

"Do car mechanics do that?"

"Some." He pulled away from the curb into traffic. "That's not the point, though. If someone asked, that's what you'd say. You were making a house call. And most people would think what you did—do car mechanics do that?—and then assume they do, cause that's what you said you were doing. People mostly believe what they're told."

Huh.

"What about the tow truck, though? That isn't something most people have sitting around."

"Would take me five minutes to get one," Rafe said and made a left turn onto Interstate Drive.

Surely not. "How?"

He shot me a look. "You walk into a body shop, you say your car broke down a mile or two down the road, and that you'll pay two hundred dollars for the use of the tow truck for thirty minutes. The guy in the shop will likely offer to do it for you, cause he wants to make more money, but you tell him you're just gonna drag the car home to your own driveway where you can work on it yourself. It'll take thirty minutes tops, you live just up the road, and then you'll bring his truck back. When he says yes, and he will when it looks like you're changing your mind and he won't make the two hundred for letting you use the truck either, you ask him to toss in the overalls hanging on the hook so you don't get grease all over your nice pants when you hook the car up, and he says that'll cost you another fifty bucks. You grumble about the gouging, he laughs, and you drive off in the tow truck, with a pair of overalls you can put on to make sure you look like you belong."

"That would work?"

"Sure," Rafe said and stepped on the gas as we merged with traffic on I-24 east. "Would take me about ten minutes."

"But you're you. You look like you'd know how to operate a tow truck and work on a car. We're talking about Walker Lamont here. Nobody would believe that he was going to tow his own Mercedes back to his own driveway to work on it himself."

"Maybe he don't look the same anymore," Rafe said and steered the Volvo into one of the two exit lanes for I-65 south. "He's been in prison for six months. It's liable to change a man."

He should know, I guess. I slanted him a look. "Did it change you?"

He shot me one back. "What d'you think?"

"I'm asking you. I didn't know you back then." Not well enough to know whether two years in prison had changed him, or just honed who he was already.

"I grew up right quick," Rafe said. "You put an eighteen-year-old kid into medium security with a bunch of criminals, he's gonna learn a lot, and not the stuff you want him to learn."

"Of course."

"I didn't really belong there, you know? I know I beat Billy Scruggs within an inch of his sorry life, but it wasn't like he didn't hit me back. And I only went after him because he'd beat on my mama."

I nodded.

"The only reason they gave me five years was 'cause I'd been in trouble before. But it wasn't any kind of serious trouble. Just stupid stuff. Borrowing someone's car and going joyriding. Partying a little too hard. You know. Stuff a lot of kids did."

He certainly hadn't been the only boy in Sweetwater to get himself into that kind of trouble. My brother Dix and Todd Satterfield got into their own share of scrapes racing Todd's new sports car. And a lot of the boys got into fights. It was something to do in a small town on a Saturday night, especially after a few beers were consumed. Rafe used to get into it with Cletus Johnson all the time, but that had never resulted in a jail sentence. For either of them.

Of course, the damage to Billy Scruggs had been a lot worse than anything he'd given Cletus, but still.

"I was lucky the TBI kept an eye on me. As soon as I got recruited by one of Hector's people, they offered me a chance outta there."

"Was it a difficult decision?" I'd never asked him any questions about this before, other than in passing, when the opportunity presented itself. We'd never sat down and actually had a conversation about it. I had always assumed it was something he didn't want to talk about, and since he'd never brought it up, I didn't know much about what that time had been like for him.

He shook his head. "When the thing with Billy Scruggs happened, I was down in Alabama working on cars. I was just coming home to visit for a couple days. I was gonna go back and keep working and prob'ly end up with a garage of my own one day. Never figured on a life of crime. So when I got the chance to get outta prison early, I grabbed it. Wasn't nothing I wanted in there."

"And it was a chance to redeem yourself." Going to work for the TBI. Catching criminals.

He glanced at me, and the corner of his mouth curled up. "Dunno that I thought about that, darlin'. I just wanted out."

"You didn't want to do something good after you almost killed Billy Scruggs?"

"I don't regret what I did to Billy," Rafe said. "If I had to do it over, I'd do it again. Except I'd make sure nobody knew it was me."

Ah. So he'd had no particular desire for redemption. And why would he, when he didn't think he'd done anything wrong?

The conversation lapsed after that. I sat in silence while Rafe maneuvered the car down Interstate 65 toward Brentwood. We exited on Old Hickory Boulevard and made our way toward Nolensville Road and the Shortstop.

I had only been at the sports bar once before, last fall, and if possible, it looked even less inviting now. At least then, there'd been leaves on the trees and some jolly green tufts of grass growing in the gravel parking lot, while now, in the gloaming, everything was reduced to black and white and shades of gray. The trees stretched skeletal branches toward the lowering sky.

The lot was full of cars. Full enough that we had to drive all the way to the back and slot the Volvo in beside a pickup with a gun rack in the bed and a bumper sticker that said "American by birth, Southern by the grace of God," next to a Confederate flag.

Rafe shot the gun rack an appreciative look. And chuckled when he saw the expression on my face. "What's the matter, darlin'?"

I gestured to the bumper sticker. "It's not that I mind the sentiment, really. I am perfectly happy to be Southern. And I have nothing against the Confederate flag. My great-great-great-grandfather fought in the War Between the States."

"Of course he did," Rafe said. "So what's the problem?"

"I just don't think it's necessary to flaunt it. It's one thing to feel that way, but quite another to go around saying so. You know?"

He shrugged. "My grandfather had a bumper sticker like that. They don't bother me."

They should. Especially if his grandfather had had one. Old Jim Collier had been a nasty piece of work, and a horrible bigot to boot. He'd beaten LaDonna almost into a miscarriage after she got herself pregnant by Rafe's father, and he'd made no bones about the fact that he despised his mixed-race grandson. The first twelve years of Rafe's life, living in a singlewide trailer with LaDonna and Old Jim, must have been pretty close to hell on earth, I imagined. I had seen the decrepit trailer in the Bog they had shared, and it had looked bad enough all on its own. When you added in Old Jim's mean streak and drunkenness, you got what amounted to a pretty rough childhood.

"Your grandfather was a horrible man."

He shrugged.

"I wouldn't have blamed you at all if you'd killed him."

He shot me a look. "I told you, darlin'. He drowned."

"I know you did."

"Maybe we coulda gone outside to check on him before the next morning, but I was just happy it was quiet."

"Of course."

"Wasn't like I held his head under or nothing. Or my mama, either. The man drowned, pure and simple. With no help from nobody."

"I wasn't saying he didn't. Just that I would have been tempted to kill him if it had been me."

"Won't say I wasn't," Rafe said with a grin, "but I was twelve. Not sure I knew how yet."

I let that 'yet' pass without comment, mostly because we'd reached the door into the Shortstop and it was time to stop talking and go to work.

The place looked just like it had six months ago. A low, dingy cinderblock room with a long bar on one end and a couple of pool tables on the other. The space between was taken up by a dozen or so Formica-topped tables surrounded by what looked like a variety of discarded kitchen chairs. A couple of TVs—not of the flat-screen variety—were showing basketball. The clientele consisted of ninety percent men, and despite the implications of the bumper sticker outside, it wasn't by any means a white bar. More than half the men present had darker skin than I did. I saw African-Americans, Hispanics, and even a couple of Asians. Most of them were dressed like Rafe, in jeans and T-shirts. Bradley must have stood out like a beacon in his expensive suit and tie.

Last time, we'd sat at a table. This time, Rafe led me to the bar. "Bottle of beer," he told the bartender as he kept a hand under my elbow to help me up on the tall chair. "Glass of sweet tea. And some information."

The man—a few years older than Rafe, with receding hair and a stomach that rounded the front of his T-shirt—arched his brows but didn't comment, just went to get the bottle of beer and glass of iced tea. By the time he put them down in front of us, Rafe had pulled out his ID.

"A friend of mine was here last night." He showed the bartender his phone, where he'd stored a picture of Manny Ortega. "D'you see him?"

"Sat at the bar. Ordered a beer." The man had a rumbling bass voice. Or maybe it just sounded rumbling because they were both speaking softly. I guess they didn't want anyone to know what they were talking about. "Something happen to him?"

"He was shot," Rafe said, pocketing the ID but leaving the phone on the bar. "Probably didn't have nothing to do with nothing, but we gotta check."

The bartender nodded.

"He was following this guy." Rafe glanced at me, and I scrambled to pull the print-outs out of my purse. The man on the other side of me glanced in my direction and away again. I did a half turn on the seat to be more circumspect when I put the picture of Bradley on the bar.

"Remember him?" Rafe asked.

The bartender shook his head. "Can't say as I do. We get a lot of people coming through here."

"He was meeting someone. Man in a suit and tie. He was waiting at a table."

They both surveyed the room; the bartender over Rafe's shoulder and Rafe in the mirror behind the bar. I did the same. The back part of the room was taken up by pool tables, so there was nowhere to sit over there. Maybe Manny had been talking about one of the tables along the sides of the room when he'd described the table as being 'in the back.'

"Marsha was on yesterday," the bartender volunteered. "You want I should get her for you?"

"When she's got a minute. No hurry. Can we get a couple cheeseburgers and fries?"

"Sure thing." The bartender moved off toward the kitchen pass-through, I assume to put in our order.

Rafe lifted his bottle and swallowed half of it. I sipped daintily on my iced tea. Both of us trying to make it look like we had all the time in the world and this wasn't a big deal. I guess Rafe didn't want to risk putting the guy's back up. To suddenly have the TBI show up on your doorstep asking questions, couldn't be a comfortable feeling. Especially with the kind of clientele the Shortstop sported. I knew for a fact that several of Rafe's former 'friends' had spent time here, because I'd met them last time I visited. Friends who were now guests of the state of Tennessee.

In fact—and I hadn't realized it until now—maybe this wasn't a safe place for Rafe. He'd been instrumental in putting those 'friends' behind bars, while he had skated through unscathed as usual, courtesy of the TBI. His incarcerated friends might have friends out here who resented that fact. As the bartender went down the bar to talk to someone else, I leaned closer to Rafe. "Is this place safe for you?"

He shot me a surprised look, and I elaborated. "Last time we were here, you were meeting those three guys you were pulling those open house robberies with. Ishmael and Antoine and whoever."

"A.J.," Rafe said. "Ishmael Jackson, A. J. Davies, and Antoine Kent. What about them?"

"They're in prison now." At least I hoped they were. "But what if they have friends? Aren't you afraid someone's going to take a potshot at you?"

"Over one of them three? Not likely."

"One of them could have had a girlfriend who depended on the income or something. Someone who didn't appreciate you helping to put them in prison."

"Nobody knows I had anything to do with putting them in prison," Rafe said mildly. And added, "till now."

Oops. I looked around. Nobody seemed interested in us, but I lowered my voice anyway. "I just don't want anything to happen to you." Especially because of me. And dragging him here had been my idea.

"I don't want nothing to happen to me either, darlin'. If I thought this was a bad idea, I wouldn't have come."

Good to know. Nonetheless, I felt a little more uneasy than I had up until now. The guy next to me on the barstool—not Rafe, the guy on the other side—was giving me the creepy-crawlies. Not that he was doing anything. He wasn't even looking at us. His attention was fixed on the TV above the bar. But just the fact that he was there, a few feet away, was enough to make my neck hair prickle. He looked like the truck outside, with the gun rack and confederate flag, could belong to him. You know the type: big and beefy, with practically no neck and less hair.

Then again, I was probably just letting my prejudices show. Most likely he was just some guy on his way home from a nine to five job in a factory or somesuch, with a tired wife and a couple of kids at home, stopping off for a beer before dealing with them.

Or not. No wedding ring. No sign of one having been removed.

Before he could turn his head and think I was checking him out, I put him out of my mind and focused on Rafe instead.

"What now?"

"We watch the game, wait for our food, and talk to Marsha when she comes over." He didn't take his eyes off the TV, although I was pretty sure he kept an eye on everything in the mirror behind the bar at the same time.

It's not like him to sit with his back to the room. He and Tamara Grimaldi both have this ingrained habit—probably born from necessity—of keeping an eye on everyone coming and going, so they won't be surprised by anyone pulling a gun. Shades of Wild Bill Hickok, or something. Whenever we go eat together, it's always a battle between the two of them over who gets the seat in the corner. They leave my posterior exposed most of the time. It's a good thing I trust both of them to have my back.

Anyway, since he couldn't keep an eye on the room from where he was sitting, I felt pretty sure he was watching it in the mirror. He straightened imperceptibly just a few seconds before the waitress with the beehive—the same one who had waited on us the last (and first) time we'd been here together—came to a stop beside him. "Whatcha need, hon?"

"Friend of mine was here yesterday." Rafe turned the phone on to show her Manny's face. "Sat at the bar, had a beer."

Marsha shrugged. "I work the floor, hon. I mighta noticed him, but then again, maybe not."

"He was following this guy." Rafe moved the printed pictures over to his other side, with the photo of Bradley on top. "Remember him? He was meeting someone. Another guy, middle-aged, both of'em in suits and ties."

Marsha nodded. "I remember. We don't get a lot of guys in suits come through here, you know? This is more of a blue collar clientele."

Indeed it was. There wasn't a tie in sight tonight. Just a lot of T-shirts, a few sweatshirts, and a Henley or two. The guy next to me—the guys on both sides of me; Rafe and the other one—were wearing jeans and T-shirts, and so were 90% of the rest of the people present. Even the women.

"Where'd they sit?"

Marsha indicated a table over by the wall, as far from the bar as it was possible to get without sitting at the pool table.

"Did they eat?"

She shook her head. "Just had a drink each. Didn't stay long."

"D'you hear what they were talking about?"

She popped a pink bubblegum bubble. She'd done that last time we were here, as well. "Didn't talk much. Stopped whenever I came close."

Rafe nodded. Obviously there was nothing unexpected here. He shuffled pictures. "Was it this guy?"

I craned my neck. The picture of Nathan Ferncliff was on top of the stack. Marsha leaned in, pressing her more than ample breast against Rafe's bicep. Since she was about the age LaDonna would have been, had his mother still been alive, I didn't mind. Much.

After a few second's scrutiny, she shook her head, setting the bouffant to swaying. "No."

"You sure?"

"There's another picture of him," I told Rafe, who shuffled the stack. "That's him. In the yellow shirt."

Marsha looked at the second picture, the one in the golf shirt with Bradley, and shook her head again. "Definitely not him. This guy, yeah." She put her finger on Bradley. "But not the other one. Similar type. Age and hair. But not the same face."

She sounded so sure we had no choice but to believe her.

"Thanks," Rafe said.

"What else you got there?" She reached past him to fan the photographs out over the counter.

Rafe put his finger on one of them. "Who the hell is this?"

I glanced over. "Haven't you met him? That's Walker Lamont. My old boss."

Rafe nodded. "Thought he looked familiar. And no, I never met him. But I saw him at the memorial service."

Brenda's memorial. Of course. He'd been there. Rafe, I mean. And Walker had gotten up to eulogize, the hypocrite.

"Why d'you add a picture of him?"

I shrugged. "It was just a hunch, I guess. Or a wild idea. But he fits the description. And he is running around Nashville causing trouble."

The guy on the other side of me slid off his stool and hit the floor with a thump. I watched him hustle toward the door while I waited for Rafe to scoff. He didn't.

"Does he know Bradley?"

I shook my head. At the door, the guy stopped to look at me over his shoulder before disappearing into the night.

"What?" Rafe said, turning in that direction.

"Nothing." I moved my attention from the now empty doorway to him. "I don't think Walker knows Bradley. We'd been divorced for two years by the time I went to work for Walker. But it wouldn't be hard to get Bradley to agree to meet him. All he'd have to do is call and say he was thinking of hiring Bradley, and he wanted to meet for a consultation."

Rafe nodded and turned back to Marsha. She shook her head. "Not him either."

No problem. I hadn't really expected it to be Walker; I was just eliminating what I assumed was a slim chance anyway.

"Who the hell's this?" Rafe wanted to know.

I leaned over. "Oh. I printed that one out by mistake. His name is Dale Vandervinder. Bradley is representing his wife in their divorce. Either that, or he's sleeping with her. But she didn't look like his type, nor he hers."

"This her?" Rafe put a fingertip on Ilona Vandervinder, next to Dale. I nodded. "No, I can see that."

"That sorta looks like the guy," Marsha said.

I shook my head. "It can't be."

Rafe glanced at me. "Why not?"

"Because Bradley is representing his wife. They're on opposing sides of a court case. They're not supposed to talk. Bradley would never violate his ethics like that."

Rafe glanced at Marsha, who shrugged. "I ain't saying it was him. Just that the guy who was here looked more like this guy than the other two. But it wasn't like I was paying a lot of attention, you know. We had a full house. I had work to do."

"Course." Rafe gathered the pictures together and pushed them in my direction. I stuffed them back in my bag. "Thanks, sugar."

"For you, hon, anything." She winked and sashayed off, posterior swinging in the tight jeans. Rafe chuckled and turned back to me.

Thirteen

We ate our burgers—which were excellent, even if I felt as though the fat and carbohydrates were bypassing my stomach and adhering themselves directly to my thighs as I chewed—and then we left the Shortstop to go home.

We had learned nothing else. The other waitress hadn't noticed Bradley last night, so she couldn't help us at all. And they all said that nothing had happened or gone wrong in any way as to explain what had happened to Manny. I hadn't expected his trip to the Shortstop to have had anything to do with his murder—how could it, when all he'd been doing was following my harmless and boring ex-husband?—but I could tell that Rafe was disappointed.

"I'm sorry." I tucked my arm through his as we navigated the rutted gravel lot in the dark. "This was a huge waste of time."

"I wouldn't say that." He grinned down at me, his teeth bright in the dusk. "Any time I get to watch you eat like a human being is a good day."

"I do eat like a human being. I just don't work out the way you do. If I keep eating like you, I'll get fat." And then he wouldn't want me anymore. As my mother—and Wallis Simpson—said, a woman can never be too rich or too thin.

"More to love." He leered exaggeratedly, and I snorted, halfway between amusement and disbelief.

"Sure."

"Darlin', if you knew what looking at you in those jeans does to me, you wouldn't doubt it."

Surely not? I twisted to look over my shoulder. "Are you sure they don't make my butt look big?"

"Positive," Rafe said. "Your butt's just the right size." He slipped a hand down my back to demonstrate, with a squeeze.

I swatted at it. "You're awful."

The leer went away and was replaced by sincerity. "I like the way you look, darlin'. Always have. But I love *you*, not what you look like. So if your butt gets twice as big, I'll still love you."

"I don't understand that," I confessed, even as I melted a little inside. "Not the butt thing. I get that. You're a man. You like women's butts. But the other part. I'm not a nice person. I spent a lot of time judging you for things you can't help."

His response was easy, and entirely free of recrimination. "You got over it."

"It took too long."

"It took as long as it needed. I'm just glad you got there. And between you and me..."

"Yes?"

We'd reached the Volvo, and he swung me around and up against the side of the car. "Between you and me," he stepped close enough that there was nothing between him and me but a few layers of fabric, "the way you look don't hurt, either."

"Glad to hear it," I said—a little breathlessly, as always when he was this close—and looped my arms around his neck.

I expected a kiss. The look in his eyes promised one, and between you and me—hah!—the way he was pressed against me didn't leave much to the imagination. He wanted to do more, but of course we couldn't, not here. But he definitely planned to kiss me.

I prepared myself, but it didn't happen. Instead he glanced down.

"What the hell?"

So much for the kiss. He dropped his arms from around me and took a step back. I followed the direction of his gaze, while I tried not to pout. "What?"

"Flat tire." He pointed.

No kidding. The rear tire was as flat as a pancake.

"We must have run over a nail or something." I looked around, vaguely, while I lamented the fact that now we'd have to take the time to change the tire before driving home, when all I wanted to do was get him into bed.

"No," Rafe said, and his voice was dangerous. So was the look on his face. "Damn."

He stalked away, to the other side of the car. I watched him, and that's when I realized that not only was the rear tire flat, the front tire was flat too.

Before I could ask about the status on the opposite side of the car, I already had my answer.

"Fuck!"

"Both of them?"

"All of 'em. Every damn one." He scrubbed a hand over the top of his head. "How the hell—?"

It wasn't really a question. Because it was obvious that we hadn't accidentally run over four different nails. That was impossible. And if someone had spiked the parking lot entrance, I think we would have noticed.

"Do you think someone did it on purpose?"

"Hell, yeah!" He looked around. I did the same. Nothing stirred. Everything was silent. Almost eerily silent, although that could be just my nerves prickling. The only sound was the hum of cars driving by on Nolensville Road, a football field's distance away.

"We'd better get back inside," Rafe said. "C'mon." He reached for me.

I let him guide me in the direction of the neon sign outside the Shortstop, with an arm around my shoulders. "Are you carrying?" I asked softly.

He glanced down for just a second, before answering in the same low voice. "Yeah. But I don't wanna pull out a gun right now. If someone's watching, he might take it as a sign I need shooting."

I suppressed a shudder. "No, please don't do that."

He gave my shoulders a squeeze. "Don't worry, darlin'. It's probably just someone having some fun."

"Fun?"

"Kids," Rafe said.

"Is this the kind of neighborhood where teenagers would hang around in bar parking lots with carving knives?"

"You never know. But it's better than the alternative."

Which was what, exactly?

I didn't ask. "What are we going to do? The car only has one spare tire."

"We're gonna call for a ride," Rafe said, "and a tow truck. And tomorrow, we'll have a look at your car and see if we can figure out who did this."

"I thought you said kids did it."

He opened the door into the bar. Light and sound spilled out into the parking lot. "It's better not to take any chances," he told me as I passed in front of him.

So we ended up back inside the bar, while Rafe made his phone calls. Twenty minutes later, Tamara Grimaldi walked in.

I turned to him. "You called a woman to come rescue you?"

He glanced at me. "I ain't proud. A woman can rescue me any day, so long as I stay alive."

Sure. Although this wasn't really a matter of life and death. At least I hoped not.

"Besides," he added, "my manhood ain't in question here. This is her case."

Of course. This might have something to do with Manny's murder. If someone had heard what we'd asked the bartender or waitress, for instance. Like the man who'd sat next to me and who had left while we'd been talking.

Although how would he know which car in the parking lot was mine? The lot was full; mine could have been any of them.

Grimaldi came to stand between us. "Good evening, Ms.... Savannah."

"Good evening, Det..." I thought better of it. "Tammy."

She scowled at me, but there was nothing she could say, of course. I'm sure she realized, as I had, that it would be better not to bandy the title about.

Rafe, meanwhile, didn't bother to hide his grin. He also didn't bother with the niceties. "D'you look at the car?"

Grimaldi nodded. "They're hooking it up. I'll have someone go over it in the morning."

"My car's a crime scene?" I said.

Both of them turned to look at me with matching expressions of disbelief that I had to ask.

"Right. Sorry."

"Let's head outside." Grimaldi made for the door. I slid off the barstool and followed, while Rafe brought up the rear.

"Any idea what happened?" Grimaldi asked when we were standing outside watching the tow truck slowly winching the Volvo up onto the flatbed. The winch squealed with every rotation.

Rafe shook his head. "We were inside maybe an hour. Sat at the bar. Ate and talked to a couple people. When we got back out, the tires were flat. We didn't hear nothing and didn't see nobody."

"Did anyone leave after you came in?"

He shrugged. "Sure. It's a bar. People come and go."

"I don't suppose you knew who they were?"

"No. Nobody here I'd ever seen before. Save the staff."

"The guy who sat next to me left," I said. "While we were in the middle of talking to the waitress. He turned around when he got to the door to look back at us."

Grimaldi glanced at Rafe, who shrugged. She returned her attention to me. "Can you describe him?"

"Forty, very little hair, stocky, thick neck. Dressed in jeans and a T-shirt."

"Bald?" Grimaldi queried.

I shook my head. "Just short. Almost shaved. Like Rafe."

Grimaldi turned again to look at him. "Black or white? Or something else?"

"The guy? White. Medium hair. Could be dark blond or light brown. Hard to tell when there was so little of it. It's kind of dark inside, too. The T-shirt was blue."

"Light or dark?"

"Navy."

"Did it say anything? Or have a picture on it?"

"It had a logo," I said, thinking back. "White letters. And a key."

"Key?"

They both said it together, and then exchanged glances.

I nodded, looking from one to the other of them. "Why? Does that mean something?" Obviously to them it did, but it meant nothing to me.

"What kind of key was it?"

What kind of key? "A skeleton one, I guess. The kind with a circle on top, and a long piece coming down. One of the letters was shaped like the circle. An O, I guess. It had something inside it..."

"Stars," Grimaldi said, her jaw tight. I blinked, and she added, "Three of them."

"Like the Tennessee state flag?"

The three stars stand for East, West, and Middle Tennessee, in case you're curious. The mountains in the east, the river delta in the west, and the Cumberland Plateau in the middle. Or to put it more officially: the mountains, highlands, and lowlands.

She nodded grimly.

"You know what kind of shirt it was?"

"I can make a good guess. Did the other letters happen to be a T, a D and a C?"

"Could be." I arranged them in my head, adding in the O. TODC? TCOD? CDOT? DCOT?

"TDOC," Rafe said.

Grimaldi nodded.

I looked from one to the other of them. "What's TDOC?"

They both turned to me, but Grimaldi let Rafe answer the question. "Tennessee Department of Corrections."

"The prison people?"

His mouth twitched. "Yes, darlin'."

"Did you see T-shirts like that when you were in prison?"

He shook his head. "The guards wore uniforms. But I've seen the logo. More than I'd like to."

Tamara Grimaldi looked up from manipulating the buttons on her phone to look at him before going back to what she was doing.

"So this guy works for the Tennessee Department of Corrections." Maybe the T-shirt was workout gear, or something. Rafe has a couple of T-shirts with the TBI logo. Grimaldi probably had MNPD ones that she used in the gym. "Did he recognize you, do you think?"

"From ten years ago? Not likely."

Not impossible, though. And it would explain the quick retreat. But— "He couldn't have known which car you arrived in. He certainly wouldn't have guessed. You don't look like someone who'd drive a Volvo."

He quirked a brow. "What do I look like I oughta drive?"

"A Harley," I said. "Or a truck. Maybe a sports car. Something muscular and sexy. Everything a Volvo isn't."

He grinned, but before he could comment, Tamara Grimaldi lifted her head again. "Is this the guy you saw?"

She handed me her phone. I looked at the photograph she had pulled up. A prison guard was staring truculently into the camera, his jaw squared and the top half of his face shaded by the brim of a blue cap. It had TDOC embroidered on it in white, the O forming the head of a skeleton key with three white stars nestled within the circle.

Rafe moved up next to me to look over my shoulder. I felt the heat of him against my side and back.

"That's the logo I saw," I confirmed. "And that could definitely be him. It's a little hard to tell with the way his face is shaded. And I didn't get a very good look at him when he was sitting next to me. I couldn't turn around and stare. But it could be him."

I tilted my head to look up at Rafe. "Have you seen him before?"

He shook his head and cut his eyes to Grimaldi. "Who's this?"

"His name is Garth Hanson," the detective said. "He's... he *was* a guard at Riverbend Penitentiary."

"Must be after my time," Rafe said.

"He's been there eleven years. But you may not have come across him while you were there. It's a big place."

Rafe nodded. "So how d'you know who he was? You know the guy?"

"Lucky guess. Or call it a hunch if you want. This is the guard who went missing along with Mr. Lamont."

There was a moment of silence while we all digested this piece of news.

I broke it. "So he isn't dead." Walker hadn't murdered him and left him in a ditch somewhere in Kentucky, in his quest to escape.

Grimaldi shook her head. "No."

"Why?"

"That's the question, isn't it? Off-hand, I can think of a few possibilities."

"So can I," Rafe said with a grin.

Grimaldi sent him a quelling look. "Obviously, if it was Garth Hanson you saw, he's neither dead nor under duress. He's moving around under his own steam and quite possibly following you. Was he inside when you arrived?"

I nodded. "Watching TV at the bar."

"Could you tell how long he'd been there?"

How was I supposed to know that? I'm not psychic.

"Did he have a drink in front of him?" Grimaldi asked.

"Glass of beer. And it was still full when we sat down. So I guess he couldn't have been there all that long. Unless it was a second or third glass."

"Did you spend any time in the parking lot before you went inside?"

I opened my eyes wide. "How did you know?"

Rafe chuckled at the look on my face. "She's good, darlin', but she ain't that good. She's thinking he was following us, and had time to go inside while we were standing in the parking lot, necking."

"We weren't necking. We were talking about—" I realized they were both laughing at me, and grimaced. "Yes, it might have happened that way."

"Besides," Rafe said innocently, "we *were* necking when we found the flat tires."

We had been. No denying that.

By now, the Volvo was on the flatbed and the tow truck was rumbling toward the road. We watched it roll by. "Ready to leave?" Grimaldi asked when it had merged with traffic in the direction of downtown Nashville, the red taillights winking out up the road.

I nodded. "Yes, please."

"Come on." She headed toward a plain, unmarked, obviously official vehicle parked in a no-parking zone in front of the building.

Rafe opened the passenger door for me, obviously intending for me to ride next to Grimaldi while he took the back seat.

"Are you sure you wouldn't be more comfortable up front?"

Last time we'd gotten a ride from Tamara Grimaldi, he'd put me in the back, where the criminals ride, on the other side of the reinforced metal grid and bulletproof glass. I'd assumed the idea of riding back there brought back bad memories for him.

He grinned. "I'll be all right."

"I really don't mind, if you and Gri... Tamara want to talk shop."

"I can talk through the bars. I've done it before."

"I'd be perfectly happy..."

"Just get in." He gave me a nudge. "The quicker you get in, the quicker we get home so we can finish what we started."

When he put it like that...

I slid into the passenger seat next to Grimaldi and let Rafe close the door behind me. He crawled into the back. "All set."

"So what do you two think is going on?" I asked when Grimaldi had reversed and was moving forward into traffic on Nolensville Road. "With Walker and this Hanson guy. I mean, Walker wasn't here. I would have recognized him."

"He coulda been in the parking lot," Rafe said. "He coulda been the one flattening our tires while the other guy went inside to make sure we were settled and not on our way back."

"So you're saying they're working together? That this guy let Walker escape?"

"Lamont didn't kill him," Grimaldi said, "so I'm leaning that way, yes."

"Why?"

"Two reasons I can think of," Rafe said from the back seat. It was weird looking at him through the metal grid separating him from the two of us. I wasn't sure I liked the sensation. "The first's money."

"Walker paid Hanson to let him escape?"

"Law enforcement isn't a job where you get rich," Grimaldi told me, while she kept her eyes on the road. "You do it because it's important."

"It's that why you became a cop? Because you wanted to do something important?"

She glanced at me. Just a quick look before turning her attention back to the traffic. "My mother was killed when I was fourteen. I wanted to grow up and make a difference."

Ouch.

I glanced at Rafe to see whether he'd known about this. The look he gave me was totally impassive, so I had no idea one way or the other. "I'm sorry," I said.

"It was a long time ago."

"Sure, but... it's probably not something you get over."

I wanted to ask what had happened, but it wasn't really any of my business, and besides, this wasn't the time or place for such a conversation. But before I could change the subject, she'd added, "They never caught who did it. I try to make sure that doesn't happen to anyone else."

Man. What do you say after something like that? "And I'm sure we're all grateful," sounds flippant, even when it isn't meant that way, and "Good for you," isn't much better. Patronizing at best, insulting at worst. But at the same time, the location and general situation didn't really invite to anything deeply emotional.

"I do it for the benefits," Rafe said.

Grimaldi snorted. "Sure."

"Hey, nothing wrong with full medical and dental." He grinned.

And he was right, there was nothing wrong with it. I didn't have either. I'd been on Bradley's policy before the divorce, but I hadn't been able to afford my own afterwards.

If I married Rafe, I could have medical insurance.

If I got pregnant before I got married, would I be covered?

While I'd been thinking, the two of them had continued the conversation. Or had brought it back to Garth Hanson.

"You checked out his place, right?"

"The first day," Grimaldi confirmed. "When we thought he was dead. Just in case Lamont was holed up there."

"But he wasn't."

"We didn't find him."

"Have you checked it again?"

"I have one of the patrol cars drive by once or twice a day to check for signs of life," Grimaldi said, navigating the intersection at Nolensville and Harding Place, "but they can't go inside. We have no reason to suspect foul play."

"D'you have a reason to suspect foul play now?"

Rafe didn't wait for her answer, just added, "Where's his place?"

"Not very far from yours, actually. He lives near the river."

"How about we stop by on the way home?"

"He probably won't be there," Grimaldi said. "And if he is, I'll need to call it in and request backup."

"I'm your backup."

"You're not..." She stopped and rolled her eyes. "Of course you are."

"Carrying? You damn well better believe it. I ain't going nowhere without a weapon these days. Too many people with guns and knives running around."

Grimaldi didn't respond, so I guess she didn't blame him. And he did, after all, have a license to kill.

Fourteen

As it turned out, Garth Hanson really didn't live very far from us at all. Maybe two miles, as the crow flies. Instead of taking a left off the exit, Grimaldi took a right, and wended her way down through the industrial district to the river. We drove past Julio Melendez's old warehouse—which actually had turned out to belong to Hector Gonzalez, now a guest of the state of Georgia. The warehouse was dark and presumably empty. Julio was still in Tennessee state custody, as far as I knew.

Beyond that point, the land rose up to the left, on the side away from the river, and small houses crowded the steep hill up into the neighborhood known as Shelby Heights. Grimaldi turned the car onto one of the numbered streets and gunned the engine. We sailed halfway up the hill before she made a sharp turn into a narrow driveway beside a standard tract house. This area was built around 1950, and it was made up of little two bedroom, one bath cottages with the same floor plan, occasionally turned around just so the homes wouldn't all look exactly the same. Over time, the owners have painted them different colors, added rooms or porches here and there, and done their best to instill some personality, but if you strip all that aside, it's still all the same house over and over.

Garth Hanson's house was the original white color, with boring black shutters and spindly landscaping. A carport with a corrugated plastic roof was attached to one end of the house, covering the back part of the driveway. It was empty, save for a brown trashcan and a green recycling bin, both Metro issue with wheels. The house was dark, all the lights off, and it looked uninhabited.

I thought about Walker's beautiful sprawling midcentury ranch in leafy Oak Hill and tried to imagine him crashing here.

It didn't quite compute, as we used to say when I was little. One of these things is not like the others...

"Looks empty," Rafe remarked from the back seat.

"So far it's been empty. Come on." Grimaldi unlocked her door and stepped out. And then she unlocked his, since he couldn't do it himself from inside.

I got out on the other side of the car and looked from one to the other of them. "Now what?"

"Now we have a look around," Rafe said, reaching for his gun. "You can stay in the car."

I rolled my eyes. "What if I don't want to stay in the car?"

"You'd be safer in the car, if someone's here."

"No one's here. He didn't flap his wings and fly to the Shortstop. He has a vehicle of some sort. And it isn't here. So he isn't here, either."

"Unless he parked it somewhere else," Grimaldi said. She had unstrapped her own gun and was holding it in her hand. We must have caught her off-duty for once, because she was dressed in jeans and a corduroy jacket instead of the usual business pantsuit.

"And now he's sitting in the dark, twiddling his thumbs?" I said. "I don't think so. It isn't even eight o'clock yet, so it isn't like he's gone to bed. And I doubt he'd park his car so far away. If someone came for him, he'd want it within easy reach if he had to make a getaway, don't you think?"

Grimaldi shrugged. "Suit yourself. If you don't want to stay in the car, you don't have to." She glanced at Rafe. "You take the back. I'll take the front."

He nodded. "Gimme a couple minutes." He faded into the darkness behind the house. Grimaldi and I stood where we were, next to the car.

"You don't think he's here, do you?" I asked after a few moments.

She shook her head.

"So he's safe." This time, the 'he' I was talking about was Rafe, and Grimaldi knew it.

"He can take care of himself. I'd put my money on him against almost anyone most of the time."

Me too. Even so, I gnawed on my bottom lip. "He isn't bulletproof. And chances are Hanson has a gun. Guards carry guns, right?"

"Not on the job."

Wow. So these guys were tasked with keeping the peace between the state's most dangerous criminals, but they weren't given guns to do it.

"Too much opportunity for one of the inmates to get it from them," Grimaldi added, which I guess made sense. Still, it seemed somewhat counterintuitive, if you asked me.

"You probably checked, right? Does Hanson own a gun?"

She nodded, reluctantly.

"So if he's inside, he could shoot Rafe." Who wasn't wearing a bulletproof vest or anything like that.

"He isn't inside," Grimaldi said.

"How do you know?"

She glanced at me. "His car isn't here."

Great.

"Has it been long enough?"

She checked her watch. "Probably. You boyfriend should have had time to get into position in the back by now. Just in case someone's inside and when I knock, he tries to go out the back door. You'd better stay here."

She left me where I was and moved up to the front door. Her feet were silent on the dry grass, and didn't scrape on the two concrete steps that led up to the stoop. I held my breath when she knocked on the door.

Nothing happened for a second, and then there was the sound of the deadbolt being shoved back. Grimaldi pulled the gun up into a firing stance, with one hand supporting the other.

The door opened on a dark shadow. There was a blur of movement and then Rafe's voice. "Don't point that thing at me."

I opened my eyes. He was holding Grimaldi's gun by the barrel, and we were probably lucky she hadn't pulled the trigger in sheer surprise when he swept it out of her hands.

She dropped them to her hips. "I wasn't going to shoot. I saw it was you."

"Sure," Rafe said. He handed the gun back and watched as Grimaldi holstered it. "The place is empty. Nobody here." He moved back to let her in.

"You weren't supposed to go inside, you know."

Rafe shrugged. "The back door was open."

Grimaldi's eyeroll made it abundantly clear what she thought of that explanation. "Any sign that they've been here?" She moved across the threshold.

They kept talking as they disappeared inside, but I could no longer hear them. After a quick look around—nobody was watching that I could see—I made my way up the steps and through the door, too.

The house was pretty much what I had expected, from what I could see of it in the dark. Big, manly leather furniture—the kind you'd expect a bachelor who works for the prison system to own—with a big-screen TV against the wall opposite the couch. The coffee table had some debris on it: newspapers and opened mail, it looked like. I heard Grimaldi and Rafe's voices in the back of the house as I picked a Metro Water bill off the top of the stack. The postmark showed a date two days ago. If the postal service stamped it then, it might have gotten here yesterday at the earliest, or today.

I put it back down and straightened as Rafe and Grimaldi came back into the living room. "Anything?"

They book shook their heads.

"Is there a reason we're not turning on any lights?" It was like a crime show on TV, with the good guys walking through the villain's pitch black abode at night instead of waiting for daylight.

"We're not supposed to be here," Grimaldi said.

"You're the police." And the TBI.

"That doesn't mean I can walk through people's houses without a search warrant."

"The back door was open," Rafe said. "Swear to God." He grinned, white teeth flashing in the dark.

I didn't bother to register my disbelief. Grimaldi didn't, either. We both knew he'd picked the lock, but we also knew there was no way to prove it.

I looked around. "Any sign that anyone's been here recently?"

"Dirty dishes in the sink," Rafe said. "Drops of water in the bathroom drain."

"Maybe the faucet drips."

He shrugged.

"So does that mean we can go?" I looked from him to her and back.

They both nodded. "There's nothing here," Grimaldi said. "And unfortunately I don't have the manpower to put someone on this house fulltime. Not when we don't know if he'll be back. But I'll put out an APB on him alive rather than dead and see if that helps."

She headed for the front door. I followed. "I'll lock up and meet you out front," Rafe said.

"Isn't there a deadbolt on the back door too?"

"I've got it. Two minutes." He locked and bolted the front door behind us and then headed in the other direction. I could hear his steps fade away across the carpeted floors before I stepped off the stoop and went to wait beside Grimaldi and the car.

The detective watched the clock. It was less than ninety seconds before Rafe came around the corner of the house. "Damn," I heard her say.

"He's good."

She glanced at me, but didn't answer. "Get in," she said instead.

SHE DROPPED US OFF IN front of the condo complex ten minutes later, and stayed at the curb until we were safely inside the building.

"Does she think you can't protect me?" I asked Rafe when the door was closed and locked behind us and we were on our way up the stairs.

He glanced down at me. "Course not. It's just her job to make sure nothing happens to you."

"What about anything happening to you?"

"I'm supposed to be able to take care of myself." He put his hand out for the apartment keys I had fished out of my purse. "I'll do it. You stand here, outta the way."

He put me with my back against the wall next to the door while he proceeded to put himself directly in front of the door while he unlocked it. When nobody put a bullet through it and into his body, he told me, "Looks all right. C'mon in."

I passed through the doorway and proceeded to remove my jacket and shoes while he walked all through the apartment, gun in hand, opening closet doors and peering behind the shower curtain and under the bed. Then he came back. "Looks like nobody's been here since we left."

"Good to know." Nonetheless, my nerves were jittery and I felt jumpy. I headed into the kitchen and over to the refrigerator. "I could use a glass of wine."

Unfortunately, we were fresh out of wine, and the refrigerator didn't magically grow any bottles, no matter how wistfully I stared into it. After a few seconds I straightened and closed the door. "I don't suppose I could prevail upon you to go get me a bottle of Chardonnay?"

"No," Rafe said. "I ain't leaving you alone."

"It's just two blocks up to Weiss's Liquors. You could be back in ten minutes."

"You don't need it that bad. Besides..." He snagged me around the waist and pulled me closer, "I've got something that'll make you nice and relaxed."

"You do?" My body fitted itself to his, soft curves against hard planes, as I melted against him.

"M-hm." He slipped his hands down my back and into my jeans pockets. When he tilted his hips to nudge me—as if I didn't already know what the 'something' was, that he had—I sank my teeth into my bottom lip to bite back what I might in other circumstances have called a moan. I swear my eyes rolled back in my head, and he chuckled. "Not that relaxed, darlin'. I ain't going to all this trouble only to have you fall asleep on me halfway through."

No chance of that. My eyelids may have been heavy, but my body was wide awake. "I'm not sleepy," I said.

"Any chance I could talk you into going to bed anyway?"

"You can talk me into anything at all. Living room sofa. Dining room table. Right here in the hallway."

"Bed's fine." He scooped me up and carried me down the hallway and through the living room, past the sofa and the dining room table.

"Are we getting settled and boring?" I asked, a little breathlessly, when my back hit the mattress.

"Hell, no." He pulled the T-shirt up and over his head and sent it flying. My gaze snagged on the ripple of muscles in his upper body, rock-hard under the silky softness of golden skin, and my tongue got stuck to the roof of my mouth. He grinned, and dropped his hands to the button of his jeans. "You were saying?"

"Nothing. I can't remember."

"You sure?"

I nodded. "Positive. Don't stop now."

"No." He pulled the zipper down. I swooned.

WE EXITED THE HOUSE THROUGH THE courtyard the next morning at a quarter of eight, bound for 101 Potsdam Street, to meet the glazer and locksmith. And we were all the way downstairs and in view of Rafe's Harley before I realized—

"I don't have a car." I stopped in the middle of the courtyard.

Rafe stopped too, per force. "I'll drive you."

"I can't ride on the back of your bike. Not in this." I gestured to my high heeled pumps and flirty A-line skirt.

Rafe looked at me. His lips curved. "Sure you can."

"The skirt will fly up. The whole neighborhood will be able to see my thighs."

"They're nice thighs."

They're fat thighs, I thought, but I didn't say it. "Thank you, but that doesn't mean I want to share them with everyone we meet."

"Believe me, I don't wanna share your thighs with anyone else, either. But we're running late. You don't have time to go change."

No. And jeans aren't appropriate business wear, anyway, even if they're perfectly suited for going riding on a Harley.

"Won't the skirt get stuck in the spokes? We might have an accident."

"It's too short," Rafe said.

Great. "Maybe I should just call a cab. Or a rental car company."

"Or maybe you should just climb on and let me take you where you need to go."

We'd been living together for going on three months by now, but so far I had avoided getting on the back of the Harley. I had a car, and it worked perfectly well. It had a roof, so when it was raining or snowing, it was more comfortable than the bike. And I wasn't dressed right. Most of the time I wasn't dressed right. I'd always managed to come up with an excuse or other why it made more sense to take the Volvo.

But now the Volvo wasn't an option. It was either crawling onto the back of the Harley or being late. And a properly brought up lady is never late. To be early is to be on time, and to be on time is to be late.

"Fine. If I have to."

"You don't have to sound like you're going to your death," Rafe said. "You'll like it. I promise. Here." He handed me his helmet.

I looked from it to him. "What about you?"

"Won't be the first time I've ridden without a helmet, darlin'. I ain't letting you do it, though."

I looked at it again. "My hair will be ruined."

"Your hair'll be ruined if you go without, too. You'll look like you stuck your head in a wind tunnel."

Good point. I sighed and put the helmet on. It took effort to yank it down.

"Cute," Rafe said, looking at me. "OK. I'm gonna get on and start the engine. Once I've got her upright, you climb on behind me."

I nodded. My head felt strangely heavy with the helmet on, and my neck seemed too weak to hold it up. My voice didn't sound right, either. "All right."

He threw a leg over the Harley and did whatever it is he does to start the beast. I had never really paid attention to the steps before, and since I could see very little and hear less through the helmet, I'm sure I missed some of the finer points. But the motorcycle rumbled to life under him. He balanced it between his legs. "C'mon. Lift your skirt, throw one leg over the seat behind me, and sit down. Put your feet on the pegs."

I did my best. Lifted my skirt enough to crawl, as demurely as I could, onto the bike behind him. After some searching, I found the pegs he'd talked about. They fit perfectly between my three inch stiletto heels and the rest of my feet. And I imagine I probably didn't look as graceful as I might have liked, because his voice was husky with laughter when he told me, over his shoulder. "Wrap your arms around my waist and hold on. When I bank, you bank, too."

"Bank?"

"You'll see. Just do what I do."

He moved forward, slowly, out of the parking space. I had my arms wrapped around his waist, and when he suddenly sped up, I squealed and tightened my grip until I came close to cutting off his air. I could feel his stomach muscles quiver, so he was probably laughing at me, but the sound itself was lost somewhere between the wind and the helmet reducing everything to a faint buzz.

After about two seconds, he turned the corner from Main Street onto Fifth, and I learned what banking meant. He leaned in the direction of the turn, and I leaned too, until it felt like we were at a forty five degree angle to the pavement. I hiccuped inside the helmet, too fearful even to scream anymore, but just when I thought we were going to overbalance and slide, sideways, across two lanes of traffic, he straightened up. I did too, right along with him, and then we shot onto the on-ramp for Ellington Parkway with a roar of exhaust. My skirt was flapping behind me, and I daresay I flashed anyone we passed a little too much leg, but while it was fast and furious and more than a bit scary, it was also exhilarating and fun and a bit like I imagine flying might be.

The wild ride didn't last long. It was only two or three minutes later that he exited the highway at Dresden Avenue and slowed down to a decorous 35 mph through the Potsdam neighborhood. We pulled into the driveway of Mrs. Jenkins's house before either the glazer or the locksmith got there, with a little spurt of gravel. Rafe pulled up in front of the steps and cut the engine. I crawled off the bike, no more gracefully than I'd crawled on, I'm afraid, and pulled the helmet off my head. My head felt too light, like it was about to float away, and my legs were a bit shaky, although between you and me, I must admit the vibrations had been rather nice. The way I'd been plastered against his back, with his butt flexing between my thighs, had been stimulating too, if we're being honest.

He grinned at me. "What d'you think?"

I pawed the hair out of my face. "It was... interesting."

One of his eyebrows arched. "Interesting?"

I flushed. "The... um... vibrations were nice."

The grin turned wicked. "You want vibrations, darlin', I'll give you vibrations."

"We don't have time," I said, and the disappointment must have come across in my voice, because he smothered a laugh.

"Sure we do. They won't be here for ten minutes."

"That isn't enough time."

"Darlin'," Rafe said, "you're forgetting who you're talking to. Gimme five minutes upstairs, and I promise I can show you paradise."

I glanced at my watch. Nine minutes and thirty seconds until eight. "You're on."

"Let's go." He grabbed my hand and headed for the stairs at a fast enough clip that I had to run to keep up. Maybe I wasn't the only one who had been motivated by being plastered together on the back of the bike on the way here.

By the time the doorbell rang, I'd been to paradise and back, and was in the process of putting my clothes on. Rafe was already dressed. "I'll get it," he told me. "Just take your time getting yourself together."

"Thank you."

He grinned at me over his shoulder on his way to the door. "No, darlin'. Thank *you*." He winked before passing out of sight.

I finished buttoning my blouse, and then I headed into the adjoining bathroom to look at myself in the mirror. Only to take a step back from the reflection that stared back at me.

It was tempting to blame the motorcycle for the nice pink color in my cheeks and the snarled mess of my hair—the hair I had carefully styled before leaving the apartment this morning, I might add. Now it hung in a messy tangle over one shoulder, and I was pretty sure Rafe's hands had had something to do with that. It was certainly his fault that I was without my carefully applied lipstick, and the roses in my cheeks and sparkle in my eyes could be firmly laid at his door too, probably.

Not that I was complaining. Paradise and back in eight minutes flat had been just as big a thrill ride as the trip on the back of the Harley, and as far as I was concerned, I'd be happy to do either activity again any time he wanted. We usually managed our lovemaking at a more leisurely pace (Rafe being determined to reassure me that I wasn't frigid, as if I had any doubts at all on that score anymore) but this breathless rush to the finish had certainly not left me wanting in any way. Other than the fact that I looked like something the (non-existent) cat had dragged in, anyway.

I did my best to smooth my hair and reapply lipstick before I headed downstairs, but I'm afraid I appeared rather the worse for wear. When I got to the foyer, the look Tamara Grimaldi gave me said it all. Her lip curled. I flushed to the roots of my still-messy hair, but since she didn't actually say anything, I couldn't either.

"I was just telling your boyfriend," she informed me, "that Mr. Hanson did not make it home last night."

"You had someone watching the place?"

She nodded. "There's also been no activity at Mr. Lamont's Oak Hill house."

"So they're staying somewhere else."

"We're looking into any other property Mr. Hanson might own. Or any family he might have, who is harboring him. Or them."

"Do you think they're together?"

"That depends," Grimaldi said. "On whether Mr. Hanson is waiting for a payoff from Mr. Lamont, as soon as Mr. Briggs gets his hands on the money."

"Have you spoken to Tim about it?"

She nodded. "He's picking up the money from the bank this afternoon. He's awaiting instructions from Mr. Lamont as to what to do with it."

"Do you think he'll tell you when he gets them?"

"I'm hopeful he will, but just in case he doesn't, we'll keep him under surveillance. I could use your help with that."

"I don't have a car," I said.

"I'm aware of that. Just out of curiosity, how did you get here this morning?"

"On the back of the bike." I glanced at Rafe, who wasn't bothering to hide his amusement.

"I see," Grimaldi said.

"That's why I look like this."

"Of course." She sounded solicitous and understanding. Maybe she'd had her own ride on the back of a Harley at some point. Just as long as it wasn't Rafe's Harley, I was fine with that. Or maybe the solicitousness was only skin deep and she knew exactly what we'd been doing since we got here. "All I want you to do as far as Mr. Briggs is concerned, is go to the office and tell me if he leaves."

"I can do that. Once we're finished here."

"I'll stick around," Rafe said, "and make sure she gets there."

"You don't have to do that. I know you have things to do."

"We're gonna figure out what happened to Manny. But I ain't risking losing you in the process." He turned to Grimaldi. "Someone tried to get into her apartment yesterday. I dunno whether she bothered to mention that?"

"No," Grimaldi said, eyeing me, "she didn't."

"It was no big deal," I said. "I was there. I scared whoever it was away."

"Did you get a look at the burglar?"

I shook my head. "I didn't open the door. But it was after I came home from here, after I realized that someone had broken the windows and left the knife in the floor. I assumed it was the same person."

"Mr. Lamont."

"I can't imagine who else it might have been. He did vandalize my office."

Grimaldi nodded. "Once you get there, I want you to stay there, OK? No wandering off on your own. Not even to go home. From now on I want you to have someone with you at all times."

"He isn't going to hurt me," I protested. "He's just angry because I put him in prison. But he isn't stupid enough to try to harm me."

"Maybe not. But if you catch him in the process of something like this," she gestured to the house and the vandalism that had taken place, "who knows what he might do. And he did try to kill you once before."

That was true. It had taken place just a handful of feet from here, as a matter of fact.

The gravel in the driveway crunched as a car turned in from the street. We watched as the glazer's truck with big plates of glass on the back made its slow way up to the front of the house.

"I'll leave you to it," Grimaldi said. "Remember to call me if Mr. Briggs looks like he's going anywhere."

I promised I would, and watched her hustle down the steps to her car while the truck from Cumberland Hardware made its slow and ponderous way up the graveled drive.

Fifteen

Rafe stuck around while the glazer did his thing with the windows, and the locksmith—who arrived a few minutes later—changed the locks. If either of them minded a six foot three inch TBI agent looking over their shoulders, they didn't mention it. Then again, I guess maybe they wouldn't.

I cleaned up the glass and fingerprint powder from yesterday, meanwhile. I had to find a new broom for the job, since the CSI tech had taken away the one that had been used to break the windows, as evidence.

We were all still at it by the time nine o'clock rolled around and the potential buyers turned up the driveway, followed by their agent and the home inspector.

In everything that had happened, I had sort of forgotten about them, to be honest. Or not really forgotten—I knew that's why we were here, scrambling to get all this done this morning. But they had sort of slipped my mind in all the excitement.

Now I watched them walk up the stairs with misgiving. Me, I mean, although it looked like they might have some misgivings of their own, given the way they looked around, and the way the female clung to the male's arm.

Their agent had point, bounding up to stand in front of me. "What's going on?"

"We had a little problem," I said, smiling brightly. *Never mind all the activity going on all around us. Ignore the man changing the locks. And the one leaning over his shoulder.* "Someone broke a few windows night before last. I didn't realize it until yesterday afternoon, when it was too late to get anyone out to fix them."

He cast a beady eye on the proceedings. "And the locks?"

"We thought it safer to change those, as well."

Behind him, his clients exchanged a glance.

The agent was about my age, and painfully trendy in skinny jeans and a band T-shirt, with a scraggly goatee and a tattoo of a skull on his forearm, surrounded by leaves and flowers. He looked positively anemic next to Rafe, who was also wearing jeans and a T-shirt, but a T-shirt that stretched tight across his shoulders and chest, before tapering to a narrow waist. The agent was built more like a fourteen year old boy, and looked like he might be a musician in his spare time. Although if you asked him, he'd probably tell you that real estate was his day job, and music his real calling.

The clients were even younger, fresh out of college by the looks of them. About the age I had been in my wedding picture. Bright-eyed, fresh-faced, and naive. This latest development seemed to have rubbed off some of the shine. The girl—a wispy little blonde—looked worried as she chewed her bottom lip, while the guy—in suit and tie—looked as imposing as he could at twenty four or so. That, also, paled in comparison to Rafe, who imposes extremely well.

The inspector took a step back, off the stairs. "I'll start outside. Give'em time to do what they need to do in here."

He walked back to his truck, where he began wrestling a big ladder down off the bed. After a moment's hesitation, when it became clear that neither the agent nor the potential buyer was going to help him, Rafe stopped hovering over the locksmith and went to assist. Between them, they lifted the ladder to the ground and carried it around the corner of the house, where I assumed the inspector planned to use it to reach the roof. I didn't envy him the job. Mrs. J's house is three stories tall, so it's a long way up.

The inspector came back around the corner with Rafe ambling behind. He caught my eye and winked. I smiled back.

Meanwhile, the inspector informed his clients, "This is gonna take a while. Y'all can leave and come back in three hours, if you want. I should be getting close to being finished by then."

"Three hours!"

"Big house," the inspector said, with a non-apologetic shrug. "Y'all want me to look at everything, right?"

The nervous blonde nodded vehemently. The husband or boyfriend snorted. "I can't leave work again in three hours to come back here."

"Y'all don't have to be here," the inspector said. "I'll send you the report when I'm done. Tomorrow."

"Tomorrow!"

"It's gonna take me a little time to fill it out. It's thirty pages long."

"Thirty!"

The blonde put her hand on the guy's arm and whispered something. He huffed, but simmered down. "Fine. We'll wait for the report. We're certainly paying enough for it."

They probably were. Home inspections don't come cheap, and I knew the name of this inspection company. I hadn't used it myself, but several of my colleagues had, and I had heard that the inspector was good and thorough and charged accordingly.

He must be used to dealing with rude clients, because all he said was, "I'll go get started."

He walked away. Maybe the money he got paid was such that he didn't mind working for jerks.

The agent turned to his clients. "We can meet back here at noon if you like."

"I can't leave work again!" Mr. Important shrieked. Rafe rolled his eyes and left, presumably to hold the ladder while the inspector climbed the three stories to the roof. The guy's wife put her hand on his arm to try to calm him down. He shrugged it off and added, viciously, "I'm not even sure I want this house anymore. You didn't tell me this was a bad neighborhood!"

Of course he hadn't. Real estate agents aren't allowed to refer to neighborhoods as 'good' or 'bad.' Those are relative terms anyway, but we're not legally free to offer our opinions on whether a neighborhood is safe or not. We can recommend that our clients check the crime statistics and determine for themselves whether it's somewhere they'd be comfortable living, but beyond that, we have no recourse. Obviously this particular client hadn't bothered to take that particular step, because if he had, he'd have known that the area around Potsdam Street was transitional at best (and high-crime at worst) before he drove here this morning.

He might not even know that Brenda Puckett was murdered here. It isn't considered a material fact, not like a leaking roof or a propensity for water intrusion in the basement, so we hadn't been required to disclose it when we listed the house for sale. And since no one had flat out asked, we hadn't mentioned anything about it.

I could only imagine what would happen when these potential buyers found out.

I squinted at the grungy agent. Maybe he didn't know, either. I had assumed he did, since the murder of one real estate agent by another just six or seven months ago seemed like it should have been of interest to him. But maybe he was so new he hadn't had his license to practice seven months yet.

I certainly wasn't about to tell him. Things were bad enough without that. The little blonde watched the locksmith and glazer with an expression sort of like Bambi watching the forest burn. She was a wispy, ethereal, fae-like girl, with soft, floaty hair and enormous eyes. Her significant other, meanwhile, tall and severe in his suit, gave the impression of being set at a constant low boil.

Now, I've had my own experiences with macho men, and not just from reading bodice rippers. Rafe is about as domineering as they come, and so, in his own understated and chivalrous way, is Todd. Bradley, not so much. I was fairly sure Shelby wore the pants in that relationship, and Bradley would do whatever it took to keep her happy. Maybe that was why our marriage hadn't been better. He was a follower at heart, same as me, so neither of us had taken charge the way we should have.

But I digress.

Rafe is strong and forceful and dominant, but he's also a born protector. So is Todd, in his overbearing, wrap-her-in-cotton-wool-and-put-her-on-a-shelf sort of way.

This guy didn't strike me as protective at all. He seemed to have all the bad qualities of the raging alpha, and none of the good. It wouldn't have surprised me if he hit her in secret. Or if he didn't, he at least made her feel like she had to walk on eggshells around him so he wouldn't raise his hand to her.

I didn't like him. I'd already been upset because my own sweet little couple—the ones with the condo to sell—weren't going to be able to get Mrs. J's house. Now his behavior made me take against him further.

Of course I didn't let it show. My mother taught me better than that. Or rather, my mother taught me to let me feelings show only when I wanted them to. In this case, I didn't. Much.

"I'll let the three of you figure this out," I told the agent, just as Rafe came back around the corner of the house.

"Darlin'."

We stepped aside to talk privately while the agent and his clients kept whispering.

"I gotta get to work," Rafe told me.

"Of course." He had a murder to solve. "You can take me to the office now. Everything seems to be up and running." I glanced around, at the glazer, the locksmith, and the inspector, plus the agent and his clients conferencing on the porch.

He shook his head. "Just stay here. Make sure everything gets done that's supposed to get done. There are plenty of people around to keep you safe. I'll just come back for you at noon. Take you to lunch and to the office."

That would work, too. "If you prefer."

He tilted his head. "You ain't afraid of being here by yourself, are you?"

I wasn't. Not with so many people around. "I won't be alone. The inspector will be here. Just go find out what happened to Manny."

A shadow crossed his face, and he nodded. "I'll see you at twelve."

He leaned in to drop a kiss on my mouth. I tilted my face up, recognizing as I did it just how far I'd come in six or seven months. The first Saturday in August, when we'd stood here in the graveled driveway outside Mrs. Jenkins's house, the thought of him kissing me—in broad daylight, in front of an audience—would have given me heart palpitations—and not the way his kisses made my heart beat faster now.

Hell—heck—the first Saturday in August, I'd been afraid that someone I knew would see me talking to him, that's how neurotic I'd been.

While now I closed my eyes, and swayed toward him, and did my best to make what had been intended as a quick peck last as long as possible.

By the time his lips—reluctantly, I thought, or hoped—left mine, my stomach had turned to liquid, and so had my knees. So, for that matter, had his eyes, but he still managed a chuckle. "Hold that thought, darlin'."

"No problem," I managed, knowing it wouldn't be.

"And maybe you should go sit down before you fall down."

Maybe I should. "I'll see you at twelve. Hurry back."

"You know it," Rafe said. He ran his knuckles down my cheek—a tender caress that never failed to turn me to mush, the very few times he's used it—before turning to straddle the Harley. "Stay inside where you'll be safe."

"Just as soon as you're gone."

"Now," Rafe said. "I don't need you waving me off, darlin'. I ain't going to war."

"If you prefer."

"Please." He pulled the helmet over his head. I turned and walked up the stairs and into the house without looking back. At least not until I heard the roar of the engine fade down the street, and then I did turn around for a last look at him driving away. No, he wasn't going off to war. He wasn't really even going off to pit himself against bad guys the way he used to. Chances were he'd be perfectly safe and would be back to pick me up for lunch when he said he would. But it was a hard habit to break. Every time he drove away, I felt a stab of that old fear that I wouldn't see him again, and I always made sure I took one last look, just in case it really turned out to be the last time, even when I was fairly certain it wouldn't be.

I SPENT THE NEXT THREE HOURS prowling Mrs. J's house. The buyers left shortly after Rafe did, the husband striding to his second-hand BMW with barely-concealed impatience while the wife scurried in his wake. He didn't even open the car door for her, just threw himself behind the wheel and cranked the engine over. They drove off down the driveway with a spurt of gravel.

I approached the agent, who looked put out as he watched them disappear in a cloud of dust. "Everything all right?"

He snorted. "What do you think?"

"They seemed a bit upset."

He shot me a look. "Wouldn't you be?"

Maybe. Coming here to the house they wanted to buy to see a glazer replacing broken windows and a locksmith changing the locks, must have been disconcerting, but between you and me, when I discovered what had happened, I wasn't happy, either. His clients should have made sure Potsdam was a neighborhood they would be comfortable in *before* making an offer to buy the house. Now it was too late. Although of course if they were reconsidering, they could withdraw based on the results of the inspection. We wouldn't have a choice but to give them their earnest money back.

"This is a neighborhood in the midst of gentrification," I told him, exaggerating more than a little. The neighborhood wasn't in the middle of gentrification so much as our renovated house was in the middle of the neighborhood, none of the rest of which had been gentrified. "If your clients aren't comfortable in a transitional neighborhood, you should have steered them to the areas on the other side of Gallatin Road." Where the prices were double but the people were less likely to have spent time in prison.

He looked at me down the length of his nose. "We wouldn't have been able to get anything in this price range over there."

I resisted the temptation to say "No shit, Sherlock." It would have been juvenile and unladylike.

Even if it was how I felt.

"Didn't it occur to you to wonder why? This house would be three quarters of a million in Edgefield or Lockeland Springs. Here it's under four hundred thousand."

The agent shrugged, pouting. I guess maybe it really hadn't occurred to him to wonder why.

"I'll be here until noon," I informed him. "You don't have to stay unless you want to. If your clients come back before you do, I'll let them in."

It was a not so polite dismissal, and he caught it, because he snorted and took himself off, down the stairs to his Jeep Wrangler. It had an '*my other ride is a Fender*' bumper sticker attached to the spare tire, so I'd been right about the music thing.

I waited until he'd left, and then I went back inside the house to find something to do.

I started by remaking Rafe's bed, since we'd rumpled the sheets in our quickie session of lovemaking earlier. That done, I ventured back downstairs. The glazer was doing his thing in the front parlor and library, so I couldn't stay in there. The locksmith had the front door hanging wide open while he was messing with the lock, so it was cold in the front of the house. And the inspector was crawling around on the roof. I'd heard the scraping when I was upstairs. Hopefully he had tied himself to the chimney, so he wouldn't accidentally roll off and plummet to his death. It was a long way down. Granted, he probably crawled around on roofs all the time, and he'd survived so far, but we were having a rather spectacular run of bad luck right now, and it would just put the icing on the cake.

I ended up in the kitchen, at the table where Rafe and I still hadn't gotten around to having sex. I could have suggested it earlier, I guess, but it had slipped my mind in the rush of getting inside and undressed.

I hadn't planned to spend all morning at Mrs. J's house, so I hadn't brought any work, or even the laptop. I ended up sitting at the table with a pen and a pad of paper I dug out of a drawer, jotting down notes old-school to try to restore some semblance of order to my life.

I had a lot on my mind. Between Manny's murder, and Bradley's possible affair, and Walker's escape from prison, and Garth Hanson slashing my car tires, and now the possibility—or more likely probability—that this set of buyers were going to walk away from buying the house, my plate was full.

So I made lists.

First things first. Manny's murder. There was nothing I could do about that. Rafe and Grimaldi—the TBI and the MNPD—were both working on it, and were a lot better equipped to handle it than I was. As far as I was concerned, they were both the best at what they did, and they'd find who did it and punish that person accordingly. There was nothing I could do to help. They thought it was connected to Manny's past, and they were probably right, so I was out of that one. No need to even think about it anymore.

I drew a line through Manny's name on the page.

The police were on the lookout for Walker, too, and now that we'd determined that Garth Hanson was alive and kicking, for him as well. He was probably waiting for Walker's delivery of cash, before getting out of town. Tim should know about that this afternoon, and the exchange would probably take place tonight, under cover of darkness—that's the way it happens in the movies—so by tomorrow, Walker and Garth Hanson would be out of my hair, too. No need to think about either of them anymore, either.

I drew a line through Walker's name, and then through Garth Hanson's, below.

Bradley.

I found it hard to believe he was sleeping around on Shelby, and not only because Ilona Vandervinder seemed like an unlikely candidate for wanting anything to do with him. He could be sleeping with someone else, I supposed, but when we spoke at Christmas, he'd seemed genuinely happy and excited about the baby.

No, I was still inclined to think something else was going on.

Something having to do with the man he'd met at the Shortstop.

A man who wasn't Nathan Ferncliff. Marsha the waitress had been adamant about that. And it hadn't been Walker. Nor Garth Hanson, I assumed, since Hanson had been sitting right next to me during the conversation—up until the moment we started talking about Walker, and then he had left, abruptly. Surely she would have realized it, if it was the same guy.

A guy who looked like Dale Vandervinder, but who couldn't be Dale Vandervinder, because Bradley meeting with Dale Vandervinder would be a huge breach of ethics when Ferncliff & Morton were representing Ilona Vandervinder in the divorce.

Except...

That would certainly explain the secrecy, wouldn't it? Why Bradley and his well-dressed companion hid away in a dive bar in a part of town as far from their usual haunts as possible?

The possibility took my breath away for a moment, before I sucked in another mouthful of air and tried to look at the situation rationally.

Was it even a possibility? Could Bradley have compromised his ethics so badly that he'd have dealings with his client's husband, the person represented by opposing counsel?

It was hard to believe. In the time I'd known him, before and during our marriage, he hadn't struck me as particularly unethical.

Then again, he was a cheater, so that argued for a certain amount of underhandedness. If he was willing to cheat on his wife, he might be willing to cheat in other ways too.

Dale was wealthy, or so I assumed. He was a music producer, and in Nashville, such people live high on the hog. Just look at Ilona's—formerly the couple's—home. It made Mrs. Jenkins's house look like a shack.

Tennessee is an equitable distribution state, so unless they had come to an agreement themselves on how to divide the marital assets, the divorce court would do that for them. Bradley and I had made our own decision. I'd given him everything we owned jointly except for a few items I'd brought into the marriage with me or bought during the time we'd been married, plus my car. He'd kept the townhouse and everything in it, including the wedding gifts, and had given me a nice settlement I had lived on for the past almost three years. It was running low, incidentally. My sister Catherine had wanted me to take him for everything he was worth, but I'd just wanted out of the marriage, so I'd been happy with the money and the few things I couldn't live without.

Dale and Ilona were probably not in the same boat. If I had to guess, I'd say that Ilona wanted as many of the marital assets as she could get, while Dale wanted to keep as much as he could for himself. Chances were they were waiting for the court to decide for them.

And it was possible that Dale had somehow bribed or blackmailed Bradley into helping him. If he knew about something Bradley had done—if, for instance, Bradley really had slept with Ilona, and Dale knew about it—he might have prevailed upon Bradley to throw his own case just so Dale wouldn't tell Shelby. Or maybe it was about the money. Bradley made decent money, but he was still just a junior partner, and Shelby did like to spend. She'd totally redecorated the townhouse since marrying Bradley, and not with cheap furniture, either. My old kitchen had been ripped out and a new one installed, one shiny with chrome and marble and bling. None of that had come cheap. And with a baby on the way, the expenditures were about to increase tenfold. Babies are expensive, or so my brother and sister keep telling me.

Much as I'd like to insist otherwise, I couldn't totally dismiss the idea that perhaps Bradley had gotten himself involved in something professionally iffy.

Sixteen

Rafe came back at noon, as promised. By then, we had new locks, new keys, and new windowpanes. And I had a distinct feeling we'd soon be looking for a new contract on the house as well. The potential buyers were not happy. Mr. Tall, Dark and Disgruntled had managed to drag himself away from work to return for the denouement, and so had his long-suffering wife. And since the results of the inspection weren't anything to worry about, not in my opinion, I think the low-slung Buick that drove by, the one with all the chrome on the wheels and the woofers thumping so loud and low it rattled the fillings in my teeth, had something to do with it. Mrs. TD&D flinched when one of the youths leaned out the window and catcalled.

The same thing had happened to me last August, on these very steps. Rafe had taken a step closer to me, to make it clear that anyone bothering me would have to deal with him. The car had sped off.

In this case, Mr. TD&D didn't move. I'm not sure he even noticed his wife's reaction. I did, and she knew it. Her cheeks turned pink when she noticed me looking at her. The gaze she turned on the car was fearful. I couldn't imagine her agreeing to buying a house here, one that maybe her unobservant husband would expect her to stay in on her own while he was out doing other things.

Not that I thought there was any chance that was going to happen, because Mr. Disgruntled was certainly very put out with this whole situation, and made sure both the agent and the inspector knew of his displeasure.

At any rate, Rafe drove up a few minutes later. By then, the glazer and locksmith were long gone, and the agent, inspector, and soon-to-be-former-buyers were huddled at the foot of the steps.

When Rafe pulled up behind the line of cars parked in the circular drive, they started making leaving-noises.

"Take your time." He brushed past them and headed up to the porch to slip a hand around my waist. "Hi, darlin'."

"Hi," I said, tilting my face up for a quick kiss.

"Everything OK?" He glanced around.

"Fine. The windows are replaced and the locks are new. I swept up the broken glass and the dust. The only thing left to do is make sure the back door is locked and all the lights are off."

"Let's do it, then. I'm starving." He pushed open the door and crossed over the threshold. Then he hesitated. "Coming?"

"Sure." I glanced over my shoulder, but the inspector was already on his way to the truck, and the agent and clients were probably taking a quick minute to discuss the preliminary results of the inspection before they parted ways. No one looked at me. Mr. TD&D was stabbing his finger in the air a scant inch from his agent's face, and the shorter, skinnier man was trying not to flinch. Meanwhile, Small, Blond and Nervous was chewing her bottom lip and casting worried glances down the road in the direction of where the Buick had disappeared.

I closed the door behind me, and after a second's hesitation, locked it.

"Nervous?" Rafe asked.

I shrugged. "This car drove by and scared the bejeezes out of the buyers. Or out of her, anyway. I don't think her husband noticed. But I doubt they'll end up buying the house after all."

He arched a brow. "That bad?"

"A bunch of young black guys in a tricked-out Buick. They rattled her." There was no point in telling him what they'd said. I probably couldn't get my tongue to shape the words anyway.

He looked me over. "You OK?"

I nodded. "I don't think they were talking to me." I had no idea why, but maybe they just liked waifish platinum blondes. I'm neither waifish nor is my hair that fair. I'm a blonde, but it's more dishwater than platinum. With some lighter streaks when I can afford it.

"I know most of the boys around here," Rafe said, as he unlocked and relocked the back door with a determined snick. "They know better than to bother you."

That explained a lot. "Thank you."

He shrugged. "Door's secure. Ready to go?"

"Sure." I glanced around the kitchen and realized I'd left my pencil and pad of paper on the table.

Rafe got there before me. "What's this?"

"Just some notes about things." I put my hands behind my back so I wouldn't be tempted to snatch it away from him.

He didn't say anything, just focused on deciphering my scrawl. I had learned the proper elegant cursive in finishing school—a well-brought-up Southern Belle sends a lot of personalized, handwritten thank-you notes—but I'm afraid it has deteriorated a little from lack of use.

Finally he lifted his head to look at me across the table, hands braced on either side of the pad and the muscles in his arms standing out. "You serious about this?"

"It's just a theory," I said. "Marsha at the Shortstop did say the man Bradley met there looked like Dale Vandervinder. And if Bradley is planning to double cross his own client, what better reason for sneaking around?"

"Guess I'll have to schedule a visit with Bradley."

Uh-oh. "How are you going to explain that?"

He shrugged, and muscles moved smoothly under the sleeves of the blue T-shirt. I have no idea how he managed to get away with wearing T-shirts and leather jackets to work, but I guess part of the point was that he didn't look like a TBI agent. He still looked like he might be balanced on the line between right and wrong, and I guess that's exactly what the TBI wanted from him.

The shirt he had on today was soft and blue with a faded Corona logo on the chest, and I realized, with a slight sense of shock, that it was the same shirt he'd worn that night in September when I'd shown up here after surprising both Todd and myself by saying no to Todd's marriage proposal.

That was the same night Rafe and I had ended up making love for the first time, so I had fond memories of that particular shirt.

It seemed particularly fortuitous that he should be wearing it today.

"You know," I said, "we never did get around to having sex on the kitchen table."

For a second or two, nothing happened. Part of me wondered whether I only thought I'd said it out loud, when I'd really only said it in my head.

Part of me worried he was ignoring me because I'd said something he didn't want to hear.

And part of me wanted to take it back. But only part.

He lifted his head to look at me. One eyebrow crept up and the corner of his mouth tilted.

I blushed. "Sorry."

"I'm not," Rafe said. He pushed the pencil and pad of paper aside before crooking his finger at me. "C'mere."

I walked around the table with my heart thudding and my stomach swooping in anticipation. I'd lost count of the times we'd made love in the last few months. At first, every time had been special and precious and rare. But since Christmas, I'd had him in bed next to me every night, and while the sex was still wonderful and semi-magical, there'd been so much of it that by now, I couldn't remember each instance individually. Nonetheless, I never did lose that knee-jerk reaction to him. When he got that look on his face, when his eyes turned dark and full of heat, and his lips softened in that certain way, my body softened, too. My skin tingled and my knees turned to jell-o.

As soon as I got close enough, he trapped me between his body and the edge of the table. His hands wandered south. "Good thing you decided to wear this skirt today."

It was spring-like and flouncy and easy to move up. Before I realized what he was doing, he had slipped his hands underneath and up to my hips. He hooked his fingers in the sides of my panties and pulled them back down. "Up you go."

I found myself boosted unceremoniously up on the edge of the table.

"Perfect." He moved a step closer, nudging my thighs apart at the same time.

"You've done this before," I said, a little breathlessly, as I looped my arms around his neck.

"No, darlin'. I've just thought about it a lot." He slipped his hands around my back. "Let go and lie back."

I swallowed hard as I unhooked my hands from behind his neck and let him lower my back to the hard surface of the table. Looked like we were really going to do this. And now that we were, I wasn't entirely sure I felt comfortable about it. We were very exposed here in the middle of the kitchen, with bright daylight shining in through the windows and back door.

And what if the agent decided to knock on the front door before leaving? I wasn't sure I could live down the embarrassment if he caught us *in flagrante delicto*. On the kitchen table, no less. Not to mention what it would do to my professional reputation if he spread the word that I was engaging in sex in the middle of the afternoon.

I had locked the front door, hadn't I?

"Darlin'," Rafe murmured, his hands busy working my skirt up, "you think too much."

"I just don't want any interruptions."

His lips curved. "With what I'm gonna do to you, I promise you won't notice if the ceiling caves in."

Having been on the receiving end of promises like that before, I had no doubt he could deliver. And anyway, that was just when his fingers did a certain something that sent my eyes rolling back in my head.

I heard his chuckle from far away. "That's my girl. Don't worry about it, darlin'. Just let me take care of you."

No problem. I watched the ceiling fan revolve slowly through half closed eyes while my ears registered the faint rasp of a zipper being drawn down.

Then he came back.

"Ready? Lift this one a little, darlin'." He draped one of my knees over his arm and nudged my legs farther apart. I caught my breath quickly when he brushed against me, and I could hear the smile in his voice. "Sometimes I wonder if Bradley has any idea what he was missing."

"Probably not," I managed.

Bradley and I had never had an enjoyable sex life, and while part of that was certainly Bradley's lack of prowess, part was my lack of desire, too. Desire for Bradley, I mean. I have no lack of desire for Rafe.

"Good thing too," Rafe said, "or I mighta had to kill him." He surged forward, and I let out something halfway between a ladylike squeal and a very unladylike moan, and then clapped a hand over my mouth, blushing.

Rafe laughed, his voice hitching, but he didn't stop long enough to comment. I tried to keep an ear out for knocking on the front door—

just in case I'd been loud enough to catch the attention of the realtor or his clients who might still be outside—but it didn't take long before I forgot everything except Rafe. They could have been hammering on the door for all I knew, or pressing their noses against the windows—although I sincerely hoped not. But I didn't see or hear anything outside our own little world.

I'd been waiting for this for six months. And while it had taken me a good chunk of that time to get used to the idea of having sex in broad daylight on the kitchen table—with Rafe Collier!—the reality was everything I could have hoped for and more. Sex with Rafe was always good, but the long, drawn-out anticipation of this—and maybe even the fact that there were people outside the house who might just decide to investigate what was going on—contributed to one of those rare experiences I wouldn't soon forget. Some of the other times we'd made love may be blurred in my mind, but this one wouldn't be.

"I like this kitchen," Rafe said when he'd gotten his breath back.

I looked around, from where I was still on my back on the table, with him standing between my thighs. "I do, too." It was nice and big, approximately four times the size of my current galley kitchen—big enough for a table!—and he had renovated it very nicely, with granite counters and stainless steel appliances and polished hardwood floors.

He had his hands braced on either side of me, and now he bent his head to brush a light kiss over my lips. "Thanks, darlin'."

"I didn't do anything," I said. "It was all you."

"Not all of it. You're very good at being flat on your back with your legs spread." He grinned.

I smiled back. "You bring out the best in me."

That made him laugh. But then he sobered. "I'm gonna have to talk to Bradley, darlin'."

"Of course." He didn't need my permission to talk to my ex-husband. Although it was nice of him to give me warning. Not that it was likely to have anything to do with me, either way. "I don't think he'll recognize you, to be honest."

"No?"

He took a step back and zipped up, before reaching out a hand. Once I was seated on the edge of the table, he retrieved the pair of my panties he'd dropped on the floor earlier and went down on one knee to help me put them on. Skimming them up my legs and into place went a long way toward making me want him all over again—and after just these few minutes!—but I squashed it.

"I doubt it. He's only seen you once, and it was dark. He was inside the car and you were outside, so he probably didn't get a good look at you. And he... um..."

I hesitated, trying to come up with a good way to say it.

"Thinks all black people look alike?" Rafe suggested.

"Something like that."

Rafe was only half black, but no sooner had the thought crossed my mind than I wished it hadn't. I wished I could stop feeling the need to point that particular fact out, since I knew it meant I still harbored some of my own racial hang-ups. Getting to know him, and falling in love with him, and making the decision that I wanted to be with him no matter what anyone else thought of it—and some people thought plenty—had only been half the battle. I was still mentally struggling with the need to justify myself.

It's not a pretty thing to realize about yourself.

In fact, it probably made me no better than Bradley. His prejudices may be closer to the surface, but the fact that mine were better hidden didn't make them any nicer to look at. It might even make them worse. At least Bradley's prejudices were out in the open.

So now I had just rationalized myself a worse hypocrite than my ex-husband, which did nothing to make me feel any better. The afterglow of wonderful love-making was fading fast, and Rafe noticed. "Darlin'?" He put his hands on my shoulders.

I dredged up a smile from somewhere and plastered it on my face before I looked up at him. "It's fine. I'm fine."

"I'll handle him with kid gloves. I promise."

That wasn't the problem, but I didn't want him to know it, so I just nodded. "We should probably go. You can drop me off at the office and get back to work."

"Food first," Rafe said. "I just worked up an appetite." He grinned at me.

I smiled back, a little more genuinely. "What are you hungry for?"

"Besides you?" He winked. "Barbecue."

Of course. Drippy, fattening stuff he could eat with his fingers.

But I had just worked off a few ounces myself, or so I fervently hoped. "I'm game."

"That's what a man likes to hear." He put an arm around my shoulders and steered me toward the front door. In the doorway he turned to look back. "I'm gonna miss that kitchen table."

So was I. I'd spent months fantasizing about it, and now that it had happened, I found I didn't like the idea of anyone else getting it on in what I thought of as our spot.

"It looks like we'll have more time than we thought to get used to the idea. I bet you anything you want that the buyers are going to pull out and we'll be left without a contract."

He glanced down at me. "You bet me what?"

"Anything you want."

"Hold that thought," Rafe said and opened the front door.

WE HAD STICKY, GOOPY BARBECUE AT Edley's, and then he took me to the office.

"Stay here until I come get you," he informed me when he dropped me off. "If I can't come get you, I'll call, and you can get a cab."

"I could walk," I said. "It's only a mile or so, straight down the road. Maybe less."

"Down East Main Street. Where the soup kitchen is and the gangbangers hang out."

"It's getting better." In fact, as I had always had to tell Todd, whenever he took me to dinner and brought me back to East Nashville afterwards, the neighborhood is getting safer and more expensive every day.

"Not good enough," Rafe said. "You got an escaped convict gunning for you, darlin'."

"I've got you to protect me."

"Not if you decide to walk home by yourself. So just stay here until I come get you."

Yeah, yeah. I promised I would, then gave him a kiss before heading into the office through the back door. I didn't hear the Harley roar off until the door had closed and safely latched behind me.

The first office to the left inside the door—the big corner office in the back of the building—used to belong to Walker. When he left us to take up residence in Riverbend Penitentiary, Tim took over the reins—and the office. As I walked down the hall past his door, his voice floated out to me. "Is that you, Savannah?"

I backtracked a few steps and stuck my head through the opening. "Something I can do for you?"

Tim sighed exaggeratedly and threw himself backwards in his chair. "You can tell your pet detective to stop bothering me. When I hear something, she'll be the first to know."

I stepped inside the room. "She's not *my* pet detective. And she's just trying to catch Walker. We'll all be happier when he's back behind bars."

Tim looked dubious, so maybe he wouldn't be.

"You better be careful," I added maliciously. "Once he gets his money, he has no reason to keep you alive anymore."

He turned a shade paler.

Tim spent a few years in New York trying to make it as a triple threat on Broadway, and although he's getting a little long in the tooth, he still has the preternaturally glossy looks of a male model or soap opera star. Gleaming blond curls, bright blue eyes, and an excess number of teeth. They're brilliantly white, and I think they're probably capped. At the moment, the ceiling light glinted off them with the brilliance of a thousand stars. Or had, until I scared him. Then he stuck his bottom lip out in a pout more suited to a five-year-old than a grown man.

"You're such a tease."

Not really, but I blushed anyway, remembering what I'd been doing just thirty minutes ago. And that brought the malicious gleam back into Tim's baby-blues. He leaned forward. "Where have you been all morning, darling? Was that Rafael's motorcycle I heard driving away?"

I admitted as much. "The police have my car."

Tim clicked his tongue. "Getting in trouble again, sweetie?"

"Someone slashed my tires last night," I said.

His eyes opened wide. "All of them?"

I nodded. "We're thinking it was Walker."

"Why?"

"Because the guard who helped him get out of prison was in the vicinity when it happened. We think Walker might have been there, too."

"Oh dear," Tim said faintly.

"The police took it in to look over. Just in case."

He didn't ask in case of what. I guess maybe he didn't want to know. I added, "I would consider it a personal favor if you could just speed Walker on his way as soon as possible. So far he's vandalized my office, my car, and my house, and tried to break into my apartment. And that reminds me."

"What?" He looked like he was waiting for the other shoe to fall.

"I don't think this second contract on 101 Potsdam is going to work out. Yesterday, someone broke several of the windows. From inside. With no damage to the locks. So when the buyers and their agent and inspector showed up this morning, there was a glazer and a locksmith there."

"Ouch."

Yes, indeed. "Hopefully something else will come along. Maybe we can get the original buyers back."

Maybe I should give them a call. Although it might be best to wait until I actually knew something for certain, one way or the other. Best not to do anything premature, or possibly unethical.

"So how is your boyfriend this morning?" Tim wanted to know. He has a bit of a crush on Rafe. Rafe doesn't seem to mind.

"He's fine."

Tim smacked his lips. "He certainly is."

I rolled my eyes. Not at him, at myself. I fall for the same line every single time, and it's getting old. "I'll be in my office if you need me."

"I won't," Tim said.

Seventeen

I stuck around for the rest of the afternoon, making frequent trips to the bathroom and kitchen so I could make sure that Tim was still stationed in his office and hadn't snuck out when I wasn't looking. Grimaldi had asked me to keep an eye on him, and I was taking the task seriously.

He didn't stir. Just sat in his ergonomic chair doing paperwork and talking on the phone. Whenever I happened to hear him, I walked more slowly to see if I could determine whether it was Walker on the other end of the line, but in most cases it just sounded like business as usual. One time I got an earful of what sounded perilously close to phone sex, and that was the time Tim noticed me eavesdropping—I stopped dead when I heard the things that were coming out of his mouth—and he glanced up and gave me a supercilious look before swiveling the chair around and putting his back to me.

"Tell me more," he cooed into the phone.

I stumbled across the threshold into the bathroom and locked the door behind me. So much for feeling adventurous and daring for having had sex on the kitchen table in the middle of the afternoon.

I did my best not to hear anything on my way back, and succeeded. And then I sat in my chair for a bit longer and wondered what to do next.

Nothing was happening. Tim wasn't going anywhere. I had no work to do. As far as Mrs. Jenkins's house went, all I could do was wait to hear what the prospective buyers thought of the inspection results and whether they wanted to move forward with the purchase. My gut feeling was that they wouldn't, but until I knew for sure, I couldn't do anything about it. Calling the former prospective buyers—the ones with the condo to sell—to tell them that there was a chance the house might become available again, would be grossly unprofessional... and very close to fishing, which is illegal. So while I desperately wanted to do something—anything!—I sat at my desk and twiddled my thumbs and waited.

The phone rang at a quarter after four. By then I was practically catatonic with boredom, so I almost dropped it when I fumbled it out of my bag. "Yes?"

"It's me," Grimaldi said. "The game's afoot."

"Really?" I hadn't heard anything from Tim. Not that he owed me a heads up or anything, but I thought he might have mentioned it when Walker called.

Her voice turned worried. "He's still there, isn't he?"

"As far as I know," I said.

"I told you—"

"I'm doing my best." It wasn't like I could camp out in the hallway outside Tim's door, after all. "I've been to the bathroom four times in the past three hours."

"I'm sorry to hear that," Grimaldi said politely.

I rolled my eyes, but Brittany was just on the other side of the lobby, some twelve feet away, so I refrained from comment. "Just tell me what you need."

"Officers Spicer and Truman will be bringing your car by in a few minutes. You have four new tires."

"Thank you." That was certainly going above and beyond the call of duty.

"Your boyfriend paid. At any rate, one of them will come inside to give you your key."

"I already have my key," I said.

"He will also give you a microphone for Mr. Briggs."

Ah. "Do you think Walker is watching?"

"I don't want to take any chances," Grimaldi said. "When you get the mic, help Mr. Briggs put it on. And then call me, so I can make sure we can hear everything."

I promised I would. "Any news on Manny Ortega's murder?"

She hesitated, and I wondered whether she'd refuse to tell me anything. She didn't have to. Sometimes, she's told me she couldn't. In this case, I guess she must have reasoned that she might as well, since Rafe probably kept me up to date anyway. "We're closing in on a couple of suspects."

"Really? That's great! Who?"

She muttered something I didn't quite catch.

"What?" I said.

"Nothing. You should know better than to ask me that."

I guess I should, at that.

When I didn't speak, she added, "I have to go. I have an escaped murderer to apprehend."

"Of course." I thought about asking her where the handoff was to take place, but I figured she'd probably just tell me it was none of my business. I'd just ask Tim instead. He didn't usually have any qualms about telling me things.

Grimaldi hung up, and I settled in to wait some more. Fifteen minutes passed, and then the front door opened and Spicer came in. He gave Brittany a friendly wave—she shrank back in her seat—and stuck his head through the door into my office-cum-coat-closet. "Afternoon, Miz Martin."

"Hi, Officer Spicer."

"Your car's parked out back." He spoke a little louder than he had to, I guess to make sure Brittany would catch every word. "Here's the key."

He put something in my hand. It wasn't a key, but I didn't want to stare at it, so I stuck it in my pocket without looking. "Anything I need to know?"

"No," Spicer said. "I have to go."

Sure. I waved goodbye and waited for the front door to close behind him, and then I grabbed my purse and jacket. "Since I have a car again, I guess I'll head out," I told Brittany on my way past the desk. She nodded, and didn't even look up from the latest issue of *Marie Claire*.

I headed down the hallway to Tim's office. "I hear the drop-off has been scheduled."

He looked startled.

"Detective Grimaldi called me." I closed the office door behind me.

Tim looked from it to me. "Darling," he bleated, "this is so sudden."

Sure. "I have your police issued microphone." I stuck my hand in my pocket.

Tim made a face. "Any chance you could get your boyfriend over here for this part? If anyone's going to tape wires to my chest, I'd rather it be him and not you."

"Not to worry," I said. "You won't have to get naked. It's a wristwatch."

It was. Basic black, with a cloth band and a bunch of buttons around the edges of the face.

"Sweetie," Tim said, looking at it and shaking his head, "there's no way Walker will believe I'm willingly wearing that."

He had a point. The watch had nothing of Tim's usual style. "I guess they were all out of Rolex. Maybe you can hide it under your cuff." It wasn't a camera, was it? Just a microphone. So if it wasn't seen but only heard, that'd likely be sufficient.

Tim took it off my palm, gingerly. "I suppose that might be possible. And advisable."

"It isn't that bad," I said.

"Speak for yourself," Tim answered, strapping the cloth band around his wrist and eyeing it with disdain. "At least it fits."

"Why wouldn't it?"

"I have slender wrists," Tim said, shaking his arm. The watch stayed in place.

I reached for my phone. "Tamara Grimaldi said to call her. To make sure she could hear."

Tim stopped shaking to stare at me. "Your pet detective has been listening to us?"

"I assume," I said, dialing. "And she isn't my pet detective."

Tim muttered something, but I ignored him, because Grimaldi answered. "The watch is here. And around Tim's wrist." Tim's *slender* wrist. "Can you hear us?"

"No," Grimaldi said. "You have to turn on the mic first."

Ah. "How does it work?"

She explained to me about the various buttons on the edges of the clockface. I passed the information on to Tim, who turned the microphone on and held it up to his mouth. "Can you hear me?"

"Loud and clear," Grimaldi's voice said over the speakerphone. "Put your arm down."

Tim looked startled. "How did you—?"

"Everyone does it," Grimaldi said. "Just forget about the mic. Pretend it isn't there. Use your hand the way you usually do. And keep talking. Both of you."

Fine. Tim and I spent a few minutes moving around the office, talking. Tim recited Shakespeare, I recited Emily Post. We had been made to memorize swatches of her *Etiquette* in finishing school, and they were still chiseled into my brain nine years later.

I have no idea what Grimaldi thought of any of it. She didn't comment, just let us know whether she could hear us or not. After a few minutes she thanked me. "Keep the watch around your wrist and the mic turned on," she instructed Tim.

"Will you call and let me know when you have Walker in custody?" I asked, and Grimaldi promised she would. I disconnected the call, not realizing until it was too late that I had missed my opportunity to ask Tim where the money drop-off was to take place. Now, with the microphone on, I couldn't. At least not straight out.

"How long until the meeting?" I asked instead.

Tim glanced at the watch, without wincing this time. "Thirty minutes."

"Do you have far to go?"

He shook his head. "Just down to the park."

Shelby Park, I assumed. Not likely to be very populated at this time on a weekday. "Another deserted place? You remember what happened last time, right?"

Tim shuddered. "Who could forget?"

The last time Tim had arranged a meeting in a deserted place—or at least the last time I knew about it—it had been to meet Rafe and me at the ruins of Fort Negley, on a hilltop just south of downtown Nashville. And while we were there, someone took a few potshots at Tim, and hit him. I had once taken a bullet to the shoulder myself, so I understood the reflexive hand he lifted to touch the now-healed wound. Being shot hurts.

"All I'm doing is leaving the money in a trashcan," Tim added. "Nobody's going to shoot at me."

I hoped not. "Good luck."

"Thank you," Tim said, and on that note, I opened the door and left.

As promised, my car was in the parking lot, and had four new tires. I walked around it once before getting behind the wheel, just to make sure that everything was OK. Not that I had any reason to believe that anything would have happened to it in the twenty minutes since Spicer dropped it off, but I was just a little bit jumpy.

Everything looked normal, though. No flat tires, no strange scratches, nothing out of the ordinary.

No bloody knife. And no shoebox sized package with wires sticking out of it in the backseat.

I got behind the wheel and inserted the key in the ignition. The car started right up.

I did think about hanging around for a while, and following Tim to Shelby Park when the time came. I would enjoy seeing Walker re-apprehended and hauled into the back of a police car, to have visual proof that he was safely out of my hair. But Tamara Grimaldi was likely to be there, and likely to give me hell if she saw me. And I was under no illusions that she wouldn't see me if I was stupid enough to go.

Safer to go home. Especially since Walker would be in the park, to take charge of his money. My apartment would be nice and empty, and I wouldn't have to worry about anyone trying to get in.

I parked on the street in front of the building. By now it was habit, and besides, there was a chance we'd end up going out again later.

It was habit to move quickly across the courtyard and into the building too, but that was all it was. Habit. I wasn't worried. My problems were almost over.

Or some of them, anyway. With Walker back behind bars, and Garth Hanson presumably right there with him, nobody would vandalize my office, my car, or Mrs. Jenkins's house again. I didn't have to worry about anyone taking potshots at me in broad daylight—not that anyone had. Mrs. J's house would suffer no more indignities, and we could sell it to someone who'd appreciate it, even if this morning's couple pulled out of the deal—as I suspected they would. It was a great house with some very nice features—including the extra-sturdy kitchen table—and someone was sure to want it.

After tonight, my biggest concern would be Bradley and Shelby, and to be perfectly blunt about it, whatever was going on there, was none of my business and less of my concern. If Bradley was cheating on Shelby with Ilona Vandervinder, that was between them. And if Bradley was a party to cheating Ilona Vandervinder out of her rightful—or maybe not rightful—settlement from her soon-to-be-ex husband, that was a matter for Ferncliff & Morton, or maybe the Tennessee Bar, but again, not my problem.

Between them, Rafe and Tamara Grimaldi would figure out who killed Manny—someone with no connection to me or Rafe whatsoever—and things would go back to normal. I was humming when I unlocked the apartment door, stepped through, and locked it behind me.

I was still humming when Walker stepped out of the kitchen, gun in hand.

IF YOU'LL PARDON THE EXPRESSION, IT was like déjà-vu all over again.

Back in August, he had done the same thing. We'd been in Mrs. Jenkins's kitchen then, and Mrs. J had been with me. And Walker had pulled out a gun.

Now I was alone. I wasn't sure whether that was good or bad. With two of us, we'd been able to distract him. Not deliberately as much as by accident, true, but it had worked out all right. With just me, and being the sole focus of Walker's attention, I wasn't sure my chances of survival were very good.

"I thought we got along," I said after a second. It was a stupid thing to say, no doubt, but I'd honestly thought that we'd had a good relationship. I could have sworn to it, right up until he pointed the gun at me the first time. And even then, I was pretty sure it hadn't been anything personal. It was just what he had to do to try to stay out of prison. The whole vandalism thing had frankly taken me aback, and the last thing I had expected, was for him to be here.

He smiled, showing lots of nice, white, straight teeth.

He's a very attractive man. A few years too old for me, at forty five or forty six, and of course he doesn't swing my way. But he's quite good looking. Six months in prison had taken its toll on him, though. His hair was too short, his skin and nails not as well-tended as I was used to. I guess the prison authorities hadn't let him stick with his usual skin care regimen while behind bars. And he had lost weight. The khakis and button-down shirt hung on his thinner frame, but they were as knife-pleated and starched as they'd always been.

The smile didn't touch his eyes, even as he assured me, "If you do as I say, we'll continue to get along."

I'd walked right into that one, in more ways than one.

"What do you want?" I asked.

Another stupid question. He wanted to get away. Somehow, he thought I could help him. Either that, or he'd decided to tie up loose ends before leaving, and I was one such.

Since I wasn't quite ready to hear that I was bound for termination in the next minute and a half, I didn't give him a chance to answer. "I thought you'd be in Shelby Park."

Walker smirked. "Garth is taking care of that."

Garth.

"You're setting him up," I said.

Walker answered, "I have no idea what you're talking about." The statement sounded palpably false.

"Is the money for him? Payment for helping you get out of jail?"

Another smirk. "It was supposed to be for both of us. Getaway money."

Supposed to be? "Getaway where? Together?"

"Costa Rica." He hummed a few bars of that old Gershwin classic. —where the living is easy.

"You were planning to go to Costa Rica together?"

"Garth wanted to go to Costa Rica," Walker said. "I just don't want to go back to prison."

That was understandable. And since I was trying to build rapport, I figured I might as well say so. "Of course. No one could blame you for that. So you and Garth were going away together."

Walker nodded.

"Together."

"Yes, Savannah," Walker said. "Together."

Right. That explained Rafe's smirk the other day, when he'd told me he could think of two reasons Garth Hanson might have helped Walker. Money had been one, but he hadn't gotten around to mentioning the other. I don't know why it hadn't crossed my mind that Garth might have helped Walker out of fond feelings, and not simply for a monetary payoff at the end.

"So Garth is in Shelby Park waiting for Tim to drop off the money."

Walker nodded.

"And you're here."

He nodded.

"I guess you figured out that your chances of getting out of the park with the money were pretty slim, huh?"

"Yes," Walker said. "I'm not stupid, you know."

I'd never thought he was. It was sheer bad luck—for him, I mean—that he'd gotten caught for murder, and he'd certainly exhibited considerable ingenuity in getting himself out of prison.

I said as much, and he simpered. Until I added, "Coming after me doesn't seem very smart, though. Wouldn't you be better off making tracks?"

"Without my money?" Walker said.

"It must be better than getting caught again."

"I won't get caught. They'll catch Garth—maybe—but he won't tell them where I'm headed."

"Are you sure about that?" With the prospect of ending up in the same prison where he'd spent years as a guard, I could imagine that

Garth Hanson might tell Detective Grimaldi pretty much anything she wanted to know in an effort to cut a deal.

"He doesn't know," Walker said.

Ah. So I couldn't count on Grimaldi breaking Garth quickly, and coming to my rescue. And Rafe wouldn't be coming, either. I realized, too late, that I hadn't even remembered to call to tell him that I had my car back and had left the office under my own steam and gone home. He'd be going to LB&A to pick me up. But not for a while yet. And when he realized I wasn't there, he still had to make his way here. There was no chance at all that he'd rush in and save the day. By the time he made it home, I'd probably be dead.

"What are you doing here? I mean, I realize you're probably upset that I had you arrested, but killing me is only going to make things worse."

"I'm not going to kill you," Walker said; I breathed a sigh of relief, as quietly as I could, "if you cooperate."

"With what?"

He looked at me as if I were stupid. "With me."

Obviously. "What is it you want me to do?"

"I want you to call Tim," Walker said, "and tell him not to drop the bag of money in the park. To drop something else instead."

"Like what?"

"His briefcase. His gym bag. What do I care?"

"I'm just concerned that he won't have another bag in the car," I said. "He's not a woman. He doesn't carry a purse."

Walker muttered something unkind. I'm not sure whether it was directed at Tim or me, or maybe both of us. "Call him. Tell him not to drop the money in the park."

I turned to my own purse, hanging from the hook. Walker stiffened.

"I have to get my phone out," I said, fumbling. My fingers brushed something that felt like a lipstick cylinder—maybe the one with the serrated blade in it, or maybe the one with the pepper spray, or perhaps just Mauve Heather #56.

I thought about pulling it out. Last time we'd done this, I had managed to fool Walker into thinking my lipstick was a gun I was pressing into his back. That probably wouldn't work a second time, but the pepper spray might.

Or maybe I'd be better off keeping it in reserve for later. I didn't seem in imminent danger of being shot, since he needed me to call Tim first. And if I brought out the lipstick and started waving it around, he probably wouldn't give me the time to get it up and aimed.

Regretfully, I left the lipstick where it was, and went for the phone instead. Once I had it in my hand, I looked back up at Walker. "What do you want me to tell him? Other than that he shouldn't let go of the money? I assume you want to meet him somewhere and take it off his hands?"

Walker's eyes narrowed. They're a gun-metal gray, cold and hard. "Don't worry about that."

"But he won't know where to go. Don't you think he'll ask?" And if he knew, perhaps he'd be able to get word to Grimaldi, somehow.

"Tell him..." Walker hesitated, as if this was a wrinkle he hadn't thought about. "Tell him to leave the park and go north on Riverside Drive."

"For how long?"

"Until you call him back!" Walker snapped.

Fine. It wasn't what I'd hoped for—I'd wanted something specific—but it was better than nothing. I dialed.

The phone rang a few times on the other end, and then Tim picked up. "Hello?"

"It's me."

"Savannah?"

Yes. Now Grimaldi would know that I was calling, since he'd used my name. She would probably not be able to hear anything I said, so I'd have to try to get Tim to repeat as much of it as possible. Assuming the wristwatch microphone was still on, that Tim hadn't turned it off.

"What's going on?"

Entirely too much to explain. "Where are you?" I asked.

"Driving down Shelby Avenue toward the park," Tim answered.

Good. I said it out loud.

"Why is that good?" Tim asked.

"There's been a change of plans."

"What kind of change of plans?" He sounded worried, and if he'd been in front of me, I would have kissed him. If I could keep him repeating everything I said, hopefully Grimaldi could hear it and know what was going on.

"Walker wants you to keep the bag of money instead of leaving it in the park."

There was a beat. "Why is Walker talking to you?" Tim asked suspiciously.

Yes! "I can't explain that," I said. "But he's here."

"He's there? With you?"

Yes! "He wants you to keep the money and leave something else in the park."

"What does he want me to leave?"

"Another bag. If you have one. Something to throw the police off and make them think you're leaving the money."

Next to me, Walker nodded approval.

"I don't have another bag!" Tim protested, a hint of panic in his voice.

"Well, do you have anything else? A towel? A blanket? Or maybe you can take the money out of the bag and leave the bag but not the money?"

There was a pause. "I can do that," Tim said.

Walker nodded.

"That's fine," I said. "Take the money out of the bag, leave the bag, and drive away."

"Drive where?"

"North on Riverside Drive. Until you hear from us again."

"OK," Tim said.

"And be careful. He has a gun."

Walker scowled at me.

"A gun?!"

"He's pointing it at me." What was the worst that could happen, after all? Walker could shoot me, but he probably wouldn't. Not while I was talking to Tim.

Who was breathing heavily on the other end of the line. "I don't like guns."

"I know." I added, to Walker, "He got shot a few weeks ago. He's a little jumpy."

"I'm not jumpy!" Tim said.

"It's OK," I told him, soothingly, "nobody blames you for being jumpy. It's natural to be jumpy when someone points a gun at you."

"Tell him not to point the gun at me. I have his money. He doesn't have to shoot me."

"I'm sure he knows that," I said. Walker was making 'hurry-up' movements with the gun and scowling, so I added, "You know what to do?"

"Drive to the park," Tim recited, "leave the bag but not the money, drive north on Riverside Drive until I hear from you again."

Thank you. "That's it. Good luck."

I disconnected the call before turning to Walker and the gun. "Now what?"

Eighteen

"Now we leave," Walker said, which was a load off my mind. I'd been afraid he'd simply shoot me and leave me for Rafe to find whenever my boyfriend made it home.

And much as I was loath to look a gift-horse in the mouth, I couldn't keep from asking, "Why?" Not that I wanted him to shoot me—obviously I didn't—but it made more sense than taking me with him did.

"You have to drive," Walker said.

"Don't you have a car?"

His brows drew down. Obviously he didn't care for the questioning. "Garth dropped me off on his way to the park. I've been here a while."

Ah. That was a bit creepy—I wondered how much exploring he'd done, and whether he'd gone through my underwear, or more likely, Rafe's underwear—but there was nothing at all I could do about it, so I put it out of my head. Not like I didn't have other things to worry about, after all.

"I could just give you my keys and my phone. That way you could do this on your own."

"If I have to leave you here," Walker said, "you'll be dead."

Ah. Yes, that put a different complexion on things. "Fine," I said. "I'll drive you. Let's go."

I reached for my jacket. Walker watched me like a hawk as I shrugged into it. Then I reached for my bag and the gun in his hand twitched.

"You won't need that."

"I'm not leaving without my bag. If we get pulled over on the way, I'll get a ticket."

If we got pulled over on the way, I'd probably get something much worse than a ticket, and I could see that knowledge in his eyes, but I didn't back down. "You can check the bag if you want. There's nothing here but the usual girl-stuff."

On impulse, I upended the bag on the floor in front of him. Lipstick cylinders bounced and pencils rolled, while business cards fluttered and a nail file hit the floor like a projectile. Walker jumped back.

It would have been a great time to jump him, but I didn't have it in me. He didn't lose his grip on the gun, and after you've been shot once—which I have been—there's this part of you that will do almost anything to avoid being shot again. Or at least that's the way it is for most of us. The normal people. Rafe has no such problem. He's been shot more than once, but he still throws himself into the fray each and every time.

Not me. I thought about it, but I didn't. Too risky. But if I could get my hands on the pepper spray...

"You stupid bitch!" Walked growled, lunging for my arm. That's when I realized this might have been a bad idea. When the bag was together, I could just sling it over my shoulder. But now I had strewn the contents all over the floor, and the chances of him allowing me to pick everything up and shove it back into the bag, were slim indeed.

I evaded the attempt to grab me and dropped to my knees, frantically gathering lipstick cylinders and stuffing them in my pockets, along with everything else I could get my hands on. My fingers had just closed around my wallet when Walker yanked me to my feet. "C'mon."

"My keys!" I dove for them. "If you want me to drive, I need my keys. And my phone. We'll need the phone to call Tim back."

I shoved it all into the pockets of my jacket as he herded me toward the door. On our way past the mirror, I glanced at myself. My pockets bulged, totally ruining the line of the outfit. But the knowledge that I had all three lipstick cylinders on my person—one Mauve Heather #56, one knife and one pepper spray—made me feel better about looking lumpy.

And then we were outside in the hallway. The door snicked shut behind us, and Walker pushed me ahead of him toward the stairs, the muzzle of the gun poking me in the back.

We didn't meet anyone on the way down. In the downstairs lobby, one of my neighbors was standing in front of the bank of mailboxes, and he looked over his shoulder at us when we came out of the stairwell. Walker nudged me in the back with the gun—I'm sure as a reminder that he had the power to shoot me if he wanted to—and I pasted a smile on my face. "Good afternoon, Mr. Sullivan."

He nodded. "Savannah."

Mr. Sullivan is older and I'm younger, so I call him by his last name and he calls me by my first. I was brought up to be polite to my elders.

He isn't ancient, though. Early fifties, maybe. Still healthy and seemingly strong. If I could get his attention, maybe he'd help me.

Or maybe not. Maybe I'd just succeed in getting him killed if I tried to open his eyes to what was happening.

The gun twitched again, an inducement to keep moving, and I crossed the lobby. "See you later, Mr. Sullivan." Or so I sincerely hoped.

And then we were outside in the courtyard. Walker slipped the gun into his pocket, not without a warning look at me.

"I know, I know. You can still shoot me." I headed for the car with him trailing behind.

When I headed for the drivers' side, he looked like he might be thinking about speaking up. "You wanted me to drive," I reminded him. "If you've changed your mind, I'll give you the keys and you can leave while I stay here."

I waited to see what he'd say. It would be nice if he'd take me up on the offer. There was no real reason for me to go with him, really. If he had a getaway car and my phone and his gun, he didn't need me. The fact that he seemed to want me along was cause for concern.

On the other hand, there was the possibility that he'd shoot me right here. When he didn't, just told me to get in, I wasn't sure whether to be relieved or the opposite. I lived to fight another day—or another fifteen minutes—but who knew if they'd be my last?

Walker slid into the seat next to me, and took the gun out of his pocket. He kept it in his lap, pointed my way, while I turned the key in the ignition and pulled away from the curb. "You know," I told him, "you don't really need that. I know you have it. But I'd drive better if you didn't point it at me."

He didn't answer. The gun stayed where it was.

We headed toward the office. When I signaled to turn right on South 10th, he told me not to. We continued straight on Main Street instead, past the East Library and the high and junior high schools.

When we were abreast of the Sherwin Williams store, he told me, "Call Tim."

"I can't call him," I said. "I'm driving. And it's rush hour. There's a lot of traffic. Besides, it's illegal to call and drive at the same time."

The look he sent me was vile. I ignored it, to dig in my pocket for the phone. "Here." I shoved it at him. "You call him. You're not doing anything else."

He had to take the phone, and for a second he fumbled both it and the gun. Then he got a better grip on both. I kept driving, sedately, as I watched him out of the corner of my eye. He opened the phone one handed, the other hand busy holding the gun steady. His eyes were on the phone, and I slipped my free hand into my other pocket and fumbled for a lipstick cylinder. It was hard to take it apart in the confines of the pocket, but I managed. Only to find that I had taken the top off my Mauve Heather #56, which would now probably create an unholy mess of the fabric inside my pocket.

But at least now there was a fifty-fifty chance I'd find the pepper spray next. I shot Walker another glance. He was busy manipulating the screen, dialing Tim's number. I turned my attention to the road—didn't want to accidentally have an accident while I was trying to save my neck—and thumbed the cover off another lipstick cylinder.

The tip of the tiny serrated blade pricked my finger. I managed to bite back an exclamation—it would have been a dead giveaway, and would have brought Walker's attention back to me. Instead, I ignored the drops of blood that were probably mixing with the mauve wax in my pocket, and fumbled for the last cylinder, which I now knew had to be the pepper spray.

Walker, meanwhile, had managed to dial Tim's number and put the phone to his ear. He was watching the street outside the windshield, too. I flipped the top off the last lipstick cylinder and felt the tiny nozzle. The tip of my thumb hurt. Hopefully I wasn't bleeding enough that my finger would slip off if I got the chance to use the spray.

"No," Walker said, into the phone, "it's me."

The phone quacked, a bit frantically it seemed to me, and Walker sighed. "No, she's still alive."

The phone quacked again. I couldn't make out what Tim was saying, just the tenor of his voice. He sounded upset.

"If you do as I say," Walker told him, "nothing will happen to you."

After a second—and more quacking—he glanced at me. His voice was annoyed. "Not to her, either."

Hah. Even under the circumstances, I couldn't keep back a smile. Sounded like Tim had asked Walker not to shoot me. That was nice of him.

"What happened in the park?" Walker asked, and Tim talked for a bit. I kept driving, while I wondered whether anyone was following Tim's car, or whether they'd all just stayed behind because they'd assumed he was dropping off the money and was out of it after that.

I also wondered whether they'd caught Garth Hanson, or whether he was on the loose somewhere, as well.

"Turn here," Walker said abruptly. It took me a second to realize that he was talking to me, and I ended up taking the turn onto Eastland Avenue with a screech. The car behind me honked angrily, and I cast a guilty look in the rearview mirror.

"Next time—!"

And then I froze when, a few cars behind, I caught sight of a motorcycle.

More accurately, I guess what I caught sight of was a head. I couldn't see the bike or the rider, just the top of a helmet above the blue roof of a car. Between me and the bike, there was a Lexus, a red compact, what looked like the rounded top of a Beetle, another compact, this one white, and then the blue car.

The Lexus was the one that had honked. It blew past me with a growl of the engine, leaving me in its dust as it sped away up Gallatin Road. The red compact made the turn behind me. The Beetle didn't. The white compact turned, but the blue car—a Honda Civic—went straight. I kept my eyes glued to the mirror and saw that the bike turned, as well. It stayed back, so it was hard to be sure, but I thought it might be Rafe. The bike seemed to be black, and the man was wearing a dark jacket.

"Next time, what?" Walker said.

I glanced at him, startled. For a second or two I'd almost forgotten he was there. I certainly hadn't noticed that he'd finished his conversation with Tim.

It took a second of thinking back before I understood what he was asking. "Next time, give me some notice when you want me to turn."

He glanced in the rearview mirror. "What's back there?"

"Nothing." It came out a little too fast.

He looked disbelieving, and I added, "The car behind me honked when I made the turn. I was just keeping an eye in the mirror."

Walker checked the mirror again, while I held my breath. Meanwhile, we approached the stop sign on the corner of North 14th Street. I slowed. "Which way?"

"Straight," Walker said.

I took my foot off the brake and went straight. "Have you decided where we're going?"

He glanced at me again, and I added, "I wasn't listening to you. I was busy driving."

I guess it must have made sense to him, because he didn't question it. "The Greenway."

"Back to Shelby Park?" Surely he didn't want me to take him back there. Did he?

"The other end," Walker said.

The Shelby Bottoms Greenway is a band of wetlands that runs along the Cumberland River from Shelby Park up to the area across from the Opryland Hotel. It has more than ten miles of trails for walking, biking, and rollerblading. Most people enter in the park, where the parking lot is and the biggest concentration of trails are. To be honest, I'd forgotten about the second entrance in the Riverwood neighborhood. There's nothing there. Not even a proper parking lot. But there is access to the Greenway.

"Why are we going to the Greenway?"

"To pick up Garth," Walker said.

I blinked. I had assumed the police would have done that.

Walker allowed himself a smirk. "He's making his way up the trail."

"How did that happen?" I made the sweeping left turn onto Porter Road. Behind me, the red car peeled away, down Eastland Avenue toward Fortland Park. The white car stayed behind me, and so did the bike, a few yards behind. Far enough that I could only faintly make out the sound of the engine.

"It was the plan all along." He looked very pleased with himself by now.

"That's interesting." I slowed down for the stop sign at Porter and Greenwood. "Can you tell me about it?"

He squinted at me.

"I'm curious," I said, as I slowed down again to bump across two sets of railroad tracks. Behind me, the white car came to a stop at the sign. Behind it, I could still see the bike approaching, slowly. "And it's not like I'll be able to tell anyone."

Walker smirked, probably because he realized that I realized that no matter what he'd told Tim, my chances of getting out of this alive were slim to none.

"I always knew we couldn't trust Tim," he told me, which didn't bode particularly well for Tim's survival either. "But there wasn't anyone else I could ask. You'd have gone straight to the police."

"Can you blame me? You tore up my office." And the only picture I had of myself and Rafe.

"Sorry about that," Walker said, without sounding the least bit sorry. "I lost my temper."

"Sure." And I suppose he'd lost his temper when he broke the windows in Mrs. J's house and slashed my car tires, too. Not to mention when he tried to get into my apartment yesterday afternoon.

He continued before I could bring up any of that. "It's your fault I went to prison."

"No, it wasn't. It was your fault. I didn't kill anybody."

"I had no choice," Walker said as I made another sweeping turn, this time to the right. "She was ruining my business."

Sure.

But we'd had this conversation before, and there was no point in having it again. "You were telling me about Garth and the Greenway."

A few seconds passed, while Walker breathed heavily in and out through his nostrils and while I made a left turn onto Riverside Drive.

"We thought there was a chance things might go wrong in the park," he said eventually, "so we made sure we had a Plan B."

The gun was still in his lap, but I got the feeling he'd mostly forgotten about it. The pepper spray was still in my pocket, with the top off. I didn't fancy using it while we were in this confined space together, though. If I sprayed him, I'd probably get a nose full of pepper spray myself, and then I'd lose control of the car and we'd crash.

No, much better to wait until we got to where we were going, and were outside in the fresh air.

"Garth got there early," Walker said, "and took his bike out of the car. And then he kept an eye on things. He was there before the cops, and saw them spread out. That's when he knew we needed to go to Plan B."

"I'm Plan B?"

He shrugged.

I slowed down for the green light and took a turn onto McGavock Pike. "So Garth left the park and started pedaling. And now we're going to pick him up?"

Walker nodded. I kept an eye in the mirror. Behind us, the bike took the turn onto McGavock, as well. I didn't want Walker to notice, though, so I didn't keep my attention on it. By now I was almost sure it was Rafe behind me, though, and the idea made me feel better. Even if Walker shot me, at least I'd get to say goodbye to Rafe before I died.

At the bottom of the next hill, I took a right onto Cooper Lane, and from there it was just a matter of following the road until it ended, beside the entrance to the Greenway.

The motorcycle disappeared just as we got there, down one of the side streets, and I experienced a moment of panic. Maybe it wasn't Rafe after all. Maybe it was just some random stranger who happened to be going home. It was unlikely that it should be him, after all. He was busy working, his mind on finding Manny's killer. He wouldn't cut out early. And he probably couldn't have made it back in time to pick up my trail anyway, even if Grimaldi had called him. And Grimaldi may not even know what was going on with me. Tim's microphone might not be switched on. He might have turned it off for some privacy until he got to the park. She might not have overheard our conversation. The police could be standing watch over the empty bag right now, waiting for Walker to show up to collect it.

"Park over here," Walker directed, and I pulled myself together to guide the Volvo to a stop on the side of the road a few yards down from the entrance to the Greenway.

I turned off the engine. "Now what?"

"Now we wait." He made himself comfortable in the seat. And he seemed to notice that he was holding the gun, because he firmed his grip on it.

"Can I wait outside?" I asked.

He squinted at me. "Why?"

"I'd just like some fresh air." It was true. The air inside the car had an uncomfortable scent of fear. I wasn't entirely sure whether it was me or Walker, and I didn't want to take a discreet sniff of either of us.

He glanced around. The place was deserted. Not a soul in sight. Just trees, the overgrown ribbon of blacktop that was the beginning of the Greenway trail, and the murky Cumberland River down at the end of the street. And then he looked at me, in my high heeled pumps and my flouncy skirt. And I guess he must have decided that the chances of me trying to run off into the brush—run off anywhere at all, really—were slim.

"Knock yourself out."

"Thank you." It just slipped out, I swear. He had abducted me, pretty much, and planned to kill me. I didn't really owe him thanks. But that's the drawback of having been brought up well.

I opened the door and got out. And felt better once I'd closed it between us.

Closing my hand over the pepper spray in my pocket, I started to edge around the car, toward the trees and brush, and the ditch that separated me from them.

Walker was right. In a flouncy skirt and three inch heels, I wouldn't normally consider pushing through the wilderness that surrounds the wetlands. I'd ruin my skirt and my shoes, not to mention that it would be uncomfortable. I'd get scratched, and my feet would bleed, and branches would hit me in the face. But getting shot would be worse. I've been shot once, and it hurt.

Being shot and having it not hurt, because I was dead, held even less appeal.

So I crept carefully around the car, trying not to look like I was planning anything, but simply like I was stretching my legs. And when a bicycle appeared at the entrance to the Greenway, with a man on it, I launched myself across the ditch and into the trees.

The man on the bike yelled. I hadn't gotten a good look at him— not good enough to recognize him—but I figured it had to be Garth Hanson, and I figured his appearance would distract Walker for a crucial second or two. As I pushed my way into the trees, feeling branches drag at my clothing and hair and scratching my legs, I waited for the sound of the shot from Walker's gun.

But he was inside the car, and it must have taken a few moments for the window to roll down. Either that, or he'd decided to open the door before he took aim. Whichever the reason, the shot came later than I expected, and it went wide.

It was still pretty scary, though. I could hear the sound of the bullet whistle past, tearing through leaves and branches, before it embedded itself in a tree trunk with a meaty thunk. I froze for a second, crouching. And that's when a body came crashing through the brush after me. A hand grabbed my arm and yanked me up and around.

I screamed, even as I went with the movement, bringing the pepper spray out of my pocket as I rose. I was already spraying by the time I recognized Garth Hanson's face, teeth bared and snarling.

The spray caught him dead in the face, and it was his turn to scream. He let go of me to claw at his eyes. I darted off again, just as another bullet tore through the trees a few feet away. If Walker wasn't careful, he'd shoot Garth by mistake.

The vegetation surrounding the Greenway path was dense, and the ground soggy from recent rains and the little bit of snow we'd had this winter. I had to push my way through brambles and vines that scratched my hands and face, my feet sinking into ice cold puddles that dotted my legs with dirty water. In less than a minute, my toes were numb.

Another shot went wide, but close enough to scare me. I hesitated for a second, heart beating fast. I was making too much noise. Walker could hear where I was by the sounds I made making my way through the brush. But if I slowed down in an effort to make less noise, I was afraid Garth Hanson would catch up to me.

There was a sound to my right. A soft plop of water, as if someone was approaching stealthily, trying not to be heard, but who had accidentally stepped in a puddle.

I swung in the other direction, my heart thudding so hard my chest hurt, and took off running. Only to stop a second later, when I slammed into a hard, male body.

Nineteen

My body recognized him before my mind did. The feel of him, the smell, the way his hands fit on my arms. And there was no mistaking that husky drawl. "Shhhh. I got you."

I sagged against him, the hand with the pepper spray falling to my side. "You have no idea how close you came to being pepper sprayed," I informed his shoulder, reassuringly warm and solid beneath my forehead.

"I figure about two seconds."

In spite of the dire situation, there was amusement in his voice. He slipped his hand down my arm and took the lipstick cylinder out of my now-limp fingers. He slipped it into his pocket, before taking my hand and tugging. I found the wherewithal to lift my head from his shoulder and follow. I even found myself issuing a warning.

"We have to be quiet so they don't hear us."

"Don't worry," Rafe said over his shoulder, "Tammy's got'em."

"Really?"

"The cops were right behind me. I figure by now they've got the situation under control."

Perhaps. There were no more shots, anyway, and no one was crashing through the brush after us.

As soon as we reached the bicycle path, he swung me up in his arms. "What happened to your shoes?"

"I kicked them off," I said. "To make it easier to run."

He nodded. "Skirt's ruined."

It was. It had a totally unintended slit all the way up the side of my thigh practically to the hip. Rafe didn't seem to mind, though. His lips curved. "That's a damn shame. But I'm enjoying the view."

I didn't bother to chastise him. I didn't even bother to blush. My feet were too cold to work the blood up to my face. Instead I just looped my arms around his neck and hung on.

My mad dash through the brush hadn't taken me all that far, so it was just a few minutes before we emerged from the path out into the road again. The scene that greeted us was very different from the one I'd left behind.

In the few minutes I'd been gone, a half dozen police cars had poured into the cul-de-sac, followed by Tamara Grimaldi in her unmarked Buick. They were surrounding my poor Volvo in a starburst pattern. Garth Hanson was facedown on the pavement, while a police officer—young George Truman, I realized—was cuffing his hands behind his back. Walker, meanwhile, was already in the back of one of the cruisers. I could see the outline of his head through the glass, but I couldn't see his expression. It wasn't necessary. I had a feeling that this time, he'd be less conciliatory if I went to visit him in prison.

Not that I had any plans—or any reason—to. If I never saw Walker again, it wouldn't be too soon.

Tim's car was also there, with Tim behind the wheel, looking limp and wrung out. When he saw us coming out of the trees, he perked up, though. The relief on his face was heart-warming. I even forgave him for the way his gaze lingered on Rafe a lot longer than it did on me.

"She OK?" Grimaldi asked.

Rafe nodded. "Just scratched up. She left her shoes behind when she ran."

"We got them." Grimaldi nodded to where my pumps were lined up by the side of the road, looking none the worse for wear. I wiggled.

"Just hang on," Rafe said. "I'll get you there."

"I'm too heavy," I said.

Rafe looked at me and arched a brow. Didn't say anything until I stopped squirming. "I said I'd get you there. Just hang on."

Fine. I hung on, even though I felt stupid being held like a child while other people were standing on their own two feet. It wasn't like it would hurt me—or hurt any more than I'd already been hurt—to cross the few yards of blacktop to slide my feet into the shoes.

But he wanted to hold me, so I let him. I listened while he and Grimaldi exchanged details about the op. They'd caught both Walker and Garth Hanson, which I'd already realized. Walker had shot at the police cars (as well as at me) so when he went back to prison, it would be with a few more attempted murder charges tacked onto the murders he was already in prison for. He didn't stand a chance of getting out again for the rest of his natural life. Unless, of course, he managed to arrange for another escape, but after this, I imagined the authorities would make it rather more difficult for him to do so.

"You two can go," Grimaldi told us.

"Don't you want a statement?"

She shrugged. "You can tell me what happened if you want to, but I have a pretty good idea. I imagine he was in your apartment when you came home?"

I nodded.

"He had a gun, and he made you call Mr. Briggs."

I nodded.

"I overheard his part of the conversation. You did a good job, getting him to repeat as much as possible."

"Thank you. I did my best."

"We were on him as soon as he entered the park. And followed him all the way here. Meanwhile, as soon as I heard what was going on, I called your boyfriend. He was close enough to pick up yours and Mr. Lamont's trail from the apartment."

I nodded. "I saw him." I caught Rafe's eye and added, "You. I saw you behind us when we were on our way up Gallatin Road. Or at least I hoped it was you."

The arms holding me tightened. "I was worried about you for a few minutes there, darlin'."

I'd been worried myself. I remembered thinking that if it was Rafe behind me, at least I'd get to see him again before I died. But I decided it was probably best not to say anything about that. "He wasn't going to shoot me while I was driving the car. We'd crash if he did. And once we got here, I got away from him."

He nodded, but there was still shadows in his eyes.

"Mr. Collier parked a block away and went through the woods," Grimaldi continued, "while the rest of us were following Mr. Briggs. When we heard the shots, we moved in."

"And got them both."

She nodded. "It's all over. They're both headed back to jail."

"I don't envy Mr. Hanson. That can't be much fun for him."

"He's already trying to work a deal," Grimaldi said, with a heavy layer of disgust in her voice. "He'll tell us everything we want to know and plead guilty to everything as long as we get him berth somewhere other than Riverbend."

"Will he get it?"

She nodded. "Sending him there is like signing his death warrant. To keep him alive, we'll have to incarcerate him somewhere else. But he'll still be behind bars for a very long time. You don't have to worry about him."

I wasn't worried about him. I wasn't even worried about Walker. Hopefully the TDOC would be able to hang on to him next time, and I wouldn't ever have to see him again.

"Can we go get my shoes now?"

Grimaldi nodded. Rafe took me over to where my shoes were parked. Truman was putting Garth Hanson into the back of a second cruiser, and Hanson looked up as we passed by. His eyes were red and puffy, but cold as ice. Truman put a hand on his head and shoved him inside.

I fought back a shiver. There was no doubt in my mind that if I hadn't sprayed him with pepper spray when he caught up to me in the woods, I'd be dead.

And then the door closed, and I couldn't see his face anymore.

"I'm glad that's over," I said, hanging on to Rafe's arm while I carefully inserted my toes back into the shoes. They felt hard and uncomfortable on my battered feet.

He nodded. "Me, too."

"Can we go home? My feet hurt."

He nodded. "I'll see if one of Tammy's minions can drive my bike back."

"Don't be silly," I said. "I'm capable of driving myself home. Go get your bike and I'll meet you there."

He squinted at me. "You sure?"

"Of course. Don't turn into Todd." Although if he wanted to worship me when we got home, that'd be just fine.

He must have seen the thought in my eyes, because he grinned. "I'll see you there, darlin'."

I told him he would, and then I made my slow and painful way toward the Volvo.

When I got even with Tim's car, I slowed down. Grimaldi was standing there, telling him to put the money back into the bank, where he'd gotten it. "You can go home, Mr. Briggs. Thank you for your assistance."

"Rafe's leaving," I told her. "So am I, if you don't need me for anything."

She shook her head. "Thanks for your help, Ms. Martin."

"Thank you for yours. You got here just in time."

A shadow crossed her face. "I'm glad everything worked out."

"Me, too." I turned to Tim. "You all right?"

He nodded. And shuddered. "Scary."

It had been. But it was over now. "I'll see you tomorrow," I said, and hobbled the rest of the way to my car.

Rafe was waiting for me at the curb outside the condo, and despite my protests, insisted on carrying me across the courtyard and up the stairs. We stopped in front of the door. "Key?"

"I'll do it."

He didn't put me down, so I had to insert the key and turn the knob from a hanging position. He stepped through. "Lock it."

"You can put me down now."

"In a minute. Lock the door."

It was easier to do as he said than argue. I locked the door. And although I was tempted to make a joke about being carried across the threshold, I didn't.

Although maybe I should have. He didn't put me down. Instead he walked through the living room, past the dining room table, and straight into the bedroom. He didn't put me down until he could set me gently on the edge of the bed.

And once he'd done that, he knelt on the floor in front of me and pulled my shoes off.

"You don't have to..." I began, and then lost my breath when he looked up at me.

"Don't tell me what I don't have to do, darlin'. I almost lost you. If I wanna take care of you, then let me."

That wasn't what I'd had in mind when I imagined him worshiping me when we got home—the worship I had imagined had had more of a carnal nature—but I wasn't about to complain. Still, I couldn't keep from telling him, "You didn't lose me."

"I could have. You were supposed to wait for me."

"Only because I didn't have a car," I said. "When Spicer brought it back, there was no reason to wait."

"If you'd waited, I would have been here with you when you walked through the door."

"If you'd been with me when I walked through the door, Walker would have shot you."

At least I was pretty sure he would have. Rafe alive would have been too much of a threat. Walker obviously thought he could handle me by waving the gun in my face, but I don't think he would have taken that risk with Rafe.

No, if we'd walked in together, Rafe would have been dead sixty seconds after he crossed the threshold. And then I would have died in the woods, since he wouldn't have been there to save me.

"I didn't save you," he told me when I said as much. "You saved yourself."

"If you hadn't been there, Hanson might have caught me again."

"The police were there by then. They got him."

I tilted my head. "You're determined to feel guilty, aren't you?"

He wouldn't meet my eyes. After a second, I was forced to reach out and cup his cheek. "Rafe? What's wrong?"

He looked up at me then, and the expression in his eyes took my breath away. His voice was hoarse. "I failed Manny. I don't wanna fail you, too."

Oh, God.

I forgot all about my sore feet and scratched legs as I slid off the bed and onto my knees next to him. "You didn't fail Manny. You had no idea what would happen. It wasn't anything you did or didn't do. And you didn't fail me. You were there with me the whole time. I saw you behind me before we'd driven five minutes. I knew you were back there and you wouldn't let him hurt me. Just like you didn't let Perry hurt me. Or Hector. Or Desmond or Neil."

I reached for him, and his arms went around me with almost bruising strength. I don't think he was crying—exactly—but I think if he'd allowed himself to, he might have been. "I was so afraid he'd hit you," he said into my hair. "I heard the shots, but I wasn't close enough to see what was going on. And then I heard you scream, and I heard Hanson yell, and more shots, and I was so afraid I'd get in there and find you dead."

I tightened my arms around him. "I'm not dead. I'm fine. Nothing happened."

"He hurt you." He stroked my upper arm, where Garth Hanson's fingers had bit in hard enough to leave bruises.

"I hurt him more," I said, and I could hear the pride in my voice. "I sprayed him with pepper spray." And it had felt good, too.

Rafe's lips curved at that. "Good job."

"He was probably lucky it was me and not you."

He didn't answer that, but he didn't have to. If Rafe had reached Garth Hanson—or for that matter Walker—before I or the police did, they would have been lucky to walk away.

"I love you," he told me.

I had to swallow the lump in my throat before I could speak. He didn't say it that often, and usually not unless I'd said it first, so when he did, it was always an emotional moment. "I love you, too."

He kissed me, and that was it. The things that were said after that weren't very coherent, and had nothing to do with Walker or Garth Hanson or anything else. I didn't give a single thought to my sore feet or scratched legs.

But all good things must come to an end, and about an hour later I returned to the real world. "I'm hungry."

"I can fix that."

"For food."

Rafe grinned. This was an exchange we had with regularity. "Want me to go get a pizza?"

"I want to go out," I said.

"Where d'you wanna go?"

"Anywhere but the Shortstop."

"Fidelio's?"

"Not there either. It reminds me of Todd."

Fidelio's Italian Restaurant on Murphy Road in West Nashville was what Todd had deemed 'our' place. I have no idea why, because as I had told him once, Bradley used to take me there, and it didn't bring back good memories. While the food was good, the place was much too fraught with memories.

"We had some good times there, as I recall," Rafe said mildly.

We had, at that. Rafe had taken me to Fidelio's once or twice himself, not to be outdone by Todd, I guess. Or maybe because he thought it was what I wanted. And yes, I had enjoyed myself. But that was more because of him than because of the place.

"We did," I agreed. "But it's a snooty, uncomfortable place. I just want to go somewhere where nobody will look down their noses at us."

He looked at me for a second and then he smiled. "FinBar?"

I smiled back, relieved. "That's great." Close by and casual, so I could put on a pair of jeans and not have to walk around with my scraped legs on display.

He tossed the covers off. "Let's go, then. The sooner we eat, the sooner we can go back to bed."

Indeed. I pushed my own half of the comforter off and followed suit.

"So you know how I spent the afternoon," I said when were sitting across from one another in a booth in the back of FinBar, "but what did you do?"

FinBar is a local sports bar, just down the street from the real estate office. It serves burgers—less greasy and more gourmet than the ones at the Shortstop—and there are lots of green plants and flat screen TVs that show golf and tennis and swimming in addition to the ubiquitous basketball and NASCAR racing.

It was March, so there was basketball on one screen and baseball on the other. Rafe was facing both of them, since he'd taken the seat with his back to the wall and the front door in view as usual. He didn't seem to get caught up in the on-screen action, though. He just glanced at it once in a while, but the rest of the time he kept his attention on me and on the door.

"Waiting for someone?" I asked.

He shook his head. "Just making sure everything's copacetic. Don't want nobody bursting in here with a gun or nothing."

"Why would anyone burst in here with a gun? Walker and Mr. Hanson are back in custody."

"Whoever shot Manny has a gun," Rafe said, "and that wasn't Walker or Hanson."

Not likely, no.

"So you know how I spent the afternoon," I said, "but what did you do?"

"Went to talk to your ex-husband." The waitress came by just then to deposit our drinks on the table—Diet Coke for me, beer for Rafe— and he gave her a smile. When she'd staggered off, overcome by lust, he continued, "He wasn't there. I ended up talking to a Mr. Ferncliff."

"Nathan. One of the senior partners."

He nodded. "He said Bradley was working outta the office today."

"What did he say about the Vandervinders? Anything?"

"Not much," Rafe said. "I couldn't really ask about it, without a good reason. I asked what Bradley's been working on. He said that Bradley's representing Mrs. Vandervinder in the divorce from her husband. When I asked him whether there was any reason to think Bradley might be more than professional with Mrs. Vandervinder, he got upset."

"I saw him outside Mrs. Vandervinder's house that morning I was down there," I said. "He was driving by. I thought he was checking up on Bradley, but maybe he was checking to see whether Mrs. Vandervinder was alone. Maybe he's the one who's been more than professional with Mrs. V." Or less than professional, as the case may be.

"Maybe so," Rafe said. "I also asked him if Bradley woulda had any dealings with Mr. Vandervinder, and he puffed up like a rooster and showed me the door."

"He's actually a pretty nice guy. At least he's always been nice to me." And I'd never gotten the impression that he took his ethics lightly. Although if he was bedding Ilona Vandervinder, I could be wrong about that. "He was probably just bothered by the suggestion."

Rafe shrugged and took a swig of beer.

"Did you tell him who you are?" I added.

"TBI. Looking into the shooting death of one of our agents. We'd identified Bradley as being present in the bar the same night as our man."

"No, I mean... did you tell him about us?"

He quirked a brow. "You and me? Now, why'd I wanna do that, darlin'?"

"I'm not sure," I admitted. I guess it had nothing to do with anything, really. "I just thought maybe it came up."

He shook his head. "No. I didn't mention you. Don't want nobody thinking I'm fingering Bradley 'cause I'm jealous."

"Nobody in their right mind would think that." There was no comparison at all. Rafe was worth fifteen of Bradley.

"Plenty of people'd think that. And I don't want it becoming an issue."

I guess I couldn't blame him for that. "So you didn't see Bradley."

He shook his head. "I guess he musta gone home after his appointment."

Guess so. I wondered whether Shelby had told him about our conversation.

But no, probably not. She wouldn't want him to know that she'd asked me for help in figuring out what was going on with him.

"And it wasn't Nathan with Bradley the other night."

"No," Rafe said. "Not unless he's a better liar than I give him credit for. He didn't look like he'd ever heard of the Shortstop."

I nodded. "I know the waitress said it wasn't him, but I thought she might have been mistaken. But I guess not."

"I don't think so, darlin'." He looked up. "Food's coming."

"Good. I'm starving."

He grinned at me across the table. "Better build your strength back up, darlin'. I've got plans for later."

No problem. I had plans for later, too.

Twenty

We left the FinBar just before eight, and headed home. It was nice to walk across the courtyard without worrying about anyone shooting at us. We held hands up the stairs, and when we reached the door, I was already thinking pleasant thoughts about peeling his T-shirt off with my teeth.

No, not really, but I was thinking of taking it off him.

Anyway, that all changed when we reached the door. Rafe pulled out his keys preparatory to unlocking the door, and froze. "Shit."

"What?" I peered around him.

"Stay back." He pushed me up against the wall with one hand and reached behind him for his gun with the other.

"What—?" I protested, even as I stood where he put me.

He didn't answer, just pushed the door open and went through the opening with the gun leading the way. Which led me to the conclusion that the door had been unlocked.

We'd locked it. I'd made sure of it. So had Rafe. There was no chance at all that one of us had forgotten.

"This is getting monotonous," I told him when he came back out into the hallway, looking grim.

"Tell me about it." He fished the phone out of his pocket and dialed. "We need a crime scene unit at Savannah's place," he said when it was answered.

I recognized the shriek on the other end as belonging to Tamara Grimaldi—and she wouldn't appreciate my calling her normally dulcet tones a shriek—but I couldn't hear what she said. It didn't matter; Rafe's response made it obvious.

"Between six o'clock and now. It wasn't Lamont or Hanson."

No, it hadn't been. They'd been in police custody since this afternoon.

"How the hell do I know?" Rafe asked, aggrieved, as I slipped past him and into the apartment. "We just came back from dinner."

I left him to explain while I walked inside, looking left and right.

It didn't take long to see the damage. It started just inside the door, with all my jackets and coats on the floor. (Rafe basically just has one. Black leather. He'd been wearing it.)

In the kitchen, the fridge had been opened and food was all over the floor, mixed with shards of glass and porcelain from the cabinets. Spatters of ketchup looked like fresh blood.

In the living room, the TV had been upended and broken, and everything that had been on the dining room and living room tables had been tossed on the carpet. And the bedroom—I didn't even want to go into the bedroom.

Rafe found me hovering the doorway with my eyes closed. "I'm afraid to look," I told him.

"It ain't that bad." His hands landed on my shoulders, squeezed reassuringly. "They blew their wad in the kitchen, pretty much. The bedroom got off easy."

I slitted one eye and then opened them both wide. "You call this easy?"

The bed was stripped and the sheets and comforter tossed on the floor. Both side table drawers were emptied onto the carpet, and the lamps that had stood on top of the tables were toppled. One bulb had broken. All the drawers in the bureau were hanging open, with the clothes strewn across the floor—Rafe's boxers mixing with my slinky satin and frothy lace—and the closet doors were gaping, showing all my dresses and skirts on the floor. Here and there I saw a glint of metal or stone, from where my jewelry box had been emptied all over everything.

He shrugged. "Don't look like they destroyed nothing."

Actually, it didn't. A broken lightbulb seemed to be the extent of it. That and the sense of violation. I'd had my bedroom invaded once before, and it had left me with mixed feelings of anger and fear, with a sense of incredulous outrage thrown in for good measure. But back then, Rafe's old admirer—whose violation it was—had slashed my nightgown and written on the wall in what looked like blood. It had turned out to be lipstick—L'Oreal Endless Kissable 16 hour No Fade, No Smudge Ruby-Ruby lipstick—but the shock of seeing it had been considerable.

Rafe was right. This wasn't so bad. Someone had just taken their anger out on my—or our—belongings. But there wasn't that edge of insanity permeating the place. This was someone throwing the adult equivalent of a child's temper tantrum, basically.

"Who...?"

"No idea," Rafe said. He pulled me back against him and wrapped his arms around my waist. The heat of his body along my back felt comforting. "Tammy's got a crime scene unit on the way. They'll look for fingerprints."

Sure, but... I looked around helplessly. "It's going to take all night, cleaning up."

His arms tightened. "I'll do it."

"You don't have to do it by yourself. It's mostly my stuff." He'd been traveling light over the past ten years, so he hadn't accumulated as much junk as I had. Besides, he doesn't like clothes as much as I do. His wardrobe consists mostly of jeans and T-shirts. A half dozen pairs of jeans, a dozen T-shirts, a couple of dress shirts, one suit...

In the closet, his clothes used four or five hangers, while mine used the rest. Forty five, or so.

"We can argue about it tomorrow. Tonight, we ain't doing nothing."

"We have to. We can't go to bed with it like this."

"We'll spend the night at the house," Rafe said. "Wait for Tammy's people to show up and then leave. It's still our house."

It *was* still our house. Or his house, more accurately. Or most accurately, Mrs. Jenkins's house. But since she was suffering from dementia and couldn't be trusted to make good decisions—she'd agreed to sell her house to Brenda Puckett for a song last August—Rafe had legal power of attorney to handle the estate. So for all intents and purposes it was our house.

"That's fine." I didn't want to stay in my apartment. Not until it was all cleaned up and back to normal. Just looking around at the mess made me feel unsettled, my stomach clenching, and I doubted I'd be able to get to sleep in the middle of it.

"Pack a bag," Rafe said. "Throw in my toothbrush and a change of clothes for me, too."

He nudged my hair aside to kiss the back of my neck and then let go. I stood for a second to let the goosebumps dissipate before I picked my careful way across the floor to gather what I needed for the night and tomorrow morning.

THE CSI CREW MADE GOOD time. It was less than thirty minutes later when they showed up, with Grimaldi bringing up the rear.

I looked up, surprised, when she walked into the living room. "What are you doing here? Aren't you interrogating Walker and Garth Hanson?"

She looked surprised, as well. "What's to interrogate them about? We know what they did."

I guess they did, at that. It just hadn't crossed my mind. When someone gets arrested, they get interrogated, or so I've always assumed.

"I was on my way out when your call came," she added, nodding to Rafe. "I'd finished writing up the report about this afternoon, and I thought maybe I'd get a full night's sleep for once."

"Sorry."

It was me who said it, not Rafe. He just smiled.

"I won't stay long," Grimaldi said. "I just wanted to see the place for myself." She looked around.

"It's a mess," I said, as if she wasn't capable of seeing that for herself, "but I don't think anything's missing. The TV's broken, of course. And the computer." It looked like someone had taken a hammer to it. They hadn't, though. I imagined the monitor had been broken with the polished stone owl—technically a bookend—that was lying on the floor beside the dining room table.

She nodded. "Any idea who was here?"

"None, I'm afraid. If you hadn't had Walker in custody, I would have blamed it on him."

He had admitted to tearing up my office, after all. But he couldn't have been here this evening. Nor could Garth Hanson.

"Need you to do something for me," Rafe told Grimaldi.

She sighed, but nodded. "I know. Check with Lamont and Hanson whether they broke into the house on Potsdam Street two nights ago. And whether they slashed the tires on the car last night."

"And whether either of them tried to get in here yesterday afternoon," I added. "Someone did. Remember I told you?"

Both of them nodded.

"Better do it now," Rafe said, "before they're moved out of the jail downtown."

"Yeah, yeah." But she didn't leave right away, just looked around, at the mess and the crime scene tech who had started fingerprinting the front door knob. By now we were old friends, the tech and I. He was probably heartily sick of me.

Grimaldi glanced at us. "You two staying here overnight?"

Rafe shook his head. "We're going to my grandma's house on Potsdam for the night. We'll deal with the mess tomorrow. It's the weekend, anyway."

It was. In all the hoopla, I'd forgotten that today was Friday.

"I'll call with what I find out," Grimaldi said. "You two can head out if you're ready. I'll stay with Zach until he's done with the door and can go inside and lock it. Don't wanna take any chances."

No, indeed. There'd been entirely too much activity in this apartment for that.

"C'mon, darlin'." Rafe took the overnight bag in one hand and me in the other. "Let's go."

We went.

It's amazing how quickly something can turn. It was just thirty minutes since we'd crossed the courtyard coming home, and I'd thought about how safe I felt, knowing that Walker and Garth Hanson were back in jail. Now I was back to being jumpy again, feeling like eyes were tracking my progress across the sidewalk. I halfway expected a rifle to spit fire. I imagine Rafe expected the same, because he was back to protective mode: keeping me close and trying to shield me with his body. Not an easy thing to do when the hypothetical shot could come from practically any angle.

And anyway, it didn't come. We made it safely across the courtyard to the sidewalk, where Rafe stopped. "Car or bike?"

"Oh." It hadn't even crossed my mind that we could take the bike. We always took the Volvo when we went somewhere together. But now that I'd ridden on the Harley a few times, it was a definite possibility. Especially dressed as I was, in jeans and halfway sensible shoes. "Um... bike?"

His grin turned wicked. "Really liked those vibrations, didn't you?"

I had. But I'd also liked the wind in my hair and the way I could plaster myself against his back and the sense of freedom that came from streaking up the interstate with no walls between me and the elements.

But... "We've got the bag. It would probably be easier to take the car."

"Live a little," Rafe said and headed for the bike.

Fine. I crawled on behind him, slung the bag over my shoulder, and held on. Now that he wasn't trying to shock me by taking off like a bat out of hell, we started out down the road at a more sedate pace, and he didn't open the throttle until we hit Ellington Parkway. After that it was just a few minutes before we had to slow down again to exit. Nonetheless, I enjoyed every second of the ride, even the moment when Rafe dropped a hand from the handlebar to squeeze my knee affectionately. I might have gotten a little short of breath—as much because of the squeeze as because he was only driving with one hand—but that was all.

The Potsdam area was quiet when we arrived. Porch lights were on up and down the street, and there was the blue glow of television screens from behind closed curtains. Mrs. J's house loomed dark and still. The gravel crunched loudly under the bike tires as we made our way up to the porch.

"Guess I forgot to turn the porch light on when we left this afternoon," I told Rafe when I'd climbed off the back of the bike and taken the helmet off my head.

He nodded. "We were a little distracted, as I recall. I'm gonna park round the corner. No sense in leaving the bike at the bottom of the stairs like a beacon."

No sense at all. It was an expensive piece of equipment, quite a bit more valuable than my six year old car, and easy to hotwire, I imagined, since whoever wanted to steal it, wouldn't even have to worry about getting inside first. Not to be crude or anything, but just like on a man, everything was on the outside.

I watched while he tucked the bike out of sight beside the porch, where the light wouldn't reflect off the chrome once I turned the porch light on. Then he came back and took the overnight bag out of my hand and threw it over his shoulder. "C'mon, darlin'. Let's do this."

I took his hand and headed up the stairs.

He made a circuit of the house as soon as we walked in, just to make sure everything was still as it should be. There was no sign that anyone had been inside since we left just before one. All the windows were intact and all the doors were locked, just as they should be. Everything looked normal.

The house was still furnished the way it had been when Mrs. J lived there with her companion-cum-nurse Marquita Johnson in the fall. Rafe had nowhere else to store the furniture he'd bought for the house, so we'd left it where it was, and figured we'd just deal with it when the house sold. As a result, all three upstairs bedrooms were furnished, as were the kitchen—obviously—the dining room, parlor and library.

We ended up in the parlor in front of the TV, where Rafe let me have my pick of viewing material, probably because he realized how rattled I was and figured I'd calm down more if he let me look at soothing things. We watched a couple of hours of mindless, calming House Hunters episodes, with people looking to buy houses in such wildly disparate but idyllic locations as St. Paul, Minnesota, and St. Johns, in the Virgin Islands. Rafe kept his arm around me, and stroked my arm.

Then we switched to the news, which included the usual mixture of death and destruction. They did mention, briefly, that the escaped prisoner Walker Lamont, responsible for several murders, had been caught and was on his way back to prison. I guess they were trying to reassure the population at large that it was safe to go to sleep tonight.

Rafe's phone rang about halfway through the news. For a second I wondered whether he was on call, that he'd have to leave me to go in to work, but then I relaxed again when he answered. "Tammy."

Grimaldi said something, and Rafe smirked. "I know."

I sat up straighter in the squishy sofa.

"What've you got?"

She spoke for a while after that, with Rafe just nodding and making go-ahead noises. Eventually he thanked her and disconnected. "That was Tammy. Lamont and Hanson deny breaking the windows. They also deny slashing the car tires."

I had begun to suspect as much, since they couldn't have broken into my apartment earlier this evening. It didn't come as a complete shock, but the news still left me feeling a bit uneasy. "Do you think they're telling the truth?"

He shrugged. "Dunno. They might think they've got enough charges filed against them anyway, that they don't wanna add more."

Maybe. That made sense, and made for a reasonable explanation for why they wouldn't own up to vandalism on top of everything else.

"Then again, with what they've already got to deal with, ain't like this is gonna make much difference."

Right.

"Who do you think did those things, then?"

"No idea. The tires coulda been anyone. There were plenty of people at the Shortstop that night. Coulda been someone who didn't like the questions we asked. Or somebody who recognized me from before. Just cause I didn't see nobody I knew, doesn't mean they couldn't have seen me."

Obviously.

He continued, "Or it coulda been someone we didn't know, but who thought the likes of you woulda been better off without the likes of me."

"I'm not better off without you," I said.

He didn't answer. "As for who broke in here, I did some research after I dropped you off."

"Research?"

"I was gonna tell you," Rafe said, "but then I got sidetracked."

That was quite the understatement, considering that what had sidetracked him—sidetracked us both—had been me getting abducted and almost killed.

"Go ahead." I braced myself.

"After I took you to the office, I came back here and did a canvass. Knocked on doors and asked if anyone had heard or seen anything."

"I thought you went to see Nathan Ferncliff."

"That was later," Rafe said. "First I talked to the neighbors."

Better him than me. I wouldn't have felt comfortable walking door to door in this neighborhood. "Did you learn anything?"

"This ain't the kinda place where it pays to be interested in anybody else's business, darlin'. That's more likely to get a body in trouble. But I did find someone who'd seen a car parked out front. A dark SUV. Maybe blue, maybe black. Maybe dark green."

Not like there's any lack of those around Nashville. Especially when we didn't have a make or model.

"I don't suppose this person happened to see who was driving the car?"

He shook his head. "Who d'you know who drives a dark SUV?"

I thought about it. It was easier to tell him who didn't. "Not Tim. Nor Heidi. Nor Brittany."

He quirked a brow. "You have a reason to think your coworkers would wanna break windows or slash tires?"

None at all, I had to admit. "None of the people who were here earlier. The inspector had a white truck. The agent had a Jeep Wrangler and the clients a sports car."

He nodded.

"But Todd drives a blue SUV."

"I know he don't like me," Rafe said, "but somehow I don't think he made the drive here from Sweetwater just to break my windows."

I nodded. Me either.

"And he wouldn't slash your tires."

No, he wouldn't. "Shelby's minivan is white. Bradley drives a dark SUV, though."

He didn't say anything for a moment. "You think Bradley mighta done it?"

"I can't imagine why he would," I said, "but I suppose it's possible. He paid for my car, so if he saw it in the Shortstop parking lot, he'd know it belonged to me. And this house isn't difficult to find. It's available for sale, with my name on the sign. He might not—or whoever broke in and broke the windows—might not have realized it was your house. It might just be because I'm the agent."

Rafe nodded slowly. "We should go talk to Bradley tomorrow."

"That ought to be fun." My current boyfriend interrogating my ex-husband in front of his pregnant wife.

"You don't have to come," Rafe said. "But I thought you might enjoy it."

I might, at that.

WE WENT TO BED SHORTLY THEREAFTER, in Rafe's bed upstairs. The same bed where we'd started the day making love this morning. The same bed where we'd started our relationship six months ago, for that matter. Just like then, he did his best to wear me out—so I'd sleep well, or so he claimed—and then he wrapped an arm around my waist and snugged me close, and fell asleep with his nose buried in my hair.

I'd been afraid I wouldn't be able to sleep—it had been a pretty eventful day, after all—but between the heavy food, the warmth of the comforter and his body, and the fact that I was with him, and he always made me feel safe, I surprised myself by dropping off to sleep almost immediately.

When I woke up it was still dark. The black beyond the window wasn't lightened by sunrise, and when I turned my head to check the glowing red digital display on the clock, it told me it was just after one.

I was about to turn around to face Rafe when his hand landed on my shoulder to hold me in place. He leaned in, his front warm against my back. "Shhhh."

"What?" I breathed.

"Not sure."

We lay in silence for a few seconds. I strained my ears, trying to discern something, anything, that might have woken us both.

Rafe is a light sleeper, always ready for trouble. I'm not, particularly, so I imagined it was probably him coming awake that had awakened me.

There was a soft sound from downstairs. Something like a scurry, from tiny feet on the floor or the brush of clothing against a doorjamb.

"Mouse?"

He shook his head. No, we probably wouldn't hear a mouse all the way up here.

Please, God, let it not be a rat!

Rafe rolled away and to his feet. I turned over, as quietly as I could, praying that the mattress wouldn't squeak and the blankets wouldn't rustle too loudly, to watch him. It was dark outside, but there was enough light from the streetlamps and the porch light to see his outline standing at the side of the bed.

For a moment I wondered whether he'd cross the floor and head down the stairs naked. The sight of all those muscles on display would be enough to put the fear of God into any evildoer who might be lurking. Unless the evildoer was female, and then she'd probably faint dead away with excitement. Either way, problem solved.

However, he tugged his jeans on and grabbed his gun before moving to the door, soundless on bare feet.

I waited until he was gone down the hallway before I swung my legs over the edge of the bed and got to my feet. I didn't want to get in his way, but I might as well get ready, just in case. In case he missed the rat when he fired at it, or something, and the rat ran up the stairs and into the bedroom. I didn't want to be in bed then. The bed was a simple platform, much too close to the ground for comfort. No, if I saw a rat, I wanted to be able to jump on top of the bureau, the tallest piece of furniture in the room, and to do it without flashing anyone my private parts.

So I fumbled my way into my own jeans and shirt and made my slow way toward the door, careful not to step on any of the creaking parts of the floor. Rafe had done his best in renovating the place, but the house was more than a hundred and twenty years old, and things do wear out over time.

I'd made it out into the hallway and had the stairs in sight when the downstairs exploded into a pandemonium of sound and fury.

Twenty-One

There were loud voices and grunts, curses and banging, but luckily no gunshots. Nonetheless, I put the idea of moving slowly and carefully out of my head and barreled down the stairs as quickly as I could. If I'd had any sense, I would have jumped on the banister and slid, but mother made it very clear early on that ladies do not slide on banisters, so that was something that didn't occur to me until it was too late and I was standing in the foyer downstairs.

The sounds were coming from the kitchen. I ran down the hallway and flipped on the light, since whatever was going on, was going on in the darkness of night.

The scene looked like something out of a bad action movie. Rafe was standing, almost literally with his bare foot on some guy's neck, pointing the gun at the back of the man's head and snarling something about making his day.

The prone fellow, meanwhile, wasn't so much as twitching a muscle. He might as well have been dead, for all the animation he showed. I could barely discern the movement of his back when he inhaled and exhaled. It was quite an achievement, since I assumed he was probably winded from going one on one with Rafe, even for just a minute.

He looked shortish and slim, with skinny arms and legs. He was dressed in black, jeans and a hoodie, and he had black hair, shaggy and in need of a cut. His hands and what I could see of his neck under Rafe's foot were white.

Rafe turned to me, a vision of smooth skin, hard muscles, and low-slung jeans, not to mention the gun and the set of his mouth. My very own romance fantasy come to life. It was all I could do not to swoon.

"You know this creep?" he wanted to know, his voice gravelly and dangerous. The man under his foot twitched nervously.

"It's a bit hard to see with him being on his stomach on the floor," I said apologetically. "Any chance I could get a better look at him?"

Rafe hesitated before taking his foot of the guy's neck. "Don't try anything."

The young man scrabbled around and out of reach, but he didn't try anything. Instead, he put his back up against the bank of cabinets on the other side of the kitchen and stared at us both, sullenly.

Rafe folded his arms across his chest, and I could see the kid's throat move as he swallowed.

He wasn't very old. Straight out of college, from the looks of it. Not that I'm particularly old myself—twenty-eight in another month or so, while Rafe is pushing thirty-one—but the intruder was about five years younger than me, at a guess. Pale skin, floppy black hair, toddler-like pout.

"No," I told Rafe. "I've never seen him before."

He nodded. "Go call Tammy."

"It's one o'clock in the morning!"

"She sleeps with one eye open," Rafe said.

I squinted at him. "How do you know that?"

He rolled his own. "Not 'cause I've ever spent the night with her. Just call."

Fine. I wandered over to the old-fashioned phone hanging on the wall beside the door, and dialed. He must have been right, because the phone only rang once on the other end before it was answered. "Grimaldi."

"It's Savannah," I said.

She immediately sounded more alert. "What's wrong?"

"Someone tried to break in."

Rafe snorted, which I took to mean that 'someone' hadn't just tried, he'd succeeded. By the time Rafe intercepted him, he'd been inside the house. In spite of our brand new locks and in spite of Walker and his handy-dandy MLS key being behind bars.

"Who?" Grimaldi asked.

"I have no idea." I glanced at him. "I've never seen him before."

He gave me a dirty look.

"Where is he now?" I heard rustling, and assumed she was getting out of bed and putting clothes on.

"Sitting on the kitchen floor with Rafe pointing a gun at him," I said.

"Tell him not to pull the trigger."

"She says not to pull the trigger," I told Rafe.

"As long as he doesn't try to move." Rafe wiggled the gun menacingly. The guy didn't stir, although I could tell he wanted to. He looked nothing at all like a hardened criminal, and had probably gotten way more than he bargained for when he found himself face to face—or nose to chin—with Rafe.

"He says he won't," I told Grimaldi, "as long as the guy doesn't try to move."

Grimaldi didn't answer that. "I'm on my way. But I'm on the other side of town, so it'll take me twenty minutes to get there."

"No problem," I said. "We've got this under control."

"Don't do anything I wouldn't do." She hung up.

I did the same. "She's on her way." For our captive's benefit, I added, "Detective Tamara Grimaldi with the Metro Nashville Police."

He turned a shade paler.

"Just in case you don't know it," I added, gesturing to Rafe, "this is Agent Collier with the TBI."

It wasn't possible for the guy to turn any paler than he already was, but he tried. "Shit," he muttered weakly.

Rafe and I glanced at each other. Rafe lips curved. After a second I smiled back. It's hard not to, with all that gorgeousness staring me in the face.

Then he turned back to the sorry specimen on the floor. "Who the hell are you?"

"Brian Bradshaw," the guy said.

Rafe shot me a look. I shrugged. The name sounded vaguely familiar, but only vaguely, and I couldn't place it.

"See? You don't even remember me." He scowled.

"I'm sorry," I said, automatically, and then I added, "Am I supposed to?"

He huffed. "I wrote the first contract on this house."

"You're the agent?"

"Yes!" He muttered something I didn't ask him to repeat.

"For that sweet little couple with the condo to sell?"

"That sweet little couple you kicked to the curb when you got a better offer!"

"It wasn't like that," I said. "Your clients had a sale of home contingency. The new buyers didn't. We could have waited around for six months for your clients' condo to sell."

Brian Bradshaw snorted. "Sure."

"It's true. It would be unethical to kick your clients out of the loop just because the other offer was higher."

"So it *was* higher?"

I hesitated. Tall, Dark & Demanding and his wife had, in fact, offered a few thousand dollars more for the house, probably to convince us to exercise the kickout clause. If they hadn't attempted to make it worth our while, we might have chosen just to take our chances with the first buyer, in the hope that their condo would sell in a timely manner. But the higher price hadn't been the main reason we'd exercised the kickout clause. That had been because we'd been afraid that after months of waiting, the original buyers wouldn't be able to sell their condo and wouldn't be able to buy the house, and we'd be left with no buyer at all.

"See?" Brian said. "Now my clients have decided not to sell after all. So I'm not getting a commission on selling their condo. And I'm not getting a commission on your house. And my car payment is due!"

"You're driving a Range Rover," Rafe told him. "Trade it in for a used Honda. Problem solved."

Brian Bradshaw stared at him. He looked like he was thinking about saying something, but then he eyed the gun and thought better of it. "You don't get it," he said instead.

"I get it," I answered. "I've been doing real estate for more than six months now, and it's hard to make a living. And you have to keep up appearances, because if you don't look successful, people won't use you to buy or sell their houses. But you can't go around breaking windows and slashing car tires just because you're not successful in your career."

Brian shrugged, pouting, so obviously he didn't think there was anything wrong with his approach.

"I assume you were trying to make the new buyers decide not to buy the house so your clients could get it back?"

"Yeah," Brian said. "So?"

"So breaking and entering is a crime," Rafe growled. "When people are home and you're armed, it becomes an automatic felony."

"I'm not armed!"

"What do you call that?" He nodded to a flashlight lying over by the fridge, lighting up the dust bunnies below. It must have rolled there in the tumult.

"It's my flashlight. I needed it to see what I was doing."

"I could kill you with that," Rafe informed him. "That makes it a weapon on the police report."

"The place was supposed to be empty!"

"It's your own fault," I informed him. "We're only here because you tore up my apartment and the CSI tech was there."

Brian folded his arms across his chest and stuck his bottom lip out.

We didn't get anything more out of him after that, and I left Rafe to stand guard while I went upstairs to put on a bra. Going without under the thin shirt made me feel exposed, and I didn't like the way Brian Bradshaw eyed me. I asked Rafe whether he wanted a shirt and shoes too, but he told me he was fine, that he'd wait. I guess maybe he figured that all those rippling muscles on display would serve as a reminder to Bradshaw not to try anything. And it wasn't like I was about to complain about the view, was it?

Tamara Grimaldi pulled up to the steps ten minutes later. She must have broken the land speed record to get here from West Nashville so fast. She told me once she lives in a little mid-century ranch in Charlotte Park, and I assumed she'd been at home and in bed when I called.

She looked perfectly put together and severe when she stalked down the hallway and into the kitchen. She'd even taken the time to put on one of those dark, masculine pantsuits she favors, with the crisply starched striped shirt underneath.

I watched her face for any response she might have to seeing so much of Rafe exposed, but beyond a quick blink when she first came face to face with him, she didn't react. Instead she turned to Brian Bradshaw, who was still pouting on the floor. "Name?"

He gave it to her.

"You're under arrest, Brian. Stand up and put your hands behind your back." She fished a pair of handcuffs out of her pocket.

"What?" Brian said, looking from her to me to Rafe and back. "But..."

"Breaking and entering is a crime. Vandalism is a crime. Tying up police resources on trying to hunt you down is a crime. On your feet. Hands behind your back."

Brian scrambled to his feet, still protesting as the handcuffs clicked shut around his skinny wrists. I actually felt a bit bad for him. I know what it's like to see the bank balance approaching zero and having no idea where your next tank of gas is going to come from.

Grimaldi glanced at Rafe. "I assume you'll be pressing charges?"

He nodded. "Hell, yeah. He broke three of my hundred year old windows and slashed four tires we had to replace. Damn straight I'm pressing charges."

Grimaldi nodded. "I'll keep him in a cell for the rest of the night. Come by in the morning and swear out a complaint."

"But..." Brian said.

"You'll have a chance to go before a judge to set bail tomorrow."

"Bail?!" I could see the expense of bailing himself out dancing in front of his eyes.

"You committed a crime," Grimaldi said. "People who commit crimes and are arrested, get the chance to post bail. If you don't have the money for bail, you can contact a bail bonding company. They'll take something as collateral. Like your house."

"I don't have a house. I live in an apartment."

"Is that your car outside?"

He nodded.

"Maybe they'll accept that. I'll give you some phone numbers when we get downtown." She herded him down the hallway toward the front door without saying anything else to us. There wasn't much to say, I guess, and I certainly didn't want her to have to interrupt her lecture on bail bonds to say goodbye. I was enjoying it too much.

So, obviously, was Rafe, who turned to me with a grin as soon as the door had shut behind them. "Looks like that Range Rover's gonna do him some good after all."

I nodded. "I feel a bit guilty. He's so young. And so worried about not making a success of real estate."

"I don't care if he's still in diapers," Rafe said. "I went to jail when I was younger than he is. And he's a criminal. Don't matter if he was just trying to sabotage the house sale. He broke our windows and flattened our tires and destroyed your peace of mind. I want him to pay."

Since he put it that way...

"I guess I do feel a bit better knowing that we won't have to worry about any more vandalism." Or about being interrupted again.

"Damn straight," Rafe said and scooped me up to carry me back upstairs and to bed.

THE NEXT DAY WAS SATURDAY. I usually do floor duty at the office on Saturday mornings. It was how I met Rafe back in August, and I tend to think of it as sort of a good luck charm or something I have to do or I'll get jinxed. If I'm not there on Saturday mornings, I worry that I'll miss out on something good, like a buyer with a million dollars to burn and no agent, calling to see a house.

This morning, Rafe talked me out of it. We woke up late, after all the excitement in the middle of the night, and then we spent another leisurely hour in bed before dragging ourselves into the shower and off to downtown to file our report.

"Are you sure you want to do this?" I asked him as we walked into Police Plaza. "He's just a kid trying to make ends meet."

He shot me a look. "He's not a kid. When I was his age, I'd spent a couple years in prison and a couple years undercover."

"I just know how he feels. It's a tough business and hard to get a break."

"That don't mean you start breaking other people's stuff," Rafe said.

"Of course not. You just feel so helpless, when it looks like everyone around you is doing so much better than you are and you're stuck in this untenable situation..."

I trailed off when I realized I'd practically described Rafe's childhood. He knew why I'd stopped, too. His lips curved. "Don't make excuses for him, darlin'. I had to learn early. It's time he learns."

Maybe so. "I think the people with the current contract on the house will probably bow out, though. Without Brian and his clients, we don't have anyone who wants to buy the house."

"So we hold onto it a bit longer," Rafe said. "Hell, with the traffic in and out of your apartment, we might be safer living there."

We might, at that. I didn't say anything about it, though, as we turned the corner into Grimaldi's office.

She looked pretty perky for someone who'd probably been up since one this morning. She was wearing the same clothes she'd had on when she walked into Mrs. J's house in the middle of the night. And I imagined that after she took Brian Bradshaw into downtown and booked him into jail and filled out whatever paperwork went with the arrest, there probably hadn't been enough left of the night for her to go home and get back into bed. But maybe she'd managed a cat nap on a sofa in a back room somewhere, or on the floor of her office, at least.

"Thanks for coming in." She gestured to the two chairs across from her desk. "I took the liberty of typing up a statement based on what you said happened. If you'll look it over and sign, we can get this thing processed."

She passed two sheets of paper across the desk to us. Rafe skimmed it and scrawled his signature on the bottom. When I didn't immediately follow suit, he gave me the evil eye. "We don't want this little punk getting off easy, darlin'. If we don't stop him now, he'll end up like Lamont one of these days, thinking he can get away with murder."

Grimaldi nodded. "I had a talk with him. He doesn't feel remorse for anything he did. He feels justified, because he was only trying to help his clients."

"And pad his own pocketbook," Rafe said.

"That, too. But the point is, he doesn't think he did anything wrong. He knows what he did was illegal and unethical, but he doesn't think it was wrong. He thinks we're wrong."

"Sign the damn thing, Savannah," Rafe said. "I want this guy behind bars. He came into *my* house, and broke *my* windows, and destroyed *my* property, and threatened *my* girlfriend. If I could, I woulda shot him. Since I can't, I want him in jail. So please do it. For me."

Since he put it like that. I scribbled my signature on the bottom of the statement and handed the sheet back to Grimaldi.

"Thank you." She gathered them together. "You might be called on to testify if this goes to court."

"No problem. Do we need to swear out a restraining order, just to make sure he stays away?"

"You can, but I don't think it'll be necessary." Grimaldi smirked. "You put the fear of God in him. He doesn't think he did anything wrong, but he's gonna think twice before he goes anywhere near the two of you again."

"Good," Rafe said. "Because if I find him anywhere near Savannah, I'll kill the little fucker."

OK, then.

"I'll be sure to mention that," Grimaldi said.

"Any news about the Ortega case?"

She gave me the beady eye and then relented, probably because Rafe was with me and had a right to know. "The hostage incident involving you and Mr. Lamont took everyone's attention yesterday afternoon. I have two uniforms contacting some of Mr. Ortega's former associates today, to see what they can learn. We're getting closer."

"Do you have a suspect?"

She hesitated again. "When Mr. Ortega was caught for grand theft auto, he informed on some of this associates to shorten his own sentence. One of them was just released from prison two weeks ago. We suspect he may have been involved."

"Name?" Rafe said.

Grimaldi eyed him. "We'll handle it, Mr. Collier."

His voice was as briskly professional as hers. "I know that, Detective. I just wanna know the guy's name."

She sighed. "Frederico Garcia. Know him?"

"We've met," Rafe said. "Couple years ago now. He was on the fringe of Hector's organization for a while. D'you know where to find him?"

"We know where he's supposed to be. If he's not there, we'll try family and known associates. We'll get him eventually."

Rafe nodded. "We'll leave you to it."

She looked surprised, but hid it quickly. "What are you two up to today?"

"We're gonna go talk to Savannah's ex," Rafe said, before I had time to get a word out. "You got a picture of Garcia I can have? I wanna see if Bradley noticed Garcia hanging around the Shortstop that night."

"Why would he have needed to hang around the Shortstop?"

"A lot of 'em do," Rafe said. "And Manny had a new place to live, away from his old hood. Garcia had to have picked him up somewhere."

Grimaldi nodded. "I'll send it to your phone."

"Appreciate it." He got to his feet. I followed. "We'll let you get to it."

"Thank you." Grimaldi hesitated a second before adding, "You won't do anything stupid, will you?"

"Who, me? We're just gonna go talk to Savannah's ex. I'll let you know what he says."

Grimaldi nodded, but from the speculative glint in her eyes, I'm not entirely sure she believed him.

Twenty-Two

I wasn't sure I believed him either, so when we were outside the building and on our way around the corner to where the bike was parked, I asked, "Where are we going?"

Rafe glanced at me. "To talk to Bradley."

"You mean you were telling the truth?"

He smiled. "Don't sound so surprised, darlin'. It happens."

"Of course. It's just... don't you want to help the police find Freddy Garcia? I'm sure Grimaldi would let you tag along if you asked."

"I ain't so sure about that," Rafe answered calmly, "but as it happens, I might know a couple things they don't. I'll just give Wendell a call."

"Sure, but... don't you want to go with him?"

He arched a brow. "You trying to get rid of me, darlin'?"

"Of course not. I love spending time with you. I just know you feel bad because of what happened to Manny. And I thought you might want to be a part of the team that brings Garcia in."

It was his turn to hesitate. "I thought maybe you'd want me to stick close today. After what happened yesterday."

"Oh." He was doing it for me, because he thought I might feel fragile after being abducted at gunpoint and having had my apartment vandalized and then being woken up in the middle of the night by a stranger breaking in. "No. I mean, yes. I would love for you to stick close." The closer the better. "But I'm not afraid. Walker's in prison and so is Brian Bradshaw. I'm perfectly safe. If you want to go try to find Freddy Garcia, I understand. I think you should."

"You sure?"

I nodded. "It might make you feel better. Or if not that, it will give you some sense of closure. And maybe the feeling that you did something to set things right."

I could see the conflict clearly written on his face. On the one hand, he wanted to make sure I was safe and felt safe. On the other, he wanted desperately to be part of taking Manny's murderer down.

"Go," I said. "Please. Do what you have to do. I'll be fine. I can walk home from here. I've done it before." It was just across the bridge and under the interstate, less than a mile to go to my apartment. And it was broad daylight and I was wearing sensible shoes, so it would be no problem.

"I'll take you home," Rafe said. "Then you can stay there or take the car somewhere. To the office or something. It's still early."

It was. Not even ten o'clock. I could go to the office and sit there for a couple hours in case the phone rang. Or I could go somewhere else. Like Green Hills to see Shelby and Bradley.

I knew it was none of my business what Bradley did. He wasn't my husband anymore, and nothing he did would reflect on me. But Shelby had asked me for help in figuring out what was going on, and although I didn't really owe her anything either, I wanted to tell her the truth. If nothing else, I could let her know that I didn't think Bradley had been cheating. That's what she'd been worried about, I fancied. She'd denied it, but that had to be it. If she'd really suspected that he was breaking every ethics law he'd sworn to uphold, she certainly wouldn't have asked for my help in exposing him.

So I let Rafe drive me home, which took a matter of two minutes to zoom across the bridge and up the road, and then I stood on the sidewalk and waved until the bike had disappeared around the corner or South Fifth Street before I fished my own keychain out of my purse and got into the Volvo.

The drive to Green Hills was also quick and easy so early on a Saturday morning. Green Hills traffic is usually difficult any time of the day or night, but early on a weekend, when people are sleeping late, it's easier to navigate than during the day or evening on a weekday. I pulled up in front of Shelby and Bradley's townhouse less than thirty minutes after I'd left home.

I had hoped to find Shelby alone, so I could talk to her privately. I didn't want Bradley to know that she had asked me to investigate him, and that I had agreed.

But when I drove up to the house, the garage doors opened and Bradley's navy blue Escalade started backing out.

By then it was too late to disappear. He recognized my car and stopped, rolling down the window. "Savannah?"

"Hi." I managed a weak smile.

He looked suspicious. "What are you doing here?"

"Oh. Um..." He was dressed in what looked like a yellow golf shirt under a windbreaker. "Going golfing?" I asked.

He nodded.

"With whom? Nathan? Or maybe Dale Vandervinder?"

Those cool gray eyes turned a shade colder. For a moment they reminded me uncomfortably of Walker, until I shook it off. This was Bradley. The man I'd shared my bed with for two years. Not very successfully, admittedly, but still. No reason to worry.

"Ferncliff & Morton represent Mrs. Vandervinder in the settlement," Bradley said, which was the equivalent of saying nothing at all.

"That didn't stop you from getting together with Mr. Vandervinder earlier this week, though, did it?"

He flushed, and then turned even paler. "I don't know what you're talking about," he told me, but his voice was half-choked.

I glanced at the door to the house. "That's fine. I didn't really come here to talk to you, anyway. I came to see Shelby."

That did it. Bradley pulled the car back into the garage and stalked toward me. If I hadn't seen it with my own two eyes, I wouldn't have thought he had it in him.

Meanwhile, I parked the Volvo and waited for him to get close enough to attempt to loom. After having been loomed over by Rafe in the early days, I must say I wasn't impressed with Bradley's effort. He was a couple of inches shorter than Rafe, and nowhere near as menacing, even though he tried to sound stern.

"What do you want to see Shelby about?"

"To tell her you aren't sleeping with Ilona Vandervinder," I said.

That took some of the wind out of his sails. "What?"

By now I figured we might as well just take it inside. He clearly wasn't going to leave, and he'd probably prefer going inside to taking the risk of one of the neighbors overhearing. I glanced at the door again. "Is Shelby home?"

Bradley nodded.

"How about we all just sit down and talk about it?"

He hesitated.

"Inside."

A door opened on the other side of the parking lot, and Bradley saw my point of view. He grabbed me by the arm and hustled me into the semi-seclusion of the garage before anyone could see me. From there, we went through the interior door into the downstairs hallway.

Bradley didn't bother to ask whether he could take my coat, just let go of my arm to put his head back. "Shelby!"

There was a clatter of noise from upstairs, and then the slow and steady thumping of Shelby making her way down the stairs to the first floor. "What?... Oh." She wrinkled those perfectly plucked brows. "Savannah?" She shot Bradley a quick glance. "What are you doing here?"

"She says she came to talk to you," Bradley said before I could open my mouth. I'd forgotten about that, his habit of answering questions for me.

"Really? About what?"

She played innocent very well, I have to say.

"I'm sorry," I said. "I figured Bradley would be out somewhere. And I realize you'd probably prefer to keep our arrangement between the two of us."

"Arrangement?" Bradley said.

Shelby threw her hands up and waddled toward the kitchen. "Since you're here," she told me over her shoulder, ungraciously, "you may as well sit down. My feet are killing me."

I eyed her butt as she moved away down the hall, doublewide in the pair of stretched-beyond-hope-of-recovery yoga pants she had on, and managed to bite back a retort. "Thank you," I said instead—taking the high road—and followed, leaving Bradley to bring up the rear. For once, I wasn't at all worried about how my derriere in the tight jeans stacked up, since there was no way I could look worse from behind than Shelby.

We arranged ourselves around the kitchen table, with Bradley still staring expectantly—and a bit worriedly—at me. "What's going on?"

"Shelby contacted me a few days ago," I said.

Shelby rolled her eyes and got up from the table. "I'm starving. I need something to eat."

Bradley and I watched as she waddled to the fridge and pulled out a plate of chicken wings and legs. Bradley had developed what looked like a permanent wrinkle between his brows. It deepened as he watched her peel back the plastic and attack the chicken. "Honey..."

"I'm eating for two," Shelby said, through a mouthful of chicken.

I raised my voice. "Shelby contacted me a few days ago. She was worried about you. She said you didn't look well and you weren't acting right."

Bradley turned his attention back to me, eyes wide.

"She wanted me to help her find out what was going on."

"Shelby...!"

Shelby shrugged, her mouth too full to respond.

"I tried to follow you from work on Monday," I told him, "but you recognized my car."

"So that's what you were doing in Germantown." He sounded a little bit triumphant, as if he had suspected I hadn't really been there for the reason I'd given him. Guilty conscience, if you ask me.

I shrugged. "Eventually I figured out that you were representing Mrs. Vandervinder in her divorce from her husband. You spent a lot of time at her place the other morning."

"We were working!" Bradley blustered.

Shelby stopped chewing, with a chicken leg halfway to her mouth, to stare at him.

"I'm sure you were. Correct me if I'm wrong, but Nathan is sleeping with Ilona Vandervinder, isn't he?"

"What?" Bradley said. Shelby started chewing again.

"Someone I know went to see Nathan yesterday. To ask about the Vandervinders. See, on Monday, when I realized I couldn't follow you myself, because you'd recognize my car, I asked someone else to follow you on Tuesday."

Bradley went still. Very still. The only sounds that could be heard were the ticking of the clock on the wall and Shelby masticating.

"He followed you to a bar in Tusculum called the Shortstop. He watched you meet with a man at a table in the back, and have a conversation with him. And then he followed you home afterwards."

Bradley looked ready to pass out.

"The man who followed you gave the TBI a description of the man you were meeting."

Bradley's eyes looked like they were about to roll out of his head. Or roll backwards, into his head. He opened his mouth, but nothing came out.

"TBI?" Shelby said.

"The Tennessee Bureau of Investigation."

She tossed her head. "I know what it stands for, Savannah. Why was the TBI following Bradley?"

Probably best not to say anything about the fact that it was all my fault. I turned back to Bradley. "They took a bunch of photographs to the Shortstop the other night, to see if the waitress could identify the man you were with."

"Why is the TBI interested in Bradley?" Shelby insisted.

I opened my mouth, but before I could say anything, Bradley croaked, "Don't tell her!"

I turned back to him. "She has to know, Bradley."

"Know what?" Shelby asked. By now, she'd become interested enough in what I had to say that she'd forgotten all about the chicken wings and legs.

"Bradley's been meeting with Dale Vandervinder."

Bradley sagged on the kitchen chair, like all the air had gone out of him.

"Bradley?" Shelby said, puzzlement mixed with a hint of displeasure on her face.

And Bradley must not be able to handle the disapproval, because he pushed the chair back without meeting her gaze—the legs scraped loudly against the tile floors—and fled with an incoherent apology. We both watched as he practically ran down the hallway and out the door into the garage. Off to take his feelings out on a golf ball, I guess. And leaving it up to me to put his wife in the picture, the coward.

"What's going on?" Shelby said, an edge to her voice now.

I took a deep breath. "The waitress at the Shortstop identified the picture of Dale Vandervinder as the man Bradley met with on Tuesday night. Dale is Ilona Vandervinder's soon to be ex-husband."

I didn't have to spell it out in any more detail than that. Shelby was a paralegal before she married Bradley. She was *his* paralegal. She knew, probably better than I did, just how illegal it was for Bradley to be meeting on the sly with his client's husband. I could see her jaw clench as she realized the implications.

"Sorry," I said. "When you asked me for help in figuring out what was going on, I had no idea it was going to be something like this. I figured he was just cheating again."

"I told you he wouldn't cheat on me." The reminder was half-hearted, as if her thoughts were elsewhere. As I'm sure they were. And besides, what he'd actually been doing, in its own way, was a lot worse than adultery. At least it isn't illegal to sleep around, horrible as it may be for his doting—and pregnant—wife to deal with. But when this got out, it might—it would probably—mean that Bradley would be disbarred. He'd lose his job, they'd lose their sole source of income, maybe they'd even lose the townhouse, and with a baby on the way, too.

The world as Shelby knew it had just taken a deathblow, and I could see her struggle to recover from the knowledge.

"I still don't understand what the TBI has to do with this."

I squirmed. "That's my fault. My boyfriend works for the TBI, remember? When I realized I couldn't follow Bradley myself, because he'd recognize my car, I asked Rafe for help. He assigned one of his rookies to follow Bradley on Tuesday night, as sort of a training exercise."

"So the TBI aren't really interested in Bradley." She sounded relieved.

"They weren't. But then—"

"What?" Shelby said, obviously alert to the sound of my voice. She pulled out a chair and sat down, with an unladylike grunt. "Tell me."

"The man who followed Bradley was named Manuel Ortega. He was shot later that night."

There was a beat of shocked silence. Then her voice rose. "How dare you accuse Bradley of shooting someone?!"

"I'm not," I protested. "Nobody thinks that."

She looked relieved until I added, "Besides, he has an alibi, doesn't he? You can verify that he was home on Tuesday night, right?"

"Of course," Shelby said. She was looking down at her empty ring finger, touching it. If there'd been a ring there, she would have been rotating it. Since there wasn't—she had probably gained too much weight for her rings to fit anymore—she was just rubbing nervously.

My next words didn't help. "It's the Tennessee Bar Association that will be interested in Bradley."

"He was really meeting with Dale Vandervinder?"

I shrugged. "I don't know. I haven't spoken to Mr. Vandervinder. I don't expect I will. It's none of my business. I just know what the waitress said. That the man Bradley was meeting, looked like the picture of Dale Vandervinder."

"So you don't know for sure that it was him." The relief in her voice was palpable now.

"Bradley didn't deny it," I reminded her gently, and watched her face cloud over again.

We sat in silence for a minute or two while Shelby thought the situation over. "What will happen to us?"

"I have no idea," I admitted. "I assume Bradley will lose his license if this comes out. And I don't see how it won't." Especially since Rafe had spoken to Nathan Ferncliff yesterday and planted the seed that Bradley might be doing something unethical.

Then again, if Nathan was doing something unethical too, in sleeping with Ilona Vandervinder, maybe he wouldn't want to pursue it.

On the other hand, if Nathan was sleeping with Ilona Vandervinder, he certainly wouldn't want her husband to get away with bribing Ilona's counsel into jeopardizing Ilona's case.

Yes, Nathan would be going after Bradley for sure. The least of it would be Bradley losing his position with Ferncliff & Morton. At the most, Nathan would have him disbarred and possibly prosecuted.

"What will happen to us?!" Shelby wailed.

Well, they'd lose their income, to start. They might have to sell their house. As Rafe had advised Brian Bradshaw last night, they might have to trade in their fancy, very expensive to maintain, luxury SUV and van in favor of something more economical. Shelby might have to go back to work after the baby was born.

I didn't think she'd want to hear me detail any of these items, though, so I didn't. She was probably just venting, anyway.

"I'm sorry to be the bearer of bad news. I just wanted you to know what I discovered. You came to me for help."

"I didn't want to know this!" Shelby shrieked.

Obviously. I pushed my chair back. "I should probably just go. Let you deal with this on your own."

"Don't you dare!" She pinned me with a furious blue gaze. "Who knows about this?"

"I do," I said. "Rafe does." Which meant the rest of the TBI did, even if I didn't say so out loud. "Nathan Ferncliff knows."

Her voice rose. "You told Nathan?!"

"*I* didn't. The TBI did."

She looked speechless, so I added, "One of their agents was shot. They're doing everything they can to find who killed him." And if Bradley and his career were casualties of that, then that was just too bad. But it was Bradley's own fault for doing something unethical in the first place.

Shelby still didn't look like she had found her voice again, and as far as I was concerned, there really wasn't much more to talk about. I had told her what I came here to tell her. She knew that her husband hadn't been cheating, at least not on her. Now it was up to the two of them to deal with this knowledge, and the knowledge that Bradley's boss knew what Bradley had done. As for me, my job was done and I just wanted to get out of there. I didn't regret telling her what I'd learned—she deserved to know—but it's never fun being the bearer of such awful news.

I got to my feet. "I should go. I'll see myself out."

Shelby nodded, so I guess she didn't have the wherewithal to bully me into staying one more time. I took off down the hallway, and looked back over my shoulder as I reached for the door to the garage. Might as well go out the way I'd come in. Shelby was sitting there at the table staring straight ahead, looking at a no doubt bleak future, with one hand protectively splayed on her stomach.

And I know I had no reason for fond feelings toward the woman who'd slept with my husband, but damn Bradley for doing this to her.

I ducked through the door into the garage and closed it softly behind me. And turned—to find myself face to face with Bradley and a gun pointed straight at my diaphragm.

Twenty-Three

Guess Bradley hadn't gone off to take his frustration out on whacking golf balls after all.

Nor had he gone to talk to Dale Vandervinder or Nathan Ferncliff. He was right here, and so was his car. Beyond him, I could see the parking lot and the tail end of my own Volvo.

"Back inside." He twitched the gun in the direction of the door.

I hesitated. The garage doors were open, and not that far away. I might be able to make a break for it. But I was at the top of a tiny staircase of three steps, while he was at the bottom. I'd have to make it past him, and past the car. And while I never would have guessed, in my wildest dreams, that Bradley would ever point a gun at me, he looked serious. Or at least he looked panicked enough to be willing to use it.

I decided to play it safe. I reminded myself that this was my ex-husband, not some crazed murderer, and that my chances of survival were probably better if I didn't give him an excuse to shoot.

So I turned around and went back into the house.

"What do you want?!" Shelby demanded when I walked back into the kitchen. "Haven't you done enough—?"

She stopped when she saw Bradley behind me, her eyes bugging out of her skull. "Bradley?"

Bradley didn't bother with more than a brief glance at her. Maybe he was afraid I'd try to jump him if he looked away. "Sit." He jerked the muzzle of the gun in the direction of the table.

"Bradley?" Shelby said again, voice quavering. "Where did that come from?" She pointed to the gun.

"It's Dale's." He added bitterly, "Although now it has my fingerprints all over it."

It was on the tip of my tongue to tell him that he shouldn't have picked it up then, but I figured it probably wouldn't help my case at all. Instead, I just sat down at the table, where he'd directed me. "How did you end up with Dale Vandervinder's gun?"

"He gave it to me the other night," Bradley said.

Uh-oh. I felt something cold skitter down my spine, like a caterpillar with cold feet, and it took effort to get my voice to cooperate. "Why?"

He looked at me, and I realized I hadn't been wrong about his eyes after all. They were just as cold as Walker's. "Dale was there waiting when I got to the bar that night. He noticed the guy following me in. He asked me about him, but I had no idea who the guy was, so we thought maybe it was a coincidence. But Dale made me leave first, just so he could see if the guy left, too. And when he did, Dale followed him. Here. And then home. And then he called me."

Shelby said, "So that's why you got so upset after that phone call."

Bradley nodded. "If Ilona found out I was working with Dale, it would ruin everything. He just wanted to keep what was his. More of what was his."

I wanted to ask about Ilona and what was hers—not to mention his legal duty to his client—but that wouldn't do any good either, so I didn't. "What happened?"

"He told me to meet him," Bradley said. "At one o'clock. He gave me an address and told me where it was and said he'd see me there."

"So you went to meet him."

Bradley nodded. "After Shelby went to sleep. It was an apartment complex. Dale told me it was where the guy lived. That he'd talked to him, and the guy was working for Ilona. And the next day he was going to tell Ilona what was going on."

"He lied," I said.

"What?"

"The guy who followed you wasn't working for Ilona. He had no idea who Dale Vandervinder was. He was only following you because your wife was worried that you were cheating and she asked me for help in finding out."

Bradley turned to Shelby. "You thought I was cheating?"

"I'm fat and ugly," Shelby said. "We haven't had sex in a month."

"You're pregnant, not fat and ugly. And we haven't had sex because you go to sleep at nine o'clock." He sounded impatient rather than loving, or I might have given him points for trying, at least.

Shelby obviously wasn't impressed either, because she sniffed.

"What happened when you got there?" I asked Bradley, to get the conversation back on track. Not that I didn't have a pretty good idea, of course, but I wanted to hear him say it.

"Dale was waiting. The place was quiet. Nobody around. We went up to the door and rang the bell. When the guy opened the door, Dale shot him."

"Dale shot him?"

"*I* wouldn't shoot anyone!" Bradley said indignantly.

I focused on keeping my voice level. If he was telling the truth, I might walk out of here. "That's good. Does that mean you can put the gun down?"

Bradley looked down, as if surprised he was holding it. For a second, it looked like he might be considering it, but then he shook his head. "Sorry. Can't do that."

"So you didn't shoot Manny Ortega, but you'll shoot me?" Shelby squeaked.

"It's all your fault," Bradley said. "Ever since I met you, you've been a pain in my butt."

That was rather rich, coming from him.

"For your information," I told him, "I only married you because you asked. If you hadn't, I wouldn't have."

"If you hadn't been frigid," Bradley shot back, "I wouldn't have had to get my needs met elsewhere!"

Better and better. That was what he'd told me back then, too.

"If you'd been any good in bed, I wouldn't have been frigid!"

That was one thing Rafe had taught me. The fact that I had been, as Bradley described it, 'frigid,' hadn't been my fault, it had been his. I was anything but frigid with Rafe, but then he knew what he was doing.

"I should shoot you right now," Bradley said and leveled the gun.

Shelby squawked. "Not in my kitchen!"

"Yes," I told Bradley, "think about the blood."

He hesitated, and I pushed my advantage. "You were there when Dale shot Manny, right? There must have been a lot of blood."

He shuddered very faintly.

"Shoot her somewhere else," Shelby said.

Thanks a lot, I thought.

"Fine." Bradley waved with the gun. "Come on. We'll go for a ride."

I got to my feet.

"You, too," Bradley told his wife. "You'll have to follow us."

Shelby pouted. "Why?"

"Because I'll have to drive her car. Or make her drive her car. I need you to take me back home."

He was talking about me as 'her,' instead of as Savannah. That probably wasn't a good sign, since Bradley's mama brought him up better than that. I eyed the knife block on the counter, to gauge whether I could make it there before Bradley shot me. The odds were not in my favor.

"Oh, fine," Shelby said. She started the process of getting to her feet, not an easy task when she was so front-heavy. "Just let me get my purse." She waddled off down the hallway toward the front door.

Bradley twitched the gun at me. "Move."

"Where?"

"Outside," Bradley said. "We're going for a ride."

"Where?" I gave him as wide a berth as I could, moving past.

"I don't know yet. I'll figure it out. Just go."

Fine. He hadn't told me whether to follow Shelby to the front of the house or whether to go out through the garage. Since he'd left it up to me, I choose the garage.

There were three steps from the kitchen door down to the concrete floor of the garage. Then there was Bradley's car to move past before getting to the open air beyond the garage doors. And then the parking lot to traverse before getting to my car.

On the hood of Bradley's car sat a motorcycle helmet.

It hadn't been there when he'd been on his way out to play golf earlier.

I didn't think it had been there when I opened the garage door to leave a few minutes ago, either.

Granted, that was when I'd come face to face with Bradley and his gun, so I might not have noticed, but there was no logical reason I could think of why it would be there.

Other than the obvious one, I mean. Rafe was here somewhere, and had put the helmet there so I'd know.

At the moment I didn't care. I grabbed the helmet and swung around on my heel and whacked Bradley on the side of the head with it.

It made a satisfying smack. Bradley staggered and dropped the gun, but not before getting off a shot. Fortunately, it didn't hit me, it only took out the Escalade's front tire. Then Bradley dropped, too, accompanied by a hissing sound from the tire, as it flattened.

"What the hell?" Rafe's voice said from behind me.

I kicked the gun out of the way, just in case Bradley was faking. I didn't think he was, but it was better not to take any chances.

Rafe came up to stand next to me, to stare down at Bradley. The sleeve of his jacket brushed my shoulder, but he didn't touch me or offer support. He just stood there, ready to catch me if I fell.

"I wish you wouldna done that," he told me. "I was looking forward to hitting him."

"Sorry." I glanced up at him. "I've been wanting to do it for a long time." And anyway, wasn't that why he'd left me the helmet?

He looked back down at me, dark eyes searching. "You OK?"

I nodded. "I don't think he would have shot me. Not really. He just panicked. Everything came crashing down around him, and he didn't know what else to do."

Rafe didn't look convinced, but he also didn't argue.

"He said Dale Vandervinder shot Manny," I added.

"You believe him?"

I shrugged. "Not sure we'll ever know for sure. His fingerprints are all over the gun now, anyway."

Rafe nodded.

"What are you doing here?" I added.

"I called Wendell and told him I knew where Freddy Garcia might be holed up. He told me not to worry about it, that Garcia had an alibi. So I decided to follow you. You have a tendency to get yourself in trouble."

"I got myself out of trouble this time."

"With my helmet."

True. I was about to thank him for leaving it when the basement door opened and Shelby stepped through. She took a look at the tableau at the bottom of the stairs—Bradley out cold on the floor, me with a no doubt murderous look on my face, and Rafe next to me with his gun in his hand. After a second, she stepped back and slammed the door behind her. We could hear the lock hitting home.

"She's probably calling 911 right now," I told Rafe.

"I already did. Tammy's on her way."

"We're keeping her busy this weekend."

He shrugged. We went back to watching Bradley.

"He isn't dead, is he?" I asked after a few seconds.

Rafe shook his head. "You didn't hit him that hard. Besides, I can see him breathe."

I could too, now that he mentioned it. "You don't think he'll suddenly jump up and attack us, do you?"

"Not if he has any sense. I've got a gun pointed at him." He made sure his voice was loud and clear enough that Bradley would hear it, in the event that he was just playing possum. "If he has any sense at all, he'll just stay there quietly until the cavalry arrives, and not gimme a reason to hit him."

Bradley must have heard him—or maybe because he really was out cold—because he didn't so much as twitch.

Tamara Grimaldi's car pulled up outside after a few minutes. She didn't even greet me, just took in the scene at a glance and shook her head. "What did you do to him?"

"I knocked him out with the motorcycle helmet," I said, brandishing it. "He was going to shoot me."

"With what?" She glanced around.

"He dropped the gun when I hit him," I explained. "I kicked it under the car. Over there." I pointed.

Grimaldi eyed the flat tire. "He shoot that?"

I nodded. "I'm lucky it wasn't me." The bullet hadn't come quite as close as the one yesterday, from Walker's gun, but it had come close enough. Anything without about fifty yards is too close for comfort.

"I'd say." She turned back to him. "How long has he been like that?"

"Couple minutes," Rafe said. "He's breathing. He prob'ly just don't wanna have to wake up and deal with reality."

Probably. "Maybe you and I should just step out for a minute and let Grimaldi deal with him," I suggested. "Maybe that would help."

Rafe quirked a brow. "You think that'd be safe?"

"He isn't stupid." Current circumstances to the contrary. "He won't attack her."

"If he does," Grimaldi said, "I'll keep him locked up for the rest of his natural life. If he's telling the truth and he didn't kill Ortega, he's not looking at serving much time. If he'll turn evidence against Vandervinder and cut a deal, he might get out in time to see his kid start kindergarten."

That sounded like a long time to me—five and a half years until any child born in the next month would start kindergarten—but perhaps to Bradley it didn't sound so bad. His eyelids flickered.

"Let's go," I told Rafe, suddenly eager to get away before I had to deal with Bradley, and watch him deal with what he'd done, and with what he'd attempted to do. He might not have to serve much time for Manny's murder, if Dale Vandervinder had been the one to pull the trigger, but Grimaldi hadn't mentioned anything about what he'd tried to do to me. And then there was the legal matter of scheming with Mr. Vandervinder behind Mrs. Vandervinder's back.

Bradley was finished, in a lot of ways, and although I had no fond feelings left for him—certainly not after this—I also didn't want to stand here and watch his world come down around his ears. I cared enough about the man I'd once married not to want him to go through that with his ex-wife as audience.

"Come on." I took Rafe's arm and tugged him away. He came reluctantly, not without several longing looks over his shoulder.

Not at Grimaldi. At Bradley. Obviously Rafe was still wishing for the opportunity to punch my ex-husband.

But it wasn't necessary. We watched from beside my car as Grimaldi got Bradley to his feet. He was weaving a little, and I wasn't sure whether I'd really hit him that hard or whether it was the realization that he was about to be arrested that made him reel. She talked softly to him, and got him into a pair of handcuffs. Then she guided him out of the garage toward the police car parked at an angle in front of the garage. Just in case Bradley had thought to make a break for it in the Escalade, I guess.

He stopped beside the car door and looked at me. "I'm sorry, Savannah."

I could hear Rafe's soft snort behind me.

I nodded. "I know, Bradley. Me, too."

He didn't say anything else, just looked at me. And looked at Rafe. And then let Grimaldi put him into the back of the car, with a hand on his head, like Truman had done with Garth Hanson yesterday afternoon. Never thought I'd see the day when my ex-husband was taken away in the back of a police car, with his hands cuffed behind him.

Funny how things turn out.

Grimaldi closed the door on Bradley and headed for the entrance to the townhouse, presumably to inform Shelby about what would happen now.

"Think I should go with her?" I muttered.

Rafe tightened his arm around my waist, either in warning or unconsciously. "No, darlin'. Let her handle it. You've done enough."

I guess I had, at that. More than enough, I'm sure Shelby would say.

"You don't owe her nothing," Rafe added.

I nodded. "I know. It's just... she asked me for help, and I brought this down on her. I feel guilty."

"Ain't your fault her husband's a screw-up. You did what you had to do."

He was right about that. Once I knew what was going on, it wasn't like I could have done anything different. Except perhaps refuse to meet Shelby in the first place, but that was water under the bridge. Spilled perfume. Whatever.

So I stayed where I was and watched as Shelby opened the door. Grimaldi spoke for a minute. Shelby nodded, looking pale and frail in spite of her pregnant girth. Then the door closed again, and Grimaldi came toward us.

"I'll need you to come back downtown and file another report," she told me. "Sometime today."

"We'll go right now." I glanced at Rafe, who nodded. At this point, I just wanted the whole thing over with, and I guess he did, too.

"I'll see you there." Grimaldi got into the cop car and drove slowly out of the cul-de-sac. So far the neighbors had been discreet in their interest—I was surprised none of them had come outside to see what was going on—but now I did see a few fluttering curtains, and one woman scurrying across the parking lot to knock on a neighbor's door across the way. We watched as they put their heads together, glancing in our direction.

"Your mama's gonna have a cow when she hears about this," Rafe said.

I nodded, my lips curving. "Oh, yes."

He turned me around and put both hands on my waist to look down into my face. "You gonna tell her?"

"Do you think I should?"

"I think you should wait for Tammy to tell your brother and let him break the news."

After a second, he added, "Though I wish I could be there to see her face."

He wasn't the only one. "We could schedule a visit."

"No offense, darlin'," Rafe said, "but I don't wanna see your mama that bad."

I didn't either, if it came to that. Although the optimist in me wondered whether my mother would look at Rafe any more kindly now that it turned out that Bradley was headed to jail.

A girl can hope.

"Let's go," the love of my life said and gave my posterior a swat. "I'll follow you there." He headed for the bike.

"Thanks for following me here," I called after him as I reached for the Volvo's door.

He turned to grin at me. "I'd follow that view anywhere, darlin'."

He winked before he pulled the helmet down over his face. I was laughing as I put the view he admired into the seat and turned the key in the ignition.

ABOUT THE AUTHOR

Jenna Bennett writes the *USA Today* bestselling Savannah Martin mystery series for her own gratification, as well as the *New York Times* bestselling Do-It-Yourself home renovation mysteries from Berkley Prime Crime under the pseudonym Jennie Bentley. For a change of pace, she writes a variety of romance, from contemporary to futuristic, and from paranormal to suspense.

FOR MORE INFORMATION, PLEASE VISIT HER WEBSITE:
WWW.JENNABENNETT.COM

CPSIA information can be obtained at www.ICGtesting.com
Printed in the USA
LVOW12s1613110215

426636LV00008B/854/P